Missing
By a Heartbeat

OTHER BOOKS BY LIZBETH SELVIG

SEVEN BRIDES FOR SEVEN COWBOYS

The Bride Wore Denim
The Bride Wore Red Boots
The Bride Wore Starlight
Betting on Paradise

LOVE FROM KENNISON FALLS

The Rancher and the Rock Star
Rescued By a Stranger
Beauty and the Brit
Good Guys Wear Black

KINDLE WORLDS-Sapphire Falls

Going Out on a Limb
Going Zero to Sixty

Lizbeth Selvig

Missing By a Heartbeat

A Chandler County Novel

LIZBETH SELVIG

Webster Publishing

Missing By a Heartbeat
Copyright 2017
by Lizbeth Selvig and Webster Publishing

Editing: Jennifer Van Vranken

Cover Design: Dana Lamothe—Designs by Dana

All rights reserved. No part of this book may be reproduced or transmitted in any form, including electronic or mechanical, without written permission from the publisher, except in the case of brief quotations embodied in critical articles or reviews.
This book is a work of fiction. Names, characters, places, and incidents are the product of the author's imagination or are used fictitiously. Any resemblance to actual events, locales, or persons, living or dead, is coincidental.
This book is licensed for your person enjoyment only. This book may not be re-sold or given away to other people. If you are reading this book and did not purchase it, or it was not purchased for your use only, then you should return it to the seller and purchase your own copy. Thank you for respecting the author's work.

ISBN: 978-0-9988564-3-8

Lizbeth Selvig

Dedication

To Dr. Jennifer Selvig, who is living her dream (and one of mine) and who handed me seeds for this plot back in the days of her own race track practice. I am so proud of you!

And to Walter Farley, The Black and Black Minx who, more years ago than I want to admit, made me want to write a race horse story.

Missing By a Heartbeat

Acknowledgements

To Jan Selvig—thank you. You know why every book is as much your accomplishment as mine. You are forever my only real romance hero.

This book would not exist without the incredible help of my smart and beautiful daughter, Jennifer Selvig Van Vranken. Not only is she a talented editor, she's an equine veterinarian who began her medical practice on the race track. She found me answers to weird questions about how to purposely harm horses, had up-to-date information on race track regulations and trainer ethics, and showed me that, in a sport that's highly controversial, there are a lot of good people who care deeply and want horseracing to be safe, humane, and fun for humans and animals.

In conjunction, thank you, too, to the Women in Equine Practice forum group who brainstormed and corroborated answers on some of those weird questions mentioned above!

I appreciate the tour guides and resources at Churchill Downs who made visiting the iconic track an adventure and led me to a wealth of information on their website *www.churchilldowns.com*. For more information on horseracing the following groups are invaluable:
The Jockey Club
The Daily Racing Form
Canterbury Park—Shakopee, Minnesota
American Association of Equine Practitioners

In the middle of this book is a fun little race day scene starring a mom and daughter who place their bets using silks colors as the determining factor. This is based on a true story shared by one of my favorite readers/friends. Thank you, Julie Oest for allowing me to use your experience! May our warped senses of humor always bind us—whether we admit to it in public or not.

The wonderful people who were the first to read the rough draft of this book are my heroes and have my undying love and gratitude: Ellen Lindseth, Tami Richie, Robin Selvig, Pete Feuk, and Jennifer Van Vranken—thank you for discovering the truck that couldn't exist, the illegal NG tube, the too-technical description, and the betting vet that would have made my honest heroine a criminal. Oh, and of course the "v"- versus "a"-fib, one of which will kill you.

Finally, but most importantly, to the two amazing women who created Chandler County—Patti Fiala and Stephany Tullis—thank you for inviting me into your world. The opportunity to write in and about this fun and sometimes crazy place is a joy.

Missing By a Heartbeat

CHANDLER COUNTY

CHAPTER
One

People who owned racehorses could be quirky as circus folk. Nobody knew that better than Tori Sterling, who worked with more horse owners than she could count. In the early morning October mist, she stood at the rail of America's most famous racetrack beside one such owner, Armand Mahler, a portly older man with a head as bald as a cue ball and a beard as cottony as Santa's. Behind her, the twin spires of Churchill Downs pointed heavenward into the gray clouds, while charming-but-superstitious Armand ignored the moisture beading on his head and dampening his "lucky" ensemble. She still got a kick from his ubiquitous plus fours—purple tweed paired with hideous blue, purple and yellow argyle stockings today. Once upon a time everyone had gawped openly at the eccentric owner with his thick German accent and English tweeds. But he'd worn his outlandish garb every visit to the track for the past three years without fail, and nobody so much as raised a brow anymore.

"Doc, he will be all right?" He begged Tori for the fifth time in twenty minutes. "Tell me again my groom is wrong. This isn't too soon."

Anxiety galloped through Tori's body as she awaited the appearance of Armand's semi-famous horse, but long practice allowed her to hide her anxiety. She patted his substantial upper arm and attempted to calm him for the fifth time in twenty minutes.

"Armand," she chided. "When did your groom go to medical school and not tell you? Sunspot's leg is healed as fully as it's ever going to heal. If you want to find out whether he's still got the speed and the will, you need to do this. Even if you waited another six months you'd worry."

"But he won't break down again?"

No vet could ever guarantee a horse wouldn't break down. Horses could get hurt in padded stalls. But Sunspot's fractured cannon bone was as healed as modern medicine and half a year of rest and rehab could make it. He'd been brought back slowly by a good trainer, and all that remained was to see if he could handle six furlongs at speed.

"I think he'll be fine," she said. "Remember. I said he *could* run. I never guaranteed he'd still *love* to run." She smiled, teasing her father's old friend despite the pounding of her own heart.

She'd staked her medical reputation on promising to bring this colt back from his career-threatening injury. Sunspot had been the talk of the racing world from day one, when Armand had randomly bred a young, little-raced mare he liked simply for her personality, to the great champion Curlin and produced a stunning blood bay colt. Curly Sunspot seemed to love running as much as he loved breathing. He also happened to be friendly as a clown. The insular world of thoroughbred racing had fallen in love with the baby who held so much personality and high potential. When after wins in two starts as a new two-year-old, Sunspot had developed a lateral condylar fracture to his cannon bone during a workout, everyone had honestly grieved, believing his hopes for a triple crown career were gone. The break in the large front leg bone was the kind that often spiraled down into the fetlock joint right above the hoof, and Sunspot's had done exactly that. Although such injuries were common, they were expensive to treat, and the chances of bringing even a talented horse back to racing condition were poor.

That's when Hugh Sterling had called in his daughter Victoria.

Now she stood watching for the result of her grand gamble, acting the part of a supremely confident, Kentucky equine veterinarian. Most of the time she was exactly that, but this morning all she could do was pray her bold treatment of Sunspot over the past half a year had been the right call.

"He'll run great."

Tori startled at the quiet voice behind her and spun from the rail.

"Dad? What are you doing here? I thought you and Mom were leaving today."

"Hey, kiddo. No way could I go before I found out what happened, once I heard your boy was testing out his new leg."

Her father had spent his career as a lawyer in Louisville, an ethical man dealing in all things horseracing—a world where boundaries between the legal, the ethical, and the questionable were sometimes blurred beyond easy recognition. A world he'd loved navigating.

Despite the satisfying career, he'd retired this past year at a young sixty-four so he and his artist-slash-interior decorator wife, Emma, Tori's Energizer Bunny of a mother, could start to travel the world. Retirement, however, had not remotely stopped Hugh Sterling from keeping his finger on the racing business's pulse.

She accepted his hug and kissed his cheek. He'd fully grayed years before, but his face remained broad and distinguished, his eyes perpetually youthful with their blue sparkle. His was the kind of face her girlfriends always told her was handsome. Now that she was in her thirties, she could admit it herself.

"Thanks for the support."

A buzz of voices from behind grabbed her attention. She looked to the glass doors behind her, leading from the clubhouse onto Millionaire's Row at the track's iconic finish line, where she and Armand stood. Her jaw went slack as one of Armand's grooms led what amounted to the population of a small country toward the rail. She groaned and glanced helplessly at her father before shooting Armand a scathing frown.

"What the heck, Armand? This was supposed to be a quiet, unannounced test."

Her client glanced over his shoulder and then shrugged. "Zey are not my people," he said simply, in his Americanized German accent. He turned back to the track.

Tori took a closer look. Sure enough, the new arrivals were journalists who'd smelled potential blood in the water: Will Starkey from the Chandler County Chronicles, Dick Foley from the Louisville Courier-Journal, and Brett Sandler from the Daily Racing Form. They were flanked by several trainers, three jockeys she recognized, and a handful of exercise riders.

"Hey, Hugh." Will said. "Hi, Tori."

Her father gave the young reporter a friendly shoulder clasp and shook his hand. "Will, my boy. What brings you here?"

Will adjusted the camera strap over his shoulder. "This is big news, Mr. Sterling. A Chandler County colt making a comeback?"

"You should have waited until you knew he was coming back." Tori scowled. "This is only one step in his rehab."

"But we've all adopted him, Doc. Everyone wants to see this turn out to be a success."

"C'mon, man, I thought you were my friend." Tori turned her saddest eyes on the guy, and he flushed.

"I am. You know I am."

"And if the colt doesn't perform? If he breaks down? You'll be right here to report on the humiliation."

"Breaks down!" Armand swung on her. "But you said—"

She hushed him once more with a soothing pat. "I'm ragging on the press, that's all," she said. "Sunspot is fine."

"You're not worried, then?" Will asked.

"I know better than to say a single thing to you, William. And you aren't to print one word of that last exchange."

"Sure thing, Tori." He winked, and she didn't believe his promise for a moment. He'd only been at the paper six months with his fresh journalism degree and big aspirations. Friendly and talented, he was, nonetheless, young, overzealous and a little too eager to find a story for his own good. His colleagues taunted him with the nickname Ringo—because of the Starkey, but she settled most of the time for calling him by his full name. It kept her in the role of a mother or big sister and, so far, had garnered her more respect.

She started to turn toward the track once more when her breath caught with unprofessional abruptness at another figure emerging unexpectedly from the clubhouse.

Winn Crosby?

She frowned as her heart both sank and skipped a beat at the same unpleasant moment. What was he doing here?

He sauntered toward the rail wearing no expression other than one brow quirked in a question, as if he'd come across the gathering by chance. But none of these men had chanced upon this spot. Ninety-nine percent of the time horses entered the track for morning workouts from the back side of the track and trainers and onlookers watched from the far rail. Tori and Armand along with his trainer Fred Gault had chosen to start from the front to see how Sunspot handled all the sights and places he'd see on a race day. He and Blue Moon, the companion horse who'd be pacing him, were the only horses arriving for their workout through the race day tunnel.

Winn Crosby had zero reason to be here.

Unless it was simply to decorate the place.

Which, she had to admit, he did to perfection in his scruffed beard, sapphire-eyed, six-foot-four, insouciant kind of way.

She blew her breath out in frustration. Since Winton Crosby's arrival in Louisville about six weeks ago, every college-aged woman working as a groom had turned moony-eyed with the longing to work for him. And every female horse owner, no matter how liberated, now joked about switching trainers. Tori considered herself unflappable, but this guy raised the heart rate of every All-American girl with a pulse, and there wasn't any use denying it. Fortunately, even though he'd been seen on race days sporting a newsboy cap to masculine perfection, he had a reputation of being aloof and silent—a man of few words and fewer smiles whose world consisted of horses and not much more.

Tori respected the horse part. However, she'd been born into a people-loving state of extroversion she couldn't alter, and it grated on her very soul to meet humans who couldn't be bothered to act friendly. Winn Crosby might bring out the worst in her pulse rate, but he didn't interest her beyond his role as window dressing.

"What's he doing here?" she whispered to her father.

"I assume watching his horse." Her dad shrugged.

"*His* horse?"

"He's got a gelding about to run his maiden race, and when Blue Moon came up sick, Winn offered to lend—"

"Blue Moon's sick?" Frustration balled in Tori's stomach. She was the dang veterinarian in charge of this spectacle today, and suddenly she knew absolutely nothing.

"A case of colic last night. He's all right this morning, but they didn't want to run him after that."

Tori fought a further rise of irritation. She only worked half time at the track, so she had no say-so over most of the horses or the procedures used on them. But even though she wasn't Blue Moon's vet, she knew his trainer well and should have gotten a heads up.

"You're telling me some horse of Crosby's is sprinting with Sunspot this morning?"

"That's my understanding." Her father peered at her. "Is that a problem?"

She took a calming breath and shored up her flagging professionalism. "I hope not. I chose Blue Moon because he's evenly matched with Sun, and they'd have paced each other well. I don't want Sun pushed; I want his rider to maintain his speed, and I want the horses to switch off leading and chasing. Fred had it all choreographed."

"I guess Armand's jockey, Derry, rides this horse of Crosby's, too, and thinks it'll be a good pairing. That's all I know."

She sneaked a look at Crosby, now standing against the rail about ten feet away. As if he sensed her gaze, he turned and met her eyes. She managed a cool nod before catching a flash of copper to her left. Sunspot danced onto the track.

An excited murmur rose from the assembled group, now five times larger than anything Tori had anticipated. Her stomach tied itself into a solid knot, and she wanted nothing more than to sink into a private cave where nobody could watch her and vice versa. The stunning colt's comeback was news enough that it had raised eyebrows and interest even within the veterinary community. Based on the extent of Sunspot's fracture, several much more experienced track vets had counseled Tori seriously not to raise hopes with a long rehab, and even if the surgery and healing looked like a success not to encourage Armand to let the colt race again. Save his high potential genes for breeding, they'd told her. Why chance his survival?

She'd staked her young reputation on defying their wisdom. Horses came back from this fairly common fracture of the cannon bone, but relatively few regained their pre-injury performance. Deep down, Tori did have confidence in her decision, but she knew if something went wrong, she'd never work on the track again.

Her father whistled softly through his teeth. "Lord he's a good-looking animal. You did a great thing bringing him back."

Tori nodded. "He's one of the rare ones. Looks *and* ability. That injury was severe, but I had a gut feeling.

He was trained perfectly; his bones are dense and strong. I think we made the right choice."

The hairs at her nape prickled and she glanced right. Winn Crosby studied her curiously.

"You're one of the vets?" His voice was deep and melodic as a jazz bass.

"Yes, *the* vet," she repeated and held out a hand. "Tori Sterling. I like to think I'm the only person who counts." She allowed a quick smile when he scowled over the perceived conceit. "It's not true, but my job would be easier if it were."

Narrowed eyes met hers. She swore he tried to mask a hint of amusement, but its flash vanished so quickly she couldn't prove it had been there. Straightening, she faced him fully and leaned hip first against the rail.

"I understand your horse is running with ours this morning. I wish I'd have known so we could have set some guidelines."

Crosby pointed, and Tori turned to watch a rangy, steel-gray gelding jig sideways onto the track. He moved with much less calm than Sunspot did, but was handled expertly by his rider.

"Fallon," Crosby said. "I have high hopes for him."

"But I hear he's never raced," she added.

He nodded. "If this goes well today, he'll run his maiden Saturday."

It was Tori's turn to narrow her eyes in irritation. "What do you think today is for? We aren't here to train a newbie you know—I need him to do a job."

"Dr. Sterling, I know how to rehab a horse." He spoke mildly. "I understand what you're attempting, and I also know what I'm looking to see in my gelding. If you stick to focusing on what you need, I'm satisfied I'll get what *I* need."

His words rolled over her like stones in a rock slide—hard, powerful, unyielding. Of all the arrogance... She put the brakes on her annoyance and took a slow breath.

"All right. Tell me about the horse."

"I promise you'll see it all once they start."

What the...? Did the man not know how to answer a question? She crossed her arms slowly across her chest.

"Fine. Who's riding him? A jock or one of your exercise boys?"

"Exercise *girls*. I believe you even know her. A tough little thing named Jocelyn Quinn. She told me she's ridden at your place."

"Little *thing*?" Tori glared at him.

"Oh c'mon. If you know her then you know 'tough thing' is almost a term of endearment. Any kind of feminine designation would sound demeaning in her case, whether it was girl, gal, tomboy... She's, what, eighteen? Barely speaks to anyone who isn't a horse. Attitude to spare. Admit it, she's a tough young thing."

He was right. Jocelyn Quinn was unique, with her nose stud, pierced brow, and tattoos. Although she'd managed to grab exercise rides for a couple of trainers, most didn't look past the cosmetics that were admittedly out of place at an august site like Churchill Downs.

"She's ridden my personal horses for me, and she catches a ride or two now and then. Because of her appearance, most trainers won't hire her. I'm surprised you did."

"I've only put her up a few times, but so far she's done exactly what I've told her. I couldn't give a flying crap about a nose ring as long as she treats the horse well."

Tori looked at him with slightly more interest—and appreciation. Track people were not generally known for being open-minded. They picked their teams warily and resisted change—in jockeys, grooms, veterinarians...

"Jocelyn is talented. She's intuitive." Tori nodded. "And she sticks like a burr on any horse I've seen her ride. Kudos to you for giving her a chance."

"Thank you."

"And so... since she obeys orders so well, what did you tell her do this time?"

He lifted a brow in mocking amusement. "Are you asking as a trainer or a veterinarian? I'll tailor my answer depending on which."

She took a step toward him, and he leaned back, surprised. "I'm *asking* because I'm an expert at what I do, and you're involved, through no choice of mine, in a course of treatment I've set out for one of my patients. So, let me ask again. What advice did you give your rider in regards to pacing Sunspot?"

Once more his brows arched. But although he towered over her five-foot-five frame, and his tropical sea blue eyes held hers in a seeming battle of wills, she didn't flinch. Her arms remained defiantly crossed. At last he allowed a short chuckle and shook his head.

"You're kind of a tough thing, too. But I guess I'd heard that. I told her to hold her horse at Sunspot's flank for a quarter, then let him out and see if she can catch your boy. If she can, let them battle for an eighth and then pull him back. No real racing. Just let us know what the horse tells her he wants. I talked to Fred, so I know Derry has approximately the same instructions."

Embarrassment rose in her chest and burned there for a long moment. She'd misjudged him. Instead of being no more than an arrogant, self-centered trainer interested in his own cause, he'd described the perfect training scenario. This exercise was simply to see how willing Sunspot was to fight for his lead, not to see how fast he could go. Winn Crosby had claimed he understood, and it seemed he did.

"Is that acceptable, Dr. Sterling?" he asked. "Or is your jockey the one who's going to screw up my horse?"

Had she not been guilty of judging him without cause she might have let his tone boil her blood again, but she could hardly be angry that he'd called her on her own game.

"Touché," she said. "Sorry. It sounds like everything's under control."

"I try to do my research."

He fixed his attention on the track and Tori did, too, forgetting her mild embarrassment when she saw Armand. He stood beside her, coiled tight as a cowboy's lariat ready to fly and rope his horse back to safely. Her heart went out to the eccentric owner. He was a little odd, a goofy dresser, but a caring man. He wanted the best for his animals and saw that they got it. That was more than could be said for many racing families.

"Relax," she whispered. "Fred's got this. Don't give yourself a heart attack."

He didn't reply, just gripped the railing until his knuckles shone white through his thick fingers.

Fallon caught up with Sunspot right before the famous finish line, and Fred Gault, standing across the track on inside rail, pushed back his baseball cap to salute Derry O'Keefe, the jockey tasked with Sun's ride. Derry returned it and turned to Jocelyn, riding on his right. From this vantage point, Tori caught the firm set of the girl's mouth, the glint of a gem in her right nostril, and a tight, barely imperceptible nod.

A rush of warm appreciation rolled through her at Jocelyn's presence. She liked the girl and knew she wore the tough persona for the public but had a soft and gentle touch for the horses. Tori truly was glad Winn had chosen the girl. Not only did she deserve the ride, she would, indeed, do exactly as instructed and care about both horses.

Derry and Jocelyn urged the horses into a canter and then an easy gallop, with instructions to start the workout at the first quarter pole. They reached the marker together and swept off as one. Derry went immediately into the lead, and Jocelyn kept Fallon's nose on Sunspot's flank. Lifting binoculars, as did Armand and Crosby, Tori switched her focus from the riders to Sunspot's gait. The colt moved like liquid copper, smooth, powerful, measured. Every hoof beat met the dirt with sure and equal cadence. Tori concentrated, trying not to search for trouble but trying equally not to ignore any warning signs that something was going wrong.

The gallop remained steady, fluid, eager. Her heart rate evened out, though it didn't slow.

"He looks good, right?" Armand's question sounded as if someone had pinched it from his throat.

"He looks wonderful," she agreed.

"I'd heard he was a mover, but I admit he's impressive."

Crosby's quiet comment surprised her, but she didn't look away from the horses. "I got a lot of criticism for this—trying to bring him back," she replied. "Now you can see why I thought it was worth the trouble."

"Well, here comes the test," Crosby said.

Tori squeezed the barrels of her binoculars tighter, watching as Jocelyn urged Fallon to move up. The leggy horse responded immediately and unquestioning, like a perfectly tuned performance car. He pulled alongside Sunspot until they were head to head. For one instant Tori thought Sun faltered, but almost immediately knew she'd imagined the missteps. The big, brown-red horse gave a surge that once again put him a neck ahead. Armand's cheer rang across the plaza, followed by a swell of excited chatter from the onlookers.

The pair passed their halfway point looking calm and smooth. When they reached the half-mile mark, Derry slowed Sunspot so Fallon could move ahead. The gray took his lead eagerly and Tori happily watched Derry fight to hold Sun behind. The big horse wanted to run.

She gave Armand a little bump with her elbow. "Check out your boy." She grinned behind her glasses.

Disaster came without warning.

"What the hell?" Winn called as Derry, jerking like a marionette cut from its strings, flew hard to Sunspot's right shoulder, then flopped back nearly horizontal onto the colt's thrusting hindquarters.

Cries rang from every onlooker as the jockey fought to stay aboard. Tori's voice deserted her. All she could do was stare, first in shock and then, as Derry balanced in the stirrups without hitting the dirt, in awful alarm as Sunspot gathered speed and headed down the home stretch at full throttle.

"What happened? What's happening?" Armand, panic-stricken beside her, could barely hold his binoculars up.

"This is not good," Winn said. "That horse is out of control."

There was not a thing anyone could do as the horses flew off the final turn where they should have been jogging out instead of racing. Derry clearly had no control over Sunspot and Jocelyn lay low over Fallon's withers keeping up. The two horses approached the finish line, Sunspot flying like a possessed bat. Jocelyn was the only one who looked remotely in control, methodically inching Fallon closer and closer to Sunspot's right side, pushing him toward the rail and forcing him to yield until she could slip in front and slow both horses.

A full quarter mile past the finish, both horses finally came to a stop. Split seconds later Tori ducked the fence and sprinted through the three-inch deep dirt. Ahead of her, almost comically, Fred Gault did the same, puffing out "shit, shit, shit" with each step. Then silently, with a graceful lope, Winn was beside her, effortless as a jungle cat.

"Can't wait to hear the excuse for this," he said, his features grim.

"Derry is a phenomenal jock." Tori ignored the unprofessional thrill she got from Winn's presence. "He wouldn't suddenly lose control of his horse. Something happened."

They reached the pair of riders coming back toward them. Jocelyn had hold of Sunspot's rein, ponying him along. Pale splotches rode high on her cheeks, and her eyes, round as half dollars, met first Tori's and then Winn's questioning gazes. Derry hunkered in his saddle, muttering angrily in a thick, incomprehensible Scottish burr. Both horses blew like miniature steam engines, snorting and jigging.

"Everyone okay?" Winn's voice stayed impressively calm, and both riders nodded. "Good. Then maybe you wanna tell us what that was about?"

Derry lifted his right hand. With tight, furious words he spit out an expletive and dangled a long string of white leather with a rubber grip.

"Somebody cut the bloody rein."

CHAPTER Two

WHAT HAD BOILED deep in Winn's gut as unadulterated anger turned to confusion and grudging admiration as Tori Sterling launched herself into working mode. She'd taken a mere five seconds for stupefaction when Derry had presented her with the broken rein. After that she'd merely handed it to Gault, Armand's trainer, and started firing off staccato orders.

"Jump off, Derry. Get that saddle off, too. Don't worry about it, dump it right here. Take him for a walk away from me; let me see how he's moving. Fred tell me if you see anything."

Once the colt had been stripped of saddle and pad, Tori fashioned the remaining rein into a lead rope and handed it to Derry. Sunspot walked away, still blowing and dancing slightly. Winn was about to comment about little you could see at the walk when she turned to him.

"You can tell more at the trot, but he needs to move out calmly. Damn, that was the last thing I wanted."

His heart tripped a little at the war of misery, worry, and anger playing across her features. This was a woman whose reputation was on the line, but all she focused on was the horse. He'd come to watch today, of course, because Fallon was on the track, but he'd also been enormously curious about Dr. Victoria Sterling. Her reputation matched her name—sterling despite the fact that she was young, a woman, and ethical as the day was long. The term "ethical" had a rather elastic meaning in the world of racing. Ninety percent of owners, trainers, and vets cared deeply about their animals, but the ten percent left would push any boundary to make money. Even some of the most reputable looked for and took any opportunity to legally—or not—stretch the rules.

But Tori Sterling no longer had a full time track practice because her ethics weren't even bouncy. She knew the rules about drugs, training, and racing inside out, and she didn't have any problem saying no to anyone. Her unwillingness to do a trainer's bidding if she didn't find the request legal had lost her many clients. Racing was a business, after all, and they needed to think about their bottom line. The owners who had retained her, however, adored her.

The miracle she'd apparently worked with Sunspot was only going to enhance her reputation—if this incident hadn't jeopardized his recovery. The question was whether this was truly intentional or just an accident.

Winn's mind flitted from thought to thought like a hawk trying to find a morsel worth pouncing on. Tori's focus shamed him—she had lasered in on the horse and his needs without letting herself waffle through a million other thoughts, which was precisely what he should be doing with Fallon. But Jocelyn had taken the gray down the track without being told, and after a dozen trot steps, Winn had seen Fallon was perfectly sound.

He wanted a look at that rein, but Fred Gault held it gathered in his hands, and he was head to head with Tori. If it had been purposely cut...Winn shook his head. It made no sense. He couldn't imagine a purpose for such a stunt. Derry's superb balance and his years of experience had kept him in the saddle. A younger jock could have been seriously injured.

Could someone be *after* Derry? Or Sunspot?

The way events had played out, the bay colt had blown through his training regimen. If it turned out he'd been reinjured—that could have been the plan. But how could anyone have known exactly what would happen? And the rein had started out strong enough to hold the horse for three and a half furlongs. No plot could have accounted for the exact moment it would break.

"He looks okay." Tori's words broke through his musings and he looked up.

Sunspot trotted toward them, calmer now beside Derry. The jockey, all five-foot-two of him, had calmed as well. He jogged beside the colt with the ground-covering strides and muscular arms straining against the T-shirt sleeves poking out from beneath his protective vest.

Just behind came Armand Mahler, red-faced and portly, winded after his quarter-mile bustle from the start line.

"The horse. Is he well? Is he injured?" he called.

To Winn's surprise, Tori caught his eyes and gave a slight eye roll as she smiled, and attraction bowled him over in a surprise attack. She was extremely pretty in the sharpening morning light, her dark hair drawn back in a thick, wavy pony tail, her wide cheek-boned face, windswept and fresh as if she spent her days in sunshine and cool breezes.

"It's okay, Armand," she said, without betraying a note of impatience. "I think he's fine. We'll get him back to the barn and cold hose the leg. Then I'll poultice and wrap him."

"You said you didn't vant him to run that fast." The man's clipped accent rushed out, frenzied and short of accusatory. "The timer said they ran the first quarter in forty-five and a fifth. That's good enough to be Derby speed."

"I know," Tori said. "There was an accident with the tack. You saw how Derry nearly lost his seat. We'll figure that part out. Meanwhile, I think Sun did fine. The good news is, he definitely still has the will to race."

Armand brightened immediately.

"He was a 'tremendous machine,' wasn't he?"

The reference to Secretariat wasn't missed by anyone. A bold statement that would have been arrogant had it not been Armand.

"He ran well," Tori agreed. She looked at Winn. "How's your horse?"

"He's jogging back." Winn had kept the horse in his side vision. "He looks fine. He ran faster than I'd have liked three days before a race, but he kept up with your boy. Maybe we'll have a rivalry on our hands."

"He's got a nice stride—a surprise after watching him walk."

"He's kind of like a giraffe that turns into a horse, isn't he?" Winn smiled at her smile. "I don't know why I like him, but I have a gut feeling."

"Gut feeling is important. I'd say your gut steered you right with that 'tough little thing' on your horse's back. She saved our bacon today."

He nodded. He had every intention of praising the girl, but he knew she was nervous about facing him. Usually quiet and slightly disinterested, she hadn't checked with him before jogging Fallon off to cool him. Winn assumed she feared she'd broken the rules he'd set out by doing her own thing, but in this case her instincts had been spot on.

"She kept it together in a potentially bad situation," Tori added. "You know, she has trouble finding rides. How did you happen to take her on?"

The same way his entire stable was filled with teens who didn't look or act remotely like they belonged on a racetrack. But he could never quite explain that.

"I identified with her." He shrugged. "We come from the same mothership."

"Oookay. I don't remotely understand that, but I accept that you're sincere."

Her smile brightened the whole cloud hovering over their group, and he marveled at her persistent calm.

"Do you have to try to be this *cheerful* in the face of potential disaster?" He couldn't quite make himself smile back, but the tension twisting across his shoulders eased.

"Yes. Am I making it look easy?"

"Way *too* easy. Are you worried about this?"

"Uh, gee…would you think me rude if I told you that was a ridiculous question?" She stared straight into his eyes, and once again heat rippled through him.

"Of course not," he admitted, rubbing the back of his neck in discomfort as well as frustration. "I'm concerned, that's all. I've never dealt with anything like this. If," he looked to Derry, "there really was somebody tampering with equipment."

Derry overheard, and with fierce impatience grabbed the white rein from Fred. He thrust it toward Winn.

"Have a wee look at that will ye, and tell me you think it snapped of its own desire."

Winn took the leather, and Tori leaned against him to peer around his shoulder. She smelled like track dust and warm horse, with a sweet hint of rose underlying both. Heat rose through his body, his brain fogged, and for a moment the seriousness of the situation dulled even though what he held in his hands pointed directly to foul play.

He all but jumped a step away from her to clear his head. He didn't do quick attractions and foggy brains. Neither was conducive to keeping horses safe and in peak condition. This was a grim case in point. Right now it was imperative to stay sharp, and big, brown doe-eyes and the scent of roses could play no part.

"Check this out." He ran his forefinger along the broken edge of the rein. "It was cut in the middle of the rein, right where the leather meets the rubber grip. It didn't simply tear from being worn out, somebody actually wanted the horse to get going and have the rein break. I don't know why or how someone could guarantee the thing would give way when they wanted it to."

"Maybe they didn't care when, they just wanted it to snap while Sun was working," Tori said.

"But that would endanger Derry more than the horse."

"Unless they thought Sun would stumble or knew he could injure himself by running full out." All of a sudden, Tori's cheeks blanched to the color of Churchill Downs' spires, as if the situation's severity had only now hit home. "Oh, God, someone actually meant for this to happen."

"It looks that way on the surface."

Her jaw worked up and down twice, like a slow ventriloquist's puppet, but nothing came out. For the first time in the twenty minutes he'd known her she looked lost. Winn wrapped his fingers gently around her upper arm.

"Doc, c'mon. Everyone's all right. We'll get to the bottom of this."

She blinked once and the color rose back into her cheeks as quickly as it had drained.

"Yeah." She nodded, and her smile returned but it was grim. "Oh yeah, you better believe we will."

Her moment of vulnerability passed. Gazing around the small group of people she gathered their attention with a low, commanding tone.

"The press is going to be all over us wanting to know what happened. I'm not saying we don't treat this like the serious episode it is, but for the moment let's all go with the story that it's an accident. The rein broke. Pure and simple. Armand? You can do that? No extrapolating on your concern until we do a little investigating back at the barn, yes?"

The owner looked mildly insulted. "Of course. I will be the soul of discretion."

"Good." She wrapped her arms around one of his sizeable biceps and hugged him, which wiped the insulted pout from his face.

"Fred, let's get the horse back and start the cold hosing. Derry? Have I told you yet what a phenomenal job of riding you did?"

"Amen to that," Fred added. "Glad you and the horse are okay."

Derry's face reflected both pride and relief. "Ta," he said. "Scared the bejasus out of me I won't lie. Wasn't a blessed thing I could do about it, but once I knew I was stickin' on, I tried talkin' to our fella, tellin' him not to panic. He wouldn't stop racin', but I don't think he was the least bit scared. He's a brave one, our Sun."

Tori gave him a hearty pat on his coppery neck. "I think he is. And strong. If he's still sound in twenty-four hours, I think we can declare the rehab a full success."

"Ahhh, here she is. The girl of the hour," Derry said, looking up as Jocelyn and Fallon reached them.

The girl held her lanky gelding to a walk, and the colt snorted in excitement when he touched his muzzle to Sunspot's flank. When the horses stood side-by-side, Derry held out his hand.

"Damn fine riding, young lady. You helped stop this laddie a good half a mile before he'd have run out of steam enough to listen to me."

The teen shrugged. "Fallon's a nice horse. Smart. He did what I asked and it all worked out. Some other horses wouldn't have been that calm about it."

Winn stroked Fallon's neck, too, and then offered his hand to Jocelyn just as Derry had. "I picked the right jock for the job today."

"Thanks."

He'd never seen her smile in the three times she'd worked for him. Now a tiny uptick in the corners of her mouth shaved two years off her appearance. The illusion caused a slight pang of concern. She was so young at eighteen. Was he putting kids like this at risk? Everyone who worked for him was between eighteen and twenty-four. And yet, he'd ridden at this age, and he'd been around horses since age fourteen.

He shook his head. Jocelyn clearly knew what she was doing. He had to trust that—she had her exercise rider's card after all.

He caught Tori's eye and she surprised him with a wide smile of her own and a thumbs up. "I'm impressed," she said.

Winn frowned. The affirmation was great, but—"Impressed?"

She didn't answer. Instead she groaned and pointed. "Great."

A kid, holding a camera and wearing a weird black cap, like a wool baseball hat with a leather brim, jogged toward them. He ran awkwardly in the furrowed dirt, in forced slow motion—like Baywatch's most inept lifeguard.

"How'd he get through the gate? Onlookers aren't allowed on the track." Winn added a scowl to the frown he already wore.

"It's Will Starkey from the Chronicles. They call him Ringo. Get it? Knowing him, he found a little hole the guards didn't see. He's actually a decent writer, but the kid is a little like an adorable puppy that won't stop chewing on what he isn't supposed to have."

"Exactly the kind of person we don't need."

"Exactly," she repeated.

"Tori!" Will called.

"Stop right there," she called back. "Stop running or you'll rile up the horses. You shouldn't be here. You know that."

"Aw, something's going on. You can't hide whatever is going on out here, so why not give someone you trust the story?"

He slowed as commanded but didn't stop.

"There's no story," she said, much more calmly than Winn would have. "A piece of equipment broke, and it spooked the horses. Fortunately, we have two great riders up so all's well. We're just checking to make sure there are no horse injuries."

For a moment Ringo-from-the-Chronicle's face fell in disappointment. Then some eager-beaver reporter genes kicked in.

"*Are* there any injuries? Is Sunspot all right? Can you comment on his Derby chances next May, Dr. Sterling?"

Winn stood back in amusement as Tori shook her head and placed a hand on the young man's shoulder as if he were a student.

"William, you know you'll be the first to know when I have a scoop for you. For now, here's your quote. Sunspot's owner Armand Mahler is pleased with his horse's recuperation. Dr. Victoria Sterling echoed the opinion saying so far things are progressing as hoped."

"Aw, Doc. That's no scoop."

"I said I had a quote, not a scoop."

"He has the heart of a champion!" Armand fisted a hand against his own chest. "I think he will—" Tori's hand shot up, fingers spread wide to stop him from saying more.

"Keep a little mystery for the future, Armand. William, you're to write exactly what I said and no more." She delivered her warning with a friendly but firm smile. "You know I'll check."

The young reporter eyed her with frustration and then shrugged. "Okay, Doc. But I'll keep checking, too. You know I'll hound you until you give me info."

"Oh boy, I sure do."

Tori shot Winn a smile, but her brown eyes carried dull bronze glints of exasperation. Between the over-eager reporter and the ebullient owner, she had her hands as full as a ring master's.

"Let's get everyone back to the barn." Winn stopped the kid's next question before it could leave his opening mouth. "We have too many people on the track. Dr. Sterling needs to check her horse and I definitely want to check mine."

"Is your horse a Derby prospect as well?" Ringo Reporter asked.

"No comment." Winn stabbed him with a glare of unequivocal firmness. "If there's anything more to tell the press, you'll be the first to know. As Dr. Sterling said."

At that Will Starkey backed off, finally intimidated. He was inexperienced and still malleable, Winn thought with some amusement, but he clearly had the makings of a tough and savvy journalist over a little time.

When their odd entourage reached the track gates, a moment of mild chaos engulfed them as the spectators barraged them with questions. Winn was grateful for Tori's edict that they all refer to the incident as an accident. It made quick responses possible and reactions more sympathetic. It also cleared their way faster. A few of the older school track folk might shake their heads at the neglect implied by having equipment break—but they were the minority, and they'd talk behind closed stall doors. Shit happened. And shit happened in a hundred forms at a racetrack. He couldn't worry about gossip—not here where he was probably the main source of it at the moment.

He stole a glance at Jocelyn and thought about Tori's amazement that he'd hired the girl. She led Fallon confidently and paid no attention to the trainers and riders who watched. A strand of blue-dyed blonde hair hung from beneath her unbuckled helmet. Her gray, short-sleeved T-shirt bore a black and white shadow picture of a girl riding a horse, which was amazingly positive compared to the skulls she usually favored. From beneath one sleeve curled a tattoo of a horse's tail which, according to his other tattooed employee, Renee, was attached to a black stallion that galloped across the whole of her back.

Renee herself was the queen of tattoos with two sleeves and a full back tat. Oddly enough the two men working for Winn had no ink, but they had their own questionable bits of wardrobe, enough so Winn got far more commentary and unwanted advice on the kind of help he hired than he wanted. The bottom line was, helping troubled kids who looked different wasn't a well-thought-of calling for a horse trainer, but he didn't give a rat's ass. The Jocelyns of the world with their hidden talents needed a place to belong and be acknowledged.

Yeah, he scoffed to himself, he'd love to be a mouse in the corner when the long-time trainers were discussing Winn-the-new-guy over lunch.

"Armand's stalls are on the opposite corner of the backside from yours." Tori's voice tore him away from his thoughts. "Thanks for everything, Winn. I'm sorry we hadn't had a chance to meet before now."

"Hey, your reputation preceded you," he said. "I've been looking forward to meeting the brilliant Victoria Sterling."

"Most people would not say brilliant." She smiled. "Stubborn. Opinionated. Too big for her inexperienced britches."

He hid his smile. He'd definitely heard all the epithets, but he wasn't going to tell her so. Not if he wanted to see more of those luminous brown eyes—and watching her the past half hour had convinced him he definitely did. It wasn't because she was pretty, however, and pretty was an understatement, it was that her clear sense of fair play, of calm expertise, of problem solving was far more attractive than her eyes and face.

"People who are good at what they do are often victims of other peoples' jealousy," he said. "Congrats on bringing Sunspot back."

"Don't say that out loud or Armand will have him racing this weekend. His first race is in three weeks. That's soon enough."

"Believe me, I know better than to comment on someone else's horse. It's a hard lesson to learn."

She half-smiled. "Yeah? Well, for a vet, too. Guess we both need big backpacks to carry our secrets in."

That was another thing he'd decided in the past few minutes. He needed a new vet, and there was little doubt in his mind she'd be an asset to his team. She was engaging—not the cool bird he'd been led to believe he'd find when he met her. And she was smart—not the inexperienced "bleeding heart" a few of his fellow trainers had claimed.

Then again, he'd learned years ago that the backside of a track was a weird, cutthroat place to live and work. Jocelyn continued on toward the stalls with Fallon.

Winn turned back to Tori. "Hey?"

"Yes?" she asked.

"What was the thumbs up for back on the track?"

She scowled a moment, thinking, then waved her hand with a light scoff. "Oh, nothing. I was impressed when you shook Jocelyn's hand like an employee you respect, that's all. I was waiting for you to pat her on the thigh or call her a good girl."

"Ah. Well, that would be another lesson learned back when I was an unreformed chauvinist. You hire someone, you treat them like they matter."

She assessed him, taking him in the way he would a new horse. For some reason he didn't mind.

"Good answer, Mr. Crosby. I don't know if you're trying to impress me, but I like it. You aren't living up to your reputation."

"That bad, huh?" He offered a wry smile.

"You're still new around here. An inaccurate reputation is part of the hazing." She smiled without apology and, once again, he found her straightforward manner refreshing.

"One more thing." He hesitated a moment but then plunged ahead. "Would you have time to stop by my barn sometime before you leave? I'd like to talk about some vet work."

"Vet work, for you? You're using Kevin Marsh. I'm not into stealing clients."

"I promise you, Kevin would gladly hand me over. I get on with him fine, but there are a few places where we butt heads. If you think you might be interested, name a convenient time."

She nodded, another smile lifting her lips. "Sure, okay. I've got about an hour's worth of work. Can I swing by after that?"

"I'll look forward to it."

"See you then."

He watched her stride off with purposeful confidence after Sunspot, who was already halfway down the aisle between white barn shed rows. Twenty feet away, an older man Winn didn't recognize joined her. He gave her an affectionate hug and continued on with her. Another owner? None of his business. Regardless, in a strange way it felt as if he'd made his first friend. The notion was ridiculous since he literally knew nothing about her beyond hearsay and what he'd seen this morning. But the conviction that he needed to persuade her into becoming Crosby Racing's veterinarian grew stronger the farther away she got.

At last he stopped watching her and made his way to the neatly raked dirt path in front his row of ten stalls. Fallon stood with Jocelyn while Leo Richards removed the saddle and cloth. In a quiet voice she couldn't quite keep emotionless, the usually taciturn Jocelyn was relating the broken rein story. Leo, a wiry, twenty-year-old with mixed-race heritage caught Winn's eye with a troubled frown.

"It's all fine." Winn gave his arm a pat. "Horses and riders are safe. Jocelyn did a heckuva job piloting Fallon and slowing down the other horse."

"Other horse?" Leo nearly squeaked with indignation. "Fallon raced against Curly Sunspot. That's not just some 'other horse.'"

The boy had gained Winn's affection by being as big a racing nerd as Winn was himself. Too tall to be a jockey, Leo had never developed the riding skill Winn had, but he was magic on the ground. Horses responded to him like bees to sugar water. They didn't care about his dreadlocks, worn long and shaggy to his collar. Nor did they care that he was serving out his last eight months of parole after four years in prison for criminal possession.

"You're right," he said. "He's quite an animal."

"And here I stayed missing it all." Leo groused, but it was over an almost imperceptible smile. He preferred being the guardian of the herd in the barn. He wasn't any more of a people person than Jocelyn was.

"No need to worry," she said. "No doubt somebody caught it on a phone camera. Check YouTube in about fifteen minutes."

Sadly, Winn thought that was likely true.

They went through the methodical routine of hosing down Fallon's legs, chest and the powerful muscles in his flanks that had powered him around the track in a time that had astounded.

By the time Fallon was cooled down, his legs wrapped, and he munched hay in his stall, another horse was ready for its workout, and Winn had lost himself in the continuous flow of tasks. When the soft "Hey, Winn Crosby" pulled him from his concentration, he couldn't believe an hour had passed. Glancing at his watch he scowled. It hadn't been an hour, but barely forty-five minutes.

"Dr. Sterling." He held up his hand, indicating Jocelyn should wait to mount the horse she was ready to take out.

"Tori," she said. "Please." But rather than smile in invitation, her mouth trembled very slightly in consternation. She was not here for the meeting he'd requested; that much was clear.

Then he noticed the two men flanking her, one wearing a white Churchill Downs polo shirt, the other the navy blue shirt and accompanying badge of a Louisville police officer. Winn tamped down the threat his heart made to start galloping in his chest.

"All right, then. Tori." He inclined his head. "What's going on?"

"Mr. Crosby?" The officer addressed him. "I'm Officer Hogan. There've been several incidents in the stables of Armand Mahler. We'd like to ask you a few questions."

With a sinking stomach Winn sighed and pressed the fingers of his left hand hard into the creases above his nose. Well, shit, he thought. So it starts.

CHAPTER Three

TORI'S STOMACH CHURNED with regret as the police officer stepped toward Winn and motioned to the track steward that he could stay back. Looking like a man with five migraines, Winn stopped rubbing his forehead and glanced behind him to where two young people stood, mouths slightly agog. Tori didn't miss his nod of reassurance to them and to Jocelyn, who stood beside a tacked-up chestnut gelding.

Then Winn looked Tori's way, and a deep, resentful question swam clearly in his eyes.

"I'm really sorry," she said, before the officer could speak again. "Armand found several more pieces of tack vandalized. He had to inform the steward, and he called the police."

"There was no option," the man beside her said. "We can't let an act of destruction go uninvestigated. It isn't fair to the other owners."

"I get that," Winn said. "But I don't get what it has to do with me or why you're here."

"We're simply ruling out anything we possibly can at this point," Officer Hogan said.

"What, precisely, needs ruling out?" Winn's voice hardened.

"I understand a saddle that was tampered with nearly caused a serious accident on the track earlier this morning. I also understand you had a horse that was a last-minute substitution to breeze with Mr. Mahler's."

"Yes. And...?" Winn crossed his arms, tense and anticipatory.

"May I ask what was at stake for you in this workout?"

"At stake? Seriously?" Winn's face registered disbelief and then steely anger. "I was *there* to determine my horse's readiness to race this weekend and to assist Mr. Mahler whose horse is healing from an injury. I'm sure Dr. Sterling explained that to you."

Again his glare cut to her, but she withstood his ire. His frustration at the veiled accusations was understandable.

"What about your employees? Where were they while this workout was happening?"

The officer stayed cool and relentless—like a Will Starkey with years more experience. Winn squared his stance.

"Here. In my shed row with nine other horses to care for."

"You have several employees with criminal records, is that right?"

"I don't keep that a secret. I also trust them implicitly."

"That's a fairly bold statement," Officer Hogan said mildly, but Tori heard the first traces of condescension.

To her surprise, Winn's blue eyes cleared despite the insinuation that his employees were one step from being suspects. Her pulse fluttered slightly when he sighed and sent another look of reassurance over his shoulder. The man did care about these teens. And he'd hired Jocelyn. That spoke volumes to Tori.

"My kids are hand chosen and thoroughly evaluated for their desire and readiness to be here," Winn said. "They know what I expect and I expect this to be a place where they get a clean start."

"How many are working this morning?"

"Two plus my exercise rider. Look, Officer, I resent what you're implying. I will vouch for these kids."

Tori took a longer look at the two grooms standing ten steps behind Winn. Both of them fought to keep their features composed and were having a far more difficult time of it than Winn.

"I'm not implying anything, Mr. Crosby. But you have to understand that when something happens and there are convicted thieves in the vicinity, we need to check it out."

"They are not thieves. They're young people who've done their time and deserve a chance to get away from the circumstances and environments that sent them to prison or to juvie in the first place. I don't deny their pasts, and they don't either. But they own their futures, and they're all crack stable hands."

He offered his first smile and confusion settled over Tori. In a matter of moments Winn had gone from furious to calm although the police questioning had grown ever more personal. She didn't understand, but she had to admire.

The steward finally stepped forward and, almost regretfully, offered his hand.

"Rob," Winn said and shook it.

"I'm sorry about this," the steward said, "but there are also a couple of items missing from Mr. Mahler's operation. Would you have any objection to us taking a look in your tack area?"

"Aw, come on!" One of Winn's grooms, the boy, finally spoke. "Why don't you come right out and accuse us of stealing?"

"Leo, hang on." Winn held his hand out behind him, palm facing the teen. "It's all right."

"It sure as hell isn't," Leo retorted.

"I have a lot of objections to having you look," Winn said, his voice back to being tight and even. Still, he remained calm. "But I won't stop you. Leo? Renee? Jocelyn? I assume you won't stop them either? Other than the disrespect there's no reason to object, right?"

All three shuffled in place, clearly angry, but they stood aside as the steward and the policeman let themselves be ushered to the tack room. That left Tori with the three kids, the horse, and a thick cloud of distrust and resentment.

"Hi," she said, finally. "I'm Tori Sterling. I'm so sorry about this. It wasn't my idea."

"Then why are you here with them?" The girl, Renee, stared her down. Tori gazed back, unflinching.

"They more or less required me to come. I could confirm details of this morning and I wasn't as angry as my client."

"Who are you working for?"

"Armand Mahler."

"But only as the vet for Sunspot." Jocelyn spoke up from her spot beside the chestnut gelding. "Doc's all right. I've exercised her horses when she's away from home. She's one of the good guys."

"You?" Renee asked before Tori could thank her young defender. Renee's eyes widened, this time in surprise rather than anger. "You're *that* vet?"

"Well, I'll only admit it if 'that vet' is not someone you want to tie behind the harrow and drag the track with." Tori raised her brows and got a smile in return.

"No!" Renee shook her head, her voice animated, her attitude a hundred and eighty degrees flipped. "You're famous around here. Sunspot is famous around here."

"He is?"

"Winn talks about him all the time. He was a fan of Curlin, Sunspot's sire. He always talked about having enough money to breed his own Curlin' colt. He was real happy last spring when we got in here for the fall season. He wanted to check Sunspot out, but then he got injured and everyone was so bummed."

Stunned by the story, Tori stared a moment before shaking the fog of surprise from her brain.

"Is that right? He never said a word about that." Not that they'd had any kind of lengthy conversation about anything, she thought. "Makes it a small world, doesn't it?"

"Yeah. And then he happened to be talking with Derry when he heard the colt who was supposed to run against Sunspot this morning was sick. He jumped at the chance to substitute Fallon. You should have seen him. You'da thought he was getting to watch Secretariat run."

Renee was tattooed and spikey-haired, with all the potential to be a surly young woman, but instead she contained all the bubbly personality Jocelyn didn't, and her spill of information amused Tori more than she'd admit. She couldn't picture the taciturn and collected Winn Crosby, with his reputation of aloof coolness, excited. Not after the stoic way he'd acted all morning or now with the police and steward. If she let herself, she could be annoyed that he knew so much about her and Sunspot and hadn't said word one—acting instead like she and the horse were no big deal.

On the other hand, she didn't like ostentatious or sycophantic people. Winn had proven he wasn't out to be some newbie fanboy complimenting and sucking up to make big name friends at Churchill Downs. She decided he got a point for discretion.

"Well that's all good information to know," she said, and put her hand out to the girl who'd offered so much insight. "Renee, you said?"

"Renee Hanley." She shook with enthusiasm. "And this is Leo Richards. And Jocelyn. She's kind of new, but I guess you know her?"

Tori shook Leo's hand. He smiled but remained the only one who hadn't spoken. Then she passed them and made her way to Jocelyn's side.

"Hey," she said.

"Hey, Dr. Sterling."

"Thanks for what you said. I appreciate the ice breaker. Not to mention the nice words."

Jocelyn shrugged and allowed the tiniest of smiles. "You've done the same for me. I wouldn't be riding if you didn't keep telling everyone I can handle it."

"You proved that today, didn't you?" Tori set one hand on the chestnut colt's neck. "Who's this handsome guy?"

"Red River Ale." Jocelyn shook her head. "Dumbest name ever."

"We call him Tipsy." Leo spoke for the first time. "He's a really friendly horse, but we hate cleaning his stall because he's such a pig. Like he's had too much ale every night."

Tori laughed. "I know that kind of horse well. I have two I wish could be trained to clean their own dang stalls. But tell me, are you two the only grooms? Do you ride as well?"

"We ride but not racehorses," Renee said. "I love horses, but going that fast scares me to death."

"The same," Leo said. "Sawyer and Mallory are the other two grooms. Sawyer can exercise, but only slow work-outs. We leave all the dangerous stuff to Jocelyn now."

"They're mean to new guys," Jocelyn said quietly.

"We warned you," Leo said with a grin, and behind it Tori saw a gleam of interest masquerading as joking.

"How's Winn Crosby to work for?" she asked.

There wasn't a moment's hesitation before all three kids spoke as one.

"Awesome."

"He's great."

"He's been really nice."

If their faces hadn't been so earnest, Tori would have thought it a rehearsed answer.

"That good, huh?" she asked.

"He doesn't just talk about kids like us needing a chance, he really gives us one. You heard him stand up for us," Renee said. "Not that he isn't tough. We don't get to screw around much. But he's fair."

"He's the first guy who's believed in me since I can remember," Leo added, his voice somber.

Tori had no time to respond. Their testimony was impressive, but when she started to say so, Winn appeared from the tack room, his face blank and hard, the two men flanking him looking like self-satisfied cats who'd snared the pet parakeet. When he reached them, Winn held up a green plastic bag shaped like a lunch sack, rolled at the top and free of any markings.

"Do any of you recognize this?"

Renee and Leo squinted at it for several seconds and both shook their heads.

"Never seen it before," Leo said. "What is it?"

"Are you certain you can't tell us?" Officer Hogan asked, as if Leo were a four-year-old trying to hide a misdeed.

"Pretty certain." Leo's voice grew icicles.

Winn placed a hand, gently Tori saw, on his shoulder. "Easy," he said.

"This guy is accusing me of something, and I don't like it," Leo said, glaring at the police officer.

"No accusations are being made," Winn said. "But this is serious."

He opened the sack and pulled out a clear, zip-top bag containing two items. At first silence reined, and then Jocelyn gasped, pulling everyone's eyes to her.

"Sorry," she mumbled. "Déjà vu."

"Would you care to explain?" Officer Hogan asked.

"It's the second piece of broken leather I've seen today, that's all."

"And do you have any further explanation as to why it was found in the tack room here?"

"I don't officially work here. I never go into the tack room."

Winn literally stepped between the officer's cold gaze and Jocelyn's hot one. "I told you in there when you came across that thing, that if my employees said they didn't recognize it I'd stand behind them. I meant it."

With enough skepticism in his eyes to sway a deadlocked jury, the steward, Rob Parsons, took the baggie from Winn and directed his next question to Tori. "Dr. Sterling, do these things mean anything to you?" He handed them over.

She stared, stunned, at the damning items, although what or whom, exactly, they damned wasn't at all clear. The four-inch piece of leather, wider than a rein, was the most disturbing, because it was cut cleanly rather than partially torn, and it lay beside a small multi-purpose tool that had its short, sharp blade extended.

"One of Armand's saddles had a stirrup leather cut. I expect this piece will match up with what's left. And that's a Leatherman tool. I carry one almost like this, and so do any number of people who work around horses."

"But you don't recognize it as belonging to anyone you know?"

"I don't."

He turned back to Winn. "You said you have two other employees."

"Yes. I'll ask them about this and if they know anything I'll contact you immediately."

"I'll need to know their work schedules." Officer Hogan pulled a small spiral notebook from his pocket.

For a moment Winn looked like he might protest, but he closed his mouth and nodded.

"Please keep yourself available for further questions, Mr. Crosby," Officer Hogan said. "We'll be comparing this piece to what's missing from the saddle in question, and we'll check the tool for fingerprints."

"Go ahead." Leo twisted around Winn and stepped forward. "And you won't have any trouble ruling any of us out because you already know you can find all our prints on file. I wouldn't expect you to believe anything but a definitive lab report."

"Leo." Winn's voice roped the boy and pulled him back from the brink of fury.

"I would imagine any of you would also know well how to wipe down a weapon," Hogan replied, cool as the morning air. "I wouldn't leave town, either, Mr. Richards."

"All right, that's uncalled for." Winn faced the officer and the steward. "Let's keep this professional. You found the evidence in my tack room, you can question my answers all you like. But you have no direct evidence that my kids have anything to do with this, so I expect you to treat them as innocent until proven guilty."

"And I expect you will cooperate and let us do our job," the confronted officer said.

"I think I've indicated I'll do that."

Hogan and the steward offered Tori a tight smile as they walked away. Before she could meet Winn's eyes, two voices burst into a thunderstorm of indignation and curses.

"The fuck was that about?" Leo cried.

"I've met some mean cops in my life, but that was one cold bastard." Renee kicked a clod of dirt that went spraying through the aisle.

"Knock it off," Winn said. "I'm totally on your side here, you know that. But we've talked about this stuff. If you don't let your better angels deal with these situations, you'll end up fighting your way back into trouble.

"To hell with our better angels," Leo said. "I'm sending mine out for coffee."

"Well call him back before he heads the wrong direction. C'mon," Winn cupped the back of Leo's neck and shook it affectionately. "Get a grip. It takes time for this kind of thing to die down. You both told me you haven't seen the bag before and that's that. I'm sure Sawyer and Mallory will tell me the same."

"What if they don't find who really did this?" Renee's anger melted into worry. "They can make up anything they want. Who'll believe us over them?"

"I would." Tori said, and four pairs of eyes met hers.

"You don't have to get involved with this," Winn said.

Tori shrugged. "I had a chance to talk to these guys while you were in the tack room. They like you. They respect you. I don't believe they'd lie."

"Yeah, I don't either." Jocelyn spoke for the first time. "I don't know any of you except Doc Sterling, but I listen. You guys don't ever say nothin' bad about

Winn. That's not normal if you hate your boss and want to do something to get him in trouble."

The man they discussed stared at the ground, his features expressionless. Only when he finally looked up did she see the emotion in his eyes.

"Thank you for the vote of confidence—for me and the kids," he said, and she nodded.

"I call 'em as I see 'em."

"All right. So here's what we're going to do. We're all going to work our anger off by checking every single piece of tack. Don't think of it as punishment because it isn't. I want to make note of every single nick, scrape, scratch, tear, loose stitch or cut you find. Saddles, bridles, yokes, girths, stirrup leathers. Everything. I have a couple of things to do, and then I'll help you."

"Do you still want this guy worked?" Jocelyn stroked Tipsy's neck.

"Absolutely." Winn nodded. "Exactly like we discussed. Should only take you ten minutes."

"Okay."

"Check everything double well before you mount up."

"Already done," she replied, and Winn nodded with a tight smile.

"You guys okay with this job?" he asked Leo and Renee. "It's drudgery, but necessary. And your butts are on the line after all."

"What isn't drudgery around here?" Renee asked.

"That's the spirit."

With that a cloud lifted and a refreshing waft of humor sailed over them all. Winn grinned at the girl and Tori's stomach did a hugely unexpected flop. The smile lit his face and softened every plane and angle in his tall, dark and handsome visage. She knew the sex appeal that flowed right along with the humor was nothing he controlled, but his attractiveness slammed her harder than usual. It wasn't hard to figure out why.

The man didn't simply give lip service to his trust. If he'd had a moment's concern about the trustworthiness of these kids he'd have kept them far away from his tack. Instead he was putting it completely in their hands.

And they knew it.

The man ran a very interesting ship, and he was an incredibly impressive captain physically and emotionally.

"I'm sorry."

It took her a minute to realize the apology was aimed at her. She lifted her eyes to his and had to swallow against a mouthful of abrupt dryness.

"Uh, sorry? What on earth for?"

"For having to be involved in all this. I'll be perfectly honest. I was going to try and talk you into taking on my horses as clients. But I understand now that would be inappropriate. It was presumptuous at any rate."

"Why?"

"You're a neutral party. If you worked on any of my horses you'd have a conflict of interest."

"I'm a veterinarian for one horse barely involved in this whole thing. There's no official neutral party and no conflict. Not that I'm saying I have time for more clients, but don't take away the chance to make your pitch."

A flash of hope lit his face again.

"You're serious?"

"I don't play games, especially when it comes to work. I'd need to hear what you want from a vet and you need to hear what I will and won't do for you. I warn you right up front, not everyone likes my rules and boundaries."

He studied her a long moment before he bobbed his head slowly. "That doesn't surprise me. I'd like a chance to hear what those boundaries are."

Something hot momentarily replaced the hope in his eyes, and Tori tried to analyze it, even while it stirred more flips in her stomach. She hated the thought that he had an agenda aside from the horses. But his body language held no threat, no advance on her space, no tension. And the smolder she'd been sure she'd seen had vanished. She had no reason to think he'd be any less honest with her than he'd been with his kids.

"Don't you need to watch Tipsy work?"

"Jeez, don't pick up that stupid nickname."

"Awww, it's cute."

He only scowled. "Yes. I need to watch him."

"Then I'll come with you. If nothing else, I'll get to see a pretty boy at work."

It was his turn to stare at the words she didn't explain, and she smiled to herself. It was true, the horse was pretty. But so was the man.

CHAPTER Four

FOR THE SECOND time that morning Tori stood next to the rail and watched a colt of Winn's get ready to work. This time use of the starting gate was part of the training workout, and Tori watched with interest to see how Jocelyn dealt with the piece of equipment so unique to horse racing.

"I like her," Winn said. "She's awfully composed for an eighteen-year-old."

"She's unusual. In a good way. I've known her family since they moved to Chandlerville ten years ago. She was this tiny little eight-year-old, but they went to our church for a short while, joined the Pony Club near us, and I babysat her and her brother a few times. She was a really talented rider right from the start."

"So with all that wholesomeness, where did all the goth touches come from?"

Tori sighed thoughtfully. "Some of the friends she kept in middle school rubbed off, I think. Plus, a lot of it is more or less her giving her ultra-conservative family the finger." She laughed. "The thing is, Jocelyn isn't an abused child, but she was raised in an extremely strict environment. I think she gets criticized quite a lot. Her parents are nice, but they have kind of a puckery lemon attitude about a lot of things."

Winn squinted as he watched the girl work patiently on loading the reluctant Tipsy. "That would explain a few things. I could tell when she first came around that she knew how to take criticism a little too well. She doesn't argue or flinch, she just keeps her head down. I thought she was simply a little introverted."

"That she is. But she's never been in trouble that I know of."

"If she keeps her head the way she did this morning, she can ride for me whenever she likes. It's tough to find anyone who can fit in with my crew. I've lost more than one assistant trainer over the years."

"Why? The kids were great."

"Because what happened back at the barns is what always happens sooner or later wherever we are. Our society, and this wealthy racing society in absolute spades, reveres appearance and performance and perfection. My kids are everything but perfect."

"I've been around the racing industry my entire life. I know what you're saying is true. And yet, there are the good guys. The ones who work tirelessly to make this sport better and safer."

"A lot of the trouble lies with the old school. Not all…"

"No. But enough so there are days I don't want this job anymore. Still, I keep coming."

On the track, Jocelyn leaned forward in her saddle and stroked Tipsy's neck. They couldn't see whether her lips moved, but Tori would have taken any odds that the girl was crooning to the gelding. Five seconds later he walked into the starting gate.

"Awesome!" For the first time since meeting him, Tori watched Winn's eyes dance in true excitement. "It isn't that he wouldn't load," he said. "But it was never quiet, never without wasting so much energy. That was worthy of a raise."

"Are you going to give her one?" Tori lifted her brows.

"No. But it was worthy."

His grin sent a fresh ripple of awareness through Tori's body. A warm caramel slide of pleasure rushed through every vein. His looks might have been the catalyst, but it was his humor and his support of a young woman who only looked for acceptance wherever she went, that had her wishing she could sit instead of trust her knees.

"Your kids," she said, not knowing why the phrase struck her now. "You call them that often. What's behind the endearment?"

He adjusted his cap thoughtfully. "Technically Jocelyn is the only 'kid.' The others are twenty-one or older. But a couple of them are mine in a sense. I'm their guardian until probation is over, so they became my kids. Everyone needs a chance to turn her or his life around. I'm trying to help the way someone once helped me. I end up feeling close to them."

"Few people are willing to take that kind of stand. I admit it, when Leo and Renee were angry, they looked as if they'd just as soon have taken a swing at the police."

"They've each had bad times with the law. I have no murderers on my staff, but I do have a jewel thief." He bit back a smile. "It'll cause some sparks when they look up his record."

"Which one is that?"

"Sawyer Hawkins. He's the oldest at twenty-four and my toughest nut. He has the outward friendliness down, and he's soft as a hot mash breakfast with the horses. He's also a really good judge of people's characters. But he's not open. He does his own thing more often than not—although he's not careless. Grew up on a ranch of some kind—he doesn't talk about it, but since he's one of the kids I'm responsible for, I know more than he knows I know."

"Oh. Well, good to…know." She smiled.

"He stole his mother's wedding ring and a couple of other expensive pieces and pawned them. Therefore, jewel thief."

"And you're still sure he didn't have anything to do with what was found?"

"I'm sure. Okay. Here she goes."

As quickly as the starting gate sprang open the conversation about the kids was over. Jocelyn broke the gelding perfectly and kept him straight, letting him stretch and settle into a breezing pace. He was another beautiful mover.

"You have a couple of really nice horses," Tori said.

"This owner is pretty savvy. She owns Fallon as well."

"How many owners do you have?"

"Three here. One has two horses, one has five, and the other one has three. Jane, Fallon's owner, is the one with the connections that got us a spot here. Churchill Downs is kind of my dream destination, I guess, so I grabbed the chance even though it's the off season and there are still tough requirements."

"Don't I know it? I keep up my track license and that's enough red tape."

"Speaking of which, I want to talk more about making some of that red tape pay off. Things got slightly off-track earlier."

"I'm sorry about that."

"Never said it was your fault." Winn checked a stopwatch. "Dang that girl is good. She's got him spot on where I want him. Yup. I like her."

"Too bad she's about three inches too tall, because I know she'd rather be a jockey instead of an exercise rider."

"She's also a willow twig. I bet she could pull it off."

"Maybe, but you know how owners are. Sometimes perception is more important to them than talent."

With the workout at an end, Winn led the way toward the track entrance.

"How about I buy us some coffee after I'm done talking to Jocelyn? I'll tell you what I have in mind. You can tell me whether you have time for more clients."

"All right."

They were nearly at their destination when Tori's cellphone rang—a lively version of "The Baby Elephant Walk" that indicated it was someone from her farm calling. "I have to get this," she told Winn. "Go ahead. I'll catch up in a second."

He nodded and she answered to hear a breathless Heidi Jennings, her best friend and part time vet assistant.

"Tori? I'm so sorry to bother you, but I think you need to come home." Heidi rarely lost her composure, so to hear her rapid-fire words underscored with anxiety, sent adrenaline surging.

"What's wrong?"

"I have no idea where they found it, but two of the dogs, Axel and Zoom, got into some fencing wire and are tangled."

"Where are they now?"

"They dragged themselves and a piece of fencepost home. I cut them apart but Zoom has some wrapped around her foot, and I'm worried about cutting it because the paw is swollen. Axel won't let me near him. He's got it all around his torso. It's the weirdest thing."

Weird was almost her middle name. She often regretted not calling her farm Bizarro Acres, but that had seemed a little fate-tempting. Somedays, though, it was accurate.

"I can be there in thirty minutes. Try and keep them calm; I know Axel is scary when he's upset but keep working at it. Stupid dogs. Now we'll have to check the fences, too."

"I know, right? Looks like a whole post got broken along with the wire."

"Thanks, Heidi."

She hung up with a sigh and trotted to meet Winn where he now talked with Jocelyn. The girl was actually smiling—a true rarity.

"Okay," Winn told her and gave Tipsy a firm pat on the neck. "Take him on back and give him to Renee to cool down. Great job. Glad you thought he went well."

"I did. He's fantastic."

"Tell the other two that I'll be back in an hour or so. I don't have any more rides this morning, I'm sorry to say, but tomorrow I'll have more if you're up for it."

Jocelyn's attempts to mask her pleasure over the request were clear in the contortions of her mouth and cheeks as she tried to keep them firm. But the sparkle in her eyes gave away the excitement.

"Tell me when you want me here."

"Early," Winn grinned. "We feed at five. I'll start half hour after that."

"I'll be here at five."

"Thanks. Got any other rides this morning?" She shook her head. "Well, you're free then. Although you're always welcome to hang out. Don't work, though. I can't pay another groom—you guys charge too much."

Another grin had Tori's nerves happily jumping again. What was it about this guy and his quick transitions from stern to jovial that turned her into a fluttery fangirl? She didn't do fluttery.

"I'll tell them that," Jocelyn said as she walked the horse off. "See you in an hour or so."

"Oh!" Tori's mind cleared and she shook herself out of the ridiculous fog of attraction that in two seconds had made her forget. "Winn, I'm so so sorry. The call I got was from my farm sitter at home. There's been an accident with two of the dogs and I need to go. Could we talk about this tomorrow? I'll be here by seven. I really do apologize."

"Hey," he said. "I'm sorry about the dogs. Are they okay?"

Well if that wasn't the perfect response.

"They got themselves wrapped in some wire—I have no idea if it's serious or nothing."

"Then go. We can talk any time. Come on, I'll walk you out."

A gentleman, too.

"I'm way out on the back side lot. No need to go that far."

"Well, as far as you like, then. So you have dogs?"

She laughed. Here came the part of the introduction that sent sane men ducking for cover. "Among other creatures."

"I assumed you have horses."

"Along with the python." Might as well get that one out of the way at the start.

"You keep a python with your horses? Why? Are the mice bothering them that much?"

She stared at him as they entered the backside community, trying to decide if he thought she was joking.

"The python lives in the house, actually. The donkeys live with the horses. The litter of pigs does, too, until I find homes for them."

"Pigs and donkeys. Okay. One thing. The python isn't Monty by chance?"

"Shaquille."

"Uhh…" He finally started to laugh.

"I'm serious," she said. "I do have animals. Too many of them, and too little time. All rescued from some bad situation or another. That's my only excuse. I guess there are thirty give or take. Most of them I rehome after a time—it's a revolving door."

"Thirty!"

"I know." She sighed. This was the reason she didn't bring guys into her life any more. The reason Dale had finally given up and packed his bags one night after three years of not-so-patiently trying to make a life with her. The reason four others had given up after much less time trying. "It's the curse of the veterinarian. Some of us anyway. I'm about three steps up from the crazy cat ladies of the world."

"Hmmmm. Well, it's a lot of animals I admit, but you don't really seem crazy."

"I have a snake, seven piglets, and dogs who wrap themselves in fencing wire. If that doesn't sound crazy to you, then maybe we're both crazy and happy not to know it."

She meant it as teasing, and from the light in his eye she believed he took it as such. But a sudden silence fell after her words, and although it hung companionably between them, it also crackled with unexpected electricity.

"Okay," she said when they reached the main road through the barn areas. "I'm going to the right, and you're to the left. You don't need to walk me to the parking lot, honest."

"Back to the salt mines," he said with an exaggerated sigh.

"Like my daddy always says, 'Manure heaps ain't gonna move themselves.' It was nice meeting you Winn Crosby. You're not what I expected."

"I'm not even going to ask what that was. You're not what I expected either." His thoughts from much earlier that morning came back to him.

"Oh, I know exactly what *you* expected. A sanctimonious, slightly judgmental, know-it-all. Right?"

"I didn't ever hear 'sanctimonious.'"

His slight discomfort made her chuckle. "Heck, that's probably the most accurate. I certainly don't know it all, but I have my opinions, and I usually think they're right."

"I'll remember not to argue with you."

"If, and it's still a big if, I ever work on your horses, I'm sure we'll butt heads. But you're not the emotionless, single-minded recluse I heard you were, so I don't see you holding a grudge if we do."

"Jeez, who called me that? And, you're right. I don't like to hold grudges. Not in this business."

She set her hand lightly on his upper arm even while debating whether it was a good idea to touch him. "People call you quiet and intense. You keep to yourself and your work, that's all. I get the impression you're taking your time to figure out who your friends will be."

After another electric silence she let her palm slide off his arm.

"I've found a few." His voice, husky and slow, washed over her like the sun that now stood halfway to noon.

"I'd better get going," she said. "What's a good time to find you tomorrow?"

"I start at five. Find me anytime. We can do midmorning coffee whenever you're free."

"Deal. I'll come by. If you're not in the stable I'll leave a note."

"Give me your phone."

"Good idea."

They switched and entered their numbers into each other's smart phones then handed them back. The simple, normal exchange was nothing, and yet it felt as intimate as a first kiss.

Sheesh the whole morning was getting out of hand. This wasn't a moment behind the bleachers at a high school football game. Tori shook her head yet again to clear it.

"I'll call if I can't find you," she said. "Have a good afternoon."

"Good luck with the dogs. Hope they're okay."

"I'll let you know."

They each waved and walked off. She glanced over her shoulder, found he'd looked back as well, and she rolled her eyes as she walked off for the final time, a twitch threatening to lift her lips into a private grin. They were as cliché as Tom Hanks and Meg Ryan in a scripted comedy.

She didn't stop musing over the dorkiness of it all until she reached her car and real life took its control back. Then worry about her two dogs kicked in and she forgot about rom coms and sexy biceps as she pushed the speed limit all the way back to Chandlerville.

CHAPTER Five

"ALL RIGHT, BIG guy. You were finally starting to trust me weren't you? And now I have to be the bad doctor. I'm so sorry, dude."

Even as she forced her mind into clinical mode, Tori's heart hurt for the huge Rottweiler-Pyrenees cross that whimpered on the floor of her home office-slash-exam room. Axel had only been with her a month, and he was a hundred and fifty pounds of pure affection mixed with abject terror rolled into one black, tan, and white canine mountain. The thin gauge fencing wire wrapped tightly around his stomach and upper right leg was twisted into his thick fur and cutting into the scruff of his neck. Had the dog been a calm and trusting animal, Tori could have easily cut the wire, but any attempt to get near the offending metal was met with snarls and snaps.

"I still wonder every day what happened to this poor dog in the seven months before we found him," Heidi said, pushing her thick, black-rimmed glassed up her nose.

"Yeah. Somebody put a lot of fear into him." Tori stroked his head, waiting for the mild tranquilizer she'd given him to take effect. "I'm sorry Axel sweetie."

She looked across the room to a row of four kennels where a sleek black and white border collie gazed mournfully out the open door of one through the tunnel of an e-collar. Poor Zoom had one paw swathed in thick, loose bandaging and belly full of painkillers and anti-inflammatories doing their best to return circulation to the foot that had been constricted by a wire tourniquet for over an hour. Anger tangled with sorrow in her stomach. Heidi had shown her the two-foot section of wooden fence post that had snapped off along with the snarl of wire attached to it. It was a rotted fence post, hit by something or collapsed by winds, and the dogs had run into the jumble, getting snared in a perfect storm of bad luck.

"I hate days like this," she said, watching Axel's eyelids droop for the first time. "Stupid stuff at the track. Stupid stuff here."

"Where there are animals there is heartache." Heidi said.

"Along with the joy." Tori sighed. "If you're going to quote me at least give the entire quote."

"This isn't the joy part. Except that you're going to make both these guys well. You've seen worse."

She had. But these injuries had happened under her care—that made them worse than abuse in her eyes. Zoom was her own dog, raised from a pup. But she'd promised Axel the day he'd arrived, huge and shivering at the slightest noise, that this was a safer place than what he'd known. If people thought her crazy so be it, but she believed even her human words had meaning to her animals. On some level they understood, and she'd broken the promise.

"Okay, baby, will you let me help you yet?"

She reached slowly to touch the wire at the dog's shoulder. He yelped and lifted his head, but it flopped back down and he groaned.

"Poor Axel," Heidi crooned. "Here are the wire cutters."

It took a full fifteen minutes to carefully snip the wire in enough places so Tori could free it from Axel's body. As each length was tossed aside, she breathed easier. Finally there was only one hunk left to unwind from around his leg. With a surprise surge Tori never saw coming, Axel growled to life and swung his head upward, jaws wide, snarls emanating in a wild animal hiss.

"Whoa! Whoa," Tori shot away from him fast enough so his teeth missed her, but not fast enough to avoid a crack to the side of her jaw from his massive swinging head.

"Tori! Are you okay?" Heidi grabbed for the leash hooked to Axel's collar.

As the immense dog, now on his feet, strained against the leash and bit at the last of the wire still trussing up his leg, Tori heard what sounded like a rap on the door. With no idea who could possibly be at her office door before noon, but not willing to take her eyes off Axel for long, she spared one quick glance over her shoulder and lost her concentration completely.

"Am I interrupting...?" he began. "Shit, it's a bear!"

Winn Crosby stood, mouth agape, knuckles against the open door, unmoving as a marble statue. Tori wouldn't have been more shocked to see Sasquatch.

"Winn?" She choked.

"Oooh boy. Looks like I came at a really bad time. I'll back out—"

Axel stopped fighting, but with one giant surge he yanked the leash out of Heidi's hand and bee-lined for

Winn. Tori forgot her throbbing jaw and leaped for the dog, her heart in her throat as she imagined Winn's attacked and bloodied body.

"Axel, no!"

She missed the leash, and the dog barreled into Winn's legs, let the impact stop him short, and then scooted around to press against Winn's calves like a toddler hiding behind its mother. The adrenaline pulsating through Tori turned to confusion and then relief. Ashen and wide-eyed, Winn looked ready to slump to the floor. Instead he propped himself up against the door.

"The latest in home security systems?" he quipped.

"Oh, Winn, I'm so sorry. The dog is frightened to death, and he blew through the tranquilizer I gave him. I should have had the muzzle on him. Should have used a bigger dose—he's a huge dog. I'm—"

She stopped mid-sentence. Winn had his hand on Axel's head and the dog leaned into him as if he hadn't a care in the world.

"What the…? Axel? What's up with this?" Tori reached the big animal and put out her hand. He didn't protest, but neither did he move from Winn's legs. "You *like* Winn?"

"Thanks for sounding so shocked." He smiled, the fear from seconds before completely gone. When he knelt, Axel let him stroke his face.

"I'm shocked. Dogs with high anxiety are many times far more afraid of men than women. This one seems to be the opposite. We couldn't calm him at all."

"I'm glad I could help but, buddy, hey, you could have warned me you weren't going to rip my face off."

Axel licked his cheek.

"Ingrate," Tori mumbled. "Well as long as he's in love with you, would you be willing to hold him while I get a muzzle and a little more tranquilizer?" She backed off several paces.

Winn checked over the wire still wrapped around the dog's torso and nodded. "Sure, but what do you think, Axel? Do you really want to get all shot up with drugs? What if I …" He slid one hand down Axel's front leg, fumbled a moment, and ten seconds later slid the last piece of wire off in a loop. "There you go, fella. Bet that feels better."

Tori let her jaw drop like a dumbfounded guppy.

"I'm pretty good with horses," he said, shrugging. "This guy is so big I think the instincts kicked in and I bamboozled him."

"Bamboozled?" Her tongue loosened, and watched the giant dog slouch at Winn's feet beneath a windfall of pats and scratches. His tale thumped at Tori in happiness—a completely changed animal. "Who uses that word?"

He gave the side of his nose a self-deprecating rub with one knuckle. "A crusty trainer named Sean McLeod was my first mentor in the horse world. He always said that the most important tool in any horseman's box was the art of bamboozling. You have to make a horse believe you're bigger and stronger than he is without scaring or forcing him. If he ever figures out you're a con artist, you're dead in the water. So I became a professional bamboozler."

"Gotta say, I've never heard it put quite that way."

"I've thought of putting it on my business cards."

She shot him a hard look and tried not to smile. "You have not."

He only smiled back as she approached him again, squatted and let Axel roll over to present his furry belly. Gently, methodically, and warily despite his change in demeanor, Tori felt all along the areas where wire had been caught. She came across two raw spots, but no swelling. The dog paid no attention, mesmerized by Winn's continued touch.

"I think you got lucky, pup." She kissed Axel's nose. "We'll put some medicine on those owies and keep you quiet for tonight, but I predict you'll make it."

Her baby talk and kissy-facing earned her multiple swipes from Axel's long, strong tongue. She laughed and managed to avoid one aimed directly at her own mouth and was reminded with a wave of dizziness of the whack she'd taken to the head.

"Whoa," she said, closing her eyes and plunking onto her butt.

"Hey, everything okay?"

Winn reached across Axel's body and grasped Tori's upper arm. She drew in a long breath, let it out slowly, and then opened her eyes only to have the air sucked right back away from her. His lean, gorgeous face, concerned and yet calm, scrutinized her from a distance that would take little effort to close for a kiss.

Oh, Lord, it's definitely a concussion.

She lost herself more long seconds in the complex scent of him. Soap and spice. Hay and horses. Some masculine pheromone no woman could accurately describe or fail to notice.

"Tori?"

She focused again and offered a sheepish smile. "I'm fine. Honestly I am. He whacked me a good one and then I spun my head away too quickly. There's no pain. I didn't black out."

"Do you need to get checked for a concussion?" Heidi stood behind her and put a hand on her shoulder.

"No, no. Truly I don't. I didn't get hit that hard. Some people would say there's not a force hard enough to shake up my brain through the thick skull anyway."

Laughter, rich and resonant, swirled around her like more of the misty haze she'd been in for long minutes now. The sound made her much too comfortable.

"You've done that a couple of times since I met you—called yourself stubborn as if it's a bad thing. There's nothing wrong with being stubborn, you know."

"If you know it's there and can turn it off once in a while." She knew this because she hadn't always possessed the art of turning it off.

"I'd think being stubborn would be necessary in this male-dominated sport."

"Mr. Crosby, are you trying to impress me?"

"Not at all. My father was an ass, and I never knew my mother, but my aunt was a tough woman, so I learned the skill of survival-by stubbornness."

"A man who puts his life lessons into practice."

"Hardly. I just don't know any better."

Her smiles came ever more easily. Standing slowly to test her head, she handed Axel's leash to Heidi, and sighed gratefully when the room stayed still.

"Let's get him dosed up and let him sleep in a kennel until tonight. He'll be okay."

Heidi nodded and headed off.

"How's the other dog?" Winn asked. "You said there were two?"

"There are actually four. I have two brand new rescues in the other room. They don't have names yet; I call them Thing One and Thing Two." Tori pointed to the kennel where Zoom watched through her sad little cone. "Here's our other injured one. The paw was without circulation for quite a long time, and I don't know if she'll get to keep it or not. We'll do our best."

Winn blanched a little. "How on earth did they find wire?"

She bristled slightly with guilt even though he'd accused her of nothing. She hated the wire fences, and there was only one pasture left that didn't have safe, brown vinyl rail fencing. The farm was a money pit as it was. Rebuilding her pastures over the past five years had been a long, slow process.

"Something broke a corner fence post and snapped the wire. The dogs must have run into it while playing. Makes me sick."

"I'm sorry."

He was. She could read it in his eyes, their brilliant blue now a regretful, overcast slate color.

"I'm working on getting vinyl fencing up all around. It takes too long to get everything done." she said.

"Hey, I'm not criticizing. It's obvious when driving in you have a beautiful place."

"Thanks."

He'd read her mind effortlessly, picking up on the defensiveness. A welling of emotion clogged her throat and sent burning tears to her eyes. She knew the sensation well. It had nothing to do with him or even her guilt. It was the loss of adrenaline now that the animals were safe. And it would be the only version of panic she'd allow herself to have.

Self-conscious, she cleared her throat and bolstered her mushy emotions.

"Speaking of driving in. What *are* you doing here? I left you barely ninety minutes ago."

He wiggled his impressively thick brows and reached into a leather jacket pocket. When he produced her cell phone with its distinctive protective case picturing running horses, she gasped and automatically slapped at her own pockets.

"What? Where was that?"

"In the road where we said good-bye. I don't know how it got dropped, but I only found it because I went back to go check on Armand. You were long gone, but I kind of figured a vet might need her phone."

"Oh man, that's an understatement. I can't believe I didn't notice right away. I can't thank you enough!"

"It was no problem."

"You could have left it with the vet office."

"It's not like they could have called to tell you it was there. I figured it would save you a drive to Lexington as well as a little panic."

"And cost you a drive to Chandlerville. I'm sorry."

He waved the apology away. "I'm the boss. I can leave when I need to. Plus, I wanted to see this alleged snake of yours. I've never known anyone with a python of her own. I'll head back to work afterward. Promise."

"You don't have to work on my account. And sure. I'll introduce you. I remodeled an old deck into a four-season porch right after I moved here so the less cuddly creatures could have a view. I've had a couple of reptiles over the years. Now it's just Shaq out here."

"You are a kind and thoughtful owner." He laughed. "But you need to finish with Axel. I can wait. Or we can do it another time."

"No, this is fine. Why don't I get Axel settled and you can meet Shaq, then we could have our meeting that got interrupted? Cassie's in Chandlerville or the Bourbonville Pub? You know them?"

"I've eaten at Cassie's once, but I haven't spent much time in either Chandlerville or Bourbonville. My hours are full, and with a room above the barn..."

"I hear you. If you choose to work and live at a race track you have no life."

His rueful, raised-brow acknowledgment reflected an emotion she shared. There really wasn't time for much of anything but work when the day started at four-thirty in the morning and could run until ten at night during race season. October was slower since there were no races until the end of the month. November and December would pick up, but she wouldn't be able to take time off from the Downs until the January and February break. If her life was full and unpredictable, a trainer's had to be more so.

"No rest for the wicked," he said. "But I'd be happy to try Cassie's with you. I have time. Like I said, I'm the boss."

Her heart gave a happy double beat in anticipation. "Awesome."

He stayed through Axel's care, remaining out of the way except to make Heidi's wide hazel eyes fill with sparkles of green when he took her hand at their official introduction. When he and Tori stood at last in front of the thirty-gallon aquarium lined with artificial turf, he gazed with obvious fascination past the large bowl containing about two inches of water in it and the corner cave to a driftwood branch, where Shaquille the python lay warming himself beneath the heat lamp.

"He's real! And he's got spots."

She searched his face quizzically at the surprise in his voice. "You thought I would make up a story of a six-foot snake named Shaquille? Why? To attract a guy?"

"Just the opposite, in fact. I'd think he would be more effective than a watchdog to some guys' minds." He chuckled. "I thought maybe you were warning me off."

"If that was my intent it didn't work very well, did it?"

He laughed. "Guess not. Curiosity got the better of my common sense."

She liked his easy joking. Even when he'd relaxed at the track he'd maintained a steady watchfulness, as if he had to keep tabs on everyone and everything around him. Here he'd left behind every bit of cool carefulness.

Raising the heavy cover off the aquarium, she reached in to stroke her unusual housemate.

"Let me dispel all your scary snake dreams," she said. "First one: Shaquille is a girl."

"Oh, come on—you can't do that to *Shaq*." He feigned disgust.

"Hmmm. Well worse, she's a ball python and even though she's a lot bigger than normal girls of her species, who get bigger than the boys by the way, she's done growing. Topped out at six feet three inches—which is kind of a mutant actually, but she's not all that big."

"But, seriously, don't pythons get to be twenty feet long?"

"The Burmese can. This is just a shy little pied python. C'mon, darling, there's someone who wants to meet you."

Shaq blinked a glossy round eye and lifted her head. She was a beautiful creature. Pure white with rich brown-black patches, she looked like a pretty pinto horse. And, she was plenty big enough at six feet and ten pounds.

"I admit freely I've never seen a snake that looks like this."

With a steady hand that pleased Tori simply because it was unusual, Winn stroked the snake's smooth, cool skin.

"They breed these guys in hundreds of colors," she told him. "Shaq is unusual in a lot of ways. The piebalds this distinctive are somewhat rare, and it's really exceptional to have a ball snake over five feet. Males rarely get over three and a half. The little girl who wanted this one when she was five, decided it was far too big and scary once she got to be six. I took it since they were talking about letting it into the wild. Don't even get me going on that subject."

Winn frowned. "Sounds like it was a bad decision from the beginning."

"Yup."

"So she's friendly?"

"Super friendly. Although these snakes are also shy and solitary. I take her out once or twice a day. The rest of the time she prefers her quiet. Want to hold her?"

"You know? It honestly wasn't on my to-do list for today, but I'm nothing if not flexible." He held out his hands.

In Tori's experience, people who were afraid of snakes couldn't ever learn to tolerate the feel of one contracting its incredibly powerful muscles around their hands or arms, but Winn's concentration on the long, slim reptile was born of pure curiosity and a growing admiration, not a speck of fear.

"Hello, Shaq," he said. "You're a pretty girl, but I still wouldn't like to meet you by surprise in the dark."

"I've had her two years and so far she's only escaped once. Took a full day to find her and I admit she slithered out from under the sofa and nearly gave me a stroke. Now there's a snap clip on her cage. I can put her around my waist and carry her there for short periods. *That* freaks people out."

Her mood flashed black as she remembered Dale's endless threats the long weeks before she'd given him back the engagement ring. The animals were barely tolerable as they were, the snake was non-negotiable. No snakes if she wanted him to stay. Especially not when he came home from a long day to find her starting dinner with a reptile for a belt.

She'd have given in had that not been one of a million straws on an extremely overloaded camel's back.

She heard Winn's voice and banished the old memory.

"Sorry. What?" she asked.

"I said I believe you. About the snake belt. It's very weird and slightly funny."

"Some people don't think it's funny at all." She shrugged off the last of her bitterness and smiled. "But it is. If you have a warped sense of humor."

"I'm starting to see that. How much more of a warped sense of humor does a person need to have around here?"

"Do you like rabbits?"

His eyes picked up shards of impish light. "I don't hate rabbits."

"I have a cat with three legs, would that count?"

"No."

"A litter of seven orphaned piglets."

"A little weirder."

"That's probably enough for you to take in for now. I can bring you through the barn another time."

"Glad you think there'll be another time." He wiggled his brows.

"Don't be weirder than my animals. It's not out of the realm of possibility that you'd be back sometime."

His deep laughter touched off sparks in her chest. She hadn't had a man around her house in three years. She never missed having to worry about another person's reaction to everything she did, but she missed the pure big presence of the opposite sex. And one like this who, at least on the surface, knew how to take life as it came, was easy to admire—for a short time at least.

Yet again she had to tell her pulse to ease up on the pounding.

Once Shaq was back in her safe home, Tori took Winn on an abbreviated tour of the farm she'd invested in right out of vet school five years before. A lot of well-meaning friends and even relatives had told her it was too soon for such a huge step, but with her parents' co-signatures and blessing, she'd taken the plunge.

"Brave girl," Winn said.

"Forty acres and a livable house, a mostly-solid barn, and fields with dilapidated fencing came a lot cheaper than the pristine farms most people imagine when they think of Kentucky. But here in Chandler County things are still growing. It's a buyer's market, so I did all right. Not that I have an extra cent to my name these days."

"Don't tell me. The animals eat before you do."

She gave an unapologetic smile. "Yes. But I don't starve either. I love boxed mac and cheese."

"My girl, sounds like you need better than restaurant food for lunch."

"Nah." She waved her hand. "I eat like royalty. My other favorite is smothered French fries and bourbon barbecue sauce with fried chicken, which Ethan at the Brass Rail in town makes better than anywhere as far as I can tell. We can go there if you'd rather."

"Good God, can you cook? Do you even like vegetables? Healthy meat?"

"Veggies when I snack on carrots with my rabbits. Real meat when I go to my parents' for Sunday dinners. And I can cook a few things. I just hate doing it."

"See now, that's actually weirder than all your animals."

"Don't mock me, or I'll force you to eat one of those few things."

"No need to get drastic. I do like to cook, and I am good at it, so I'll cook for you."

"Hey, you don't know me. More importantly I don't know you. You can't ask me out on a cooking date yet." She grinned, loving the stupid banter, loving even more the strange feeling that she could say anything to him.

"Sure I can. You've already asked *me*. Aren't we going on our first date to lunch?"

"Business meeting."

"Ah. Then I'll repeat my invitation after the business meeting. Maybe we'll know each other better. Deal?"

She chose to interpret his laconic smile as him having as much fun as she was. It almost made her forget the bad start from that morning.

"Deal."

CHAPTER Six

WINN FOLLOWED HER to downtown Chandlerville and into Cassie's Cafe, which was bustling with lunch business. It seemed like a dream to have the bright, beautiful woman across from him in a corner booth. He ordered a half-pound burger and she chose a black and blue steak salad, even though he promised he'd been kidding about her lack of vegetable-eating. He ordered a Coke and she an imported ginger beer, and then they chatted about nothing—the café's décor, what it was like to rent one of the rooms above the stables at the track, the race schedule, the fact that they both like Keeneland in Lexington almost but not quite as much as the Downs.

It was all incredibly, surprisingly, comfortable. He couldn't remember the last time he'd been willing to take two hours away from the track and do something enjoyable. It was work, he told himself, necessary time away, but Tori's perpetual smile and her personal questions that stopped plenty short of being invasive, made their "business lunch" feel a lot more like pleasure. It took all his willpower to steer the conversation away from jobs they'd had as kids—lemonade stands in the front yard for her to selling hotdogs at Arlington Park in Chicago for him—and back to their current jobs at the racetrack.

"You said I might not want a vet like you to work for me," he said. "I thought maybe I could say the same about you wanting to work for me. I don't do things some vets think are good prevention."

"Well, here's my bottom line. There'll never be a question that I'll sneak an illegal drug into a horse—whether it can be tested for or not." She said. "I believe that should be everyone's bottom line, but we both know it isn't."

"We do, but it is mine," he said simply, and let her smile of satisfaction warm him for the hundredth time that day.

"No milkshaking, no nerve blocks or shockwaving the day of a race ... Don't even ask."

"Tori, Tori..." He reached across the table to put his hands on hers. "That would never be an issue. Here's my question. Do you have strong feelings about running on Lasix? Pro or con?"

The use of the diuretic that was banned everywhere but in the United States, and which kept thoroughbred horses from bleeding in their lungs during a race, was a source of controversy. But some vets promoted it as good prevention.

"I don't have a problem with it," she said.

"What if I said I don't ever use it prophylactically on my two-year-olds, and rarely on my three-year-olds until I know whether or not they have any issues? Studies show—"

"I know the studies well." She cut him off gently. "I think you're doing a good thing. Why use it if it's not needed?"

"So you aren't on the ban Lasix bandwagon but you also don't push it?"

"There have never been negative side effects shown—it's a safe drug. Thoroughbred lungs are unique, and they can naturally bleed after exertion. Until we breed our horses differently, I have no trouble using it. But, I'd rather not use any drugs that aren't necessary."

"I'd like to see that happen—the breeding part."

"I agree."

"All right, Dr. Victoria Sterling. I think we agree on the basics, don't you? I want you on my team." He squeezed her hand again and released it. "On the surface it sounds like our philosophies are compatible."

"What are you looking for in terms of services? Would I take over your horses completely or be a backup?"

"Definitely be our vet—take over the barn . Like I told you, Kevin Marsh and I don't see eye-to-eye on a lot of the things we've just talked about, and I'm small potatoes to him as well as being a very new client. I haven't needed much vet work in the few weeks I've been here, but I know I will eventually. I'm pretty knowledgeable, but I've always said that I didn't go to vet school so that's not my area of expertise."

"Definitely not every trainer feels that way. You might have the makings of a decent client." A teasing light made her brown eyes shine.

"So I'm passing the interview so far?"

"So far."

"Despite what I asked you, I have three horses running on Lasix. I have another I'm watching for a mild recurring lameness. I have two I want to enter in a couple of Derby qualifying races come spring, and a filly I honestly think has a shot at the Oaks. Those are my most important horses, and I want someone I totally trust looking after them. But…" He hesitated. He didn't want to jeopardize their budding work partnership, but he wanted to be honest. "There's a more selfish reason I need you."

"Oh?"

"I want a professional I trust to know my operation. To know how I run it and how I want things done. If fortune happens to smile, and my horses were to make it to the stakes races, there'll always be questions about me because of my staff. You've already seen what can happen. Your no tolerance for cheating reputation is well known. I think if, in the end, you can say you believe Crosby Racing and its employees don't cheat, it'll go a long way if I need help."

Her eyes clouded, briefly and worryingly. Winn forced himself to be patient. He'd said his piece. It was up to her to decide if he was being reasonable or sadly paranoid.

And then she laughed. She had a great warm laugh, infused with bells and charm.

"You're right, that is selfish," she said. "And smart. I love it, and I'm honored you've asked me. Here's the thing, though. I don't blindly endorse people; that would be stupid on my part, don't you think?"

"I do."

"So. A trial period. If this really doesn't ruffle Dr. Marsh's feathers I'll take over. I'll get to know your horses, and we'll go from there. You have a race in two days?"

"Fallon's first and my first here at Churchill."

"I'm really excited for you, Winn. Let's see how it goes."

She held out her hand over the table, and he took it. Her grip was as strong as she was, her shake as bright as her words, and he felt its power to his toes. He'd fallen into fascination with her, and he was pretty sure that wasn't a good idea. There was no time in his world for fascination with anything but work.

"Thanks," he said. "You made my morning."

She withdrew her hand. "You need better mornings, my friend."

"I—"

"There you are! I've been looking for you!"

Winn looked up to see a slender slip of a woman wearing a black felt floppy hat over thick, curly black hair, and a determined hunter's look in her eyes, moving toward them with the speed of a New Yorker hailing a cab. She fixed her gaze on his. Why in the world she honed in on him he had no idea. He didn't think he knew this person from the Princess of Timbuktu, but had he met her some time on the track and forgotten?

"Hey, Rachel! You look like you're on a mission," Tori said.

After a flirty smile for him, "Rachel" turned to Tori, and Winn relaxed. He definitely didn't know her, so he wasn't going to look like an idiot for forgetting her.

"I am. I have deadlines hitting from every direction, but I'm also working on birthday bash stuff."

"I keep telling you. Stop volunteering." Tori shook her head. "Winn, this is Rachel Blakely, the editor of the Chandler County Chronicle. Rachel, this is Winn Crosby—he's new to Chandler County. He's got horses at the Downs."

"Oooh, owner or trainer?" Rachel held out her hand.

"Trainer. Happy to meet you, Ms. Blakely."

"Rachel, for goodness sake. And I can't tell you how pleased I am to meet you. Tell me, Winn Crosby. Are you married?"

Thoroughly nonplussed by the personal question, he blinked at the smiling woman. "Uh, no ma'am."

"Wonderful! I have the perfect way for you to get involved with your new town. I'm in charge of a fantastic fund-raiser we hold during the Chandler County birthday celebration in November."

Tori's eyes sparkled suddenly with way too much enjoyment. "Oh, Rachel, don't put him on the spot yet!"

His neck hairs rose in warning. "Spot? What spot?"

"We hold a bachelor auction each year and you would be a stunning addition."

"Oh, now, Miss Blakely. Rachel." Winn held both hands up. "Thank you for the compliment, but I don't think so. That's not my kind of thing."

"Oh, please. You think about it. A handsome man like you who knows his horses? You'd be an asset to the event and rake in a whole lot of charity dollars, believe me. We'll talk later. Tori, I want to make sure you're willing to run the petting zoo again."

"Of course. I have some piglets this year that will be just the right age."

"Fantastic. Okay—two things checked off my list. So nice to meet you, Winn. I'm serious about my request. You'd have fun and so would some lucky lady."

Oh hell no, he wouldn't have fun. It sounded one hundred percent like his idea of a nightmare. But Rachel Blakely was gone before he could do more than raise another finger in protest.

"What the hell was that?" he demanded.

Tori busted out laughing. "That was a force of nature. Rachel's amazing—as an editor and a go-getter. And the paper, for its relatively small circulation, is really good. She knows how to get what she needs and wants. You'll be in that bachelor auction, mark my words."

"How much do you want to bet?" He grumbled a little more fiercely than he intended, still rocking from the hurricane that had been the local newspaper editor telling him what to do.

"Doc!"

Another call interrupted them, and this time he looked up to a familiar figure.

"Cripes," Tori said. "It's Will. What could he possibly want?"

"Doc!" The young reporter literally broke into a run. "Did you hear?"

"Hear what, William?"

"At the track. Three more trainers have reported vandalism. There's an epidemic."

"Really? What on earth?" Her voice pitched upward, half in disbelief.

"And," he announced to Winn, way too eagerly, "everyone's looking for you."

Winn's stomach lurched. He yanked his phone out of his jacket pocket, and dismay turned a gut-feeling into definite acid-fueled panic. Eight messages? Why hadn't he heard them? Once more he found Tori's eyes and saw his own new fear mirrored in their depths.

"Let's go," she said. "I'll come with you."

"Don't you have appointments?"

"Nothing that can't be rescheduled."

They stood, and Winn signaled for the waitress, pulling bills out of his pocket as she approached. She'd thanked him for waving off change and Winn stood for Tori to go ahead of him. "Want to ride with me? I'll bring you back here as soon as you need to come."

She didn't hesitate. "I hate to make you drive all those miles, but okay."

"Hey, guys, I can take you right to the people involved." Will grasped the camera bag strap crossed over his chest. "Let me ride in the back seat. I can come back when Doc comes back."

The request actually stopped Winn dead in his rush to the door. He stared at the reporter who was one step from becoming thoroughly annoying.

"Thanks, Mr. Starkey, but I think I can find the information I need, without you making the trip all the way back."

"I'll be there no matter what," Will said, unperturbed at Winn's rebuke. "I'm only trying to help."

"Hey, Ringo, where did you run off to?" Yet another voice heralded a new person joining their revolving door party. A tall, slender, good-looking black man sauntered up, a scowl aimed at Will. "You left lunch like a kid followin' a jack rabbit. Oh, hey, Tori."

"Andy."

She leaned into Winn and her whispered breath sent micro tremors pouncing through every nerve in his body. "Anderson Matthews, the other Chronicles reporter."

"What the hell?" he whispered back. "Is there some secret society for Chandler County journalists we accidentally fell into?"

"I think this is all of them—save a few high school stringers Rachel calls on once in a while. These two have a minor jealous feud going."

"Don't tell me. I'm sure I can't handle the drama." Winn curled his upper lip.

"You need to get over to the Jones farm and cover that pumpkin pie contest rivalry," Andy-Anderson was saying. "You've spent your time at the track."

"The track is my beat," Will retorted. "I have full power to do what I think I need to when it comes to sports. I'm going back out there."

"You're chasing shadows trying to manufacture a story, Ringo. You've got a deadline on that pie story."

"I'll write the pie story in my sleep," Will said. "And stop calling me Ringo or I'll hack into your computer and steal your story. What's the latest for you? Someone saw a UFO north of Bourbonville? That should show me how a real investigative reporter does his job, right?"

Andy shook his head, clearly holding back another retort. Finally he checked his watch and blew out a breath. "Go chase your imaginary track story, but I'll be expecting that copy first thing in the morning."

"Since when does it go to you?"

"Since today. That's what lunch was about—a slight shift in newsroom hierarchy. Half your stuff goes through me now, since there's so much copy Rachel can't get to it all."

"Well, hey, congrats on the promotion. Better you than me," Will said, his voice breezy as ever. "You'll have the copy. You won't need to edit it. I write clean."

Andy clucked a warning. "A haughty spirit goeth before a fall, Ringo. You won't find my password—I'm not worried."

Tori elbowed Winn and nodded at the door.

"Let's go. Rachel says they've been on each other's cases from day one. Don't wave; they aren't paying attention to us."

When they'd slipped out unnoticed, Winn couldn't stop a snort of laughter.

"I don't know about this place, Doc. It's a little like living in a sitcom."

"Some days. Welcome to small town life."

"I do like 'Ringo' though. Starkey, Starr, Ringo. Clever."

"Andy has an arrogant streak and a quick tongue. He'll push that name until it's overused and no fun anymore and then find something else. Or get over it and adopt the kid. I think of Will more as Jimmy Olsen myself. He kind of fits that 'Gosh, Mr. White, I'll go find Superman for you,' persona."

"Poor kid. He's in over his head."

"I don't know. He's either too naïve or too smart to let any of it bother him. We'll find out."

"Speaking of finding out—let's get a move on. I'm worried about my kids again."

"I'm sure they're fine."

"Thanks. I need a good optimist at the moment."

***

To Tori, the scene in front of Winn's tack room was like a calm moment in a bank heist stand-off. Three police officers chatted in a standing huddle across the aisle from the stalls. Leo stood in the tack room doorway, arms crossed, features black as a wall cloud, Renee and Jocelyn sat in canvas chairs on either side of Leo, legs crossed, faces set, eyes glued on the police.

"Mr. Crosby." Officer Hogan stepped from the group when Winn approached.

"Would you like to tell me what the hell is going on here?" Friendly Winn was gone. Back was the cool, flint-eyed trainer. "What right do you have to create a scene in front of my barn?"

"Everything is perfectly quiet, Mr. Crosby," the officer said. "We need to have another look at your equipment and ask a few more questions of your employees. Unfortunately, they're refusing to cooperate. A scene would have been us arresting them for obstruction."

"On what grounds would that be?"

"They're adults. If they refuse to cooperate, we can arrest them. However, all they wanted was to wait for you, so in the name of good will we've waited."

Tori knew full well she wasn't involved in Winn's troubles, nor should she be, but because of their brand new partnership, she felt a spark of ownership in his concerns. As much as she was supposed to remain neutral and interested only in the health of the horses, she couldn't stop herself from slipping toward the three youths ardently holding their ground.

"Hey," she whispered. "You guys okay?"

"Yeah, they haven't done anything but ask questions," Renee said.

"And the horses? Nothing weird with them?"

Leo eyed her. "Why?"

"Sorry," she said. "You don't know me. I just agreed to do some vet work for you all. I guess I can't help worrying more about the horses than I should."

That elicited a smile at least from Jocelyn. "They're fine, right Renee?"

"All good. So you're gonna be our vet?"

"On a trial basis. If you like me. And vice versa."

"Good. I don't like Dr. Marsh." Renee made a face.

"He's a good doctor," Tori said. "He's been here a long time."

"Too long. He's old fashioned and rude."

"He kind of is," Jocelyn agreed.

"Well, he's a colleague, so I'll keep my opinions to myself." Tori winked. Kevin Marsh had been one of her most vocal critics when it had come to Sunspot's surgery, and he still was when it came to bringing him back. "You okay, Leo?"

"Other than being royally pissed off?" The boy shot eye daggers across the aisle.

"I get it. But I see you know how to stay cool."

The boy visibly relaxed. "I know better than to get into shit-slinging with cops."

Rough around the edges, she thought. But he had definitely kept his head.

"Hey guys, I'm really sorry." Winn approached, his eyes angry but his face calm. "My ringer was turned down, but I have no idea how that happened. I always have it on. I missed all your calls."

"You aren't in trouble because of us, are you?" Renee asked. "We weren't going to let them in here without you, but we didn't know what to say. The questions they asked seemed like they had no good answers."

"You did exactly the right thing. Are you okay talking to them now that I'm back?"

"Sure," Renee said. "We've got nothing to hide."

The kids were a thousand percent loyal. Tori could hear it in every word. She didn't understand why the authorities had decided to focus so hard on them. They couldn't be that prejudiced toward tattoos and piercings.

Then again, of course they could be. This was a racetrack.

"Doc. Doc!"

As the police moved in to start talking with the three kids, Tori groaned at the sound of Will's voice.

"Jeez Louise, William. What are you doing here?"

"I told you I'd be here. I thought you'd like to know who's lodging complaints."

She pushed him out of earshot and faced him with a grimace. "What are you talking about?"

"I know the three trainers who found sabotaged tack. The police aren't going to tell you until they clear these guys." He nodded toward Leo, Renee, and Jocelyn. "So I help you and you tell me what you know about this."

"Look, William, I swear I know absolutely nothing. On the surface it looks like they're targeting Winn. Probably because he's new and his staff is a little unusual. But maybe they're questioning everyone like this, so I can't give you a statement. Tell me who the three trainers are, and I'll tell you if I know them. That's the best I have. Then you get your butt out of here. If the police think we're talking to you, they'll have even more reason to grill the kids."

"There's a story here. I can feel it."

"For crying out loud, you'd find a story in your oatmeal right now. Don't make a scandal where there is none." She narrowed her eyes.

"Fine. Mock me. But you'll come running when you need me. Here."

He handed her a piece of paper. "I knew you'd want these. But you owe me. If something turns up…"

"Seems like a reporter who's looking for quid pro quo is asking for trouble."

"I'm not. I'm cultivating my sources. That's all."

"I'm changing your nickname from Ringo to Wile E. Coyote. Now get lost." This time she grinned at him. "Thanks for this."

"I'll be back."

"I would bet my farm on that."

When Tori returned, the questions were following very similar lines to what had been asked that morning. Where had they all been? What work were they doing here? Had anyone come by? Had the barn ever been left unattended? Who could corroborate stories?

She listened to the sincere answers for a while before wandering away to think. She believed Winn. She had to. No way could she misjudge a person so completely. She wouldn't believe he'd put these kids through this kind of game playing and lying. He'd hate that Renee and Leo no longer looked like grooms with a professional job, but instead looked like kids who knew how quickly life could deal them a crappy hand.

"You need to tell me what exactly you think you're looking for." She heard Winn's question and stepped closer again.

One of the officers emerged from the tack room and held out a small box the size of cell phone. "We were looking for these." He removed a cover and held it in front of Winn, who studied the contents silently.

"Scissors." When he spoke, he nearly spat the word. "A seam ripper for pulling out stitching? This is ridiculous."

It *was* ridiculous, Tori thought. It couldn't be coincidence that tack was breaking all through the backside, all on the same day, all on the day Sunspot had come back to the track, and everything pointed to Winn and his young employees. Nothing about the disasters seemed like they should or could be related. And yet they were.

Her thoughts spun.

What did she honestly know about Winn Crosby? Her heart dropped like an anchor. He was cool under pressure. He'd been thoughtful to bring her phone to her. On the surface he treated his workers well, and his workers were disadvantaged kids who were being given a second chance. To top everything off, her suspicious dog liked him. How dishonest could such a person be?

He couldn't be.

Then again, maybe it would be smarter to back away from the whole mess until it got cleared up. She had enough trouble maintaining her professional reputation without getting tangled in a trainer's scandal.

"I'm not going to take you or anyone here in, Mr. Crosby." Hogan had the box back and was putting it into a plastic evidence bag held by Officer Two. "But I strongly suggest you don't leave before we come back to speak with the rest of your workers."

"Oh trust me. I'm not going anywhere."

Winn's voice finally held the strain from holding back anger and worry. At least whatever doubts Tori had, she also had an advantage. She could walk away this minute since the accusations had nothing to do with her. Winn, on the other hand, was in a world of hurt. The burden of proof that the materials found in his tack room weren't his, was on him. Short of hiring a forensics team from *Law and Order* that could get fingerprinting done in fifteen minutes plus commercials, she didn't see how he could prove anything. He needed more expert help than she had to offer.

For long moments she listened to the back and forth between Winn and the police as they gave him orders on what to say and not say to his staff that wasn't there. It angered her so much she finally walked away from the group, ducking into the main aisle and leaning wearily against the side of a shed row. What little she could still hear bothered her in a way she didn't understand. Winn was cooperating; why should that make her angry? The kids were deathly quiet; why did that worry her?

They were being too passive. Too accommodating. Too much like good actors?

For God's sake, Victoria, stop. You're making up a story exactly like you accuse Will Starkey of doing. Use your brain. They didn't do this.

Will.

She dug into the pocket of her jeans and took out the crumpled piece of paper she barely remembered stuffing there. Smoothing it flat she read the scribbled note for the first time and with each short line, her breath came faster. Will had given her three names she knew well. But one of them stood out: the only man in

Churchill Downs' entire backside who she would have said actually hated her. Next to his name, Will had scribbled one line. "Told cops he had reason to suspect Crosby."

And because only one person in the world had known how to help her handle those past run-ins that had caused such bad blood, Tori knew she had to ask for his help again. With unsteady fingers, she pulled the cell phone Winn had returned to her off her belt holder and found the number. When the warm, familiar voice greeted her, her hands and her breathing steadied.

"Hey, Dad," she said. "Please tell me you haven't left town yet."

CHAPTER
Seven

IN HIS ENTIRE life Winn couldn't remember a day that had dragged on so long. This interminable one seemed hell bent on leading him straight to a cliff edge where it would be easier to fling himself off than figure out what to do next.

By 4:00 p.m. neither Sawyer nor Mallory was anywhere to be found. Their phones weren't being answered and messages weren't returned. Winn wasn't worried—Sawyer lived in a two room apartment he shared with Leo. The girls were a mile from the track in a private home with an older woman who knew the situation and had agreed to have them stay. Sooner or later they'd find each other. Until then, however, their MIA status looked suspicious—as if perhaps the pair had skipped town.

He laughed miserably and, as he did once or twice a year, asked his warped, do-gooder self what was wrong with his mind. He should have settled for marrying Rae that lifetime ago, and building a small place with horses and kids and a couple of foster teens he could mentor. He'd have had actual time to be a husband, and a father figure to kids who needed one.

Instead he was an employer, constantly fighting a battle against the world on behalf of young adults who would only ever look to him as a paycheck provider and the warden of a place to bide time until they could get off on their own again. Young people who were good, but who needed constant tending. There would never be time for a real life.

What he'd give for a place like Tori's.

A dull ache filled his stomach at the thought of her. This ridiculous turn of events had obviously turned her off. She'd disappeared for ten minutes during the police questioning only to return with distant and angry eyes. She'd hung around long enough to console the kids and help straighten the tack room the three claimed to have gone over with all but white gloves and a bomb sniffing dog. During it all she'd given Winn little attention much less sympathy. In fact, she looked at him with such sadness he'd wanted to shake her. After the great time together that afternoon, how could she suspect he would orchestrate anything illegal or harmful?

Half an hour ago she'd left again, claiming she had a couple of patients she could check on as long as she was at the track. Winn had promised to bring her back to town for her off track appointments, but she'd insisted he shouldn't leave until the police told him they were finished talking to him. She'd find a way home if need be. She was fine.

Well he *wasn't* fine. And it annoyed as well as pained him that Tori Sterling was partially at fault for that. She was only the vet, damn it. Her opinion should not matter.

Except even after one day with her, it did.

"How do you know I didn't do it?"

He popped his head up from the saddle he was rubbing with a polishing cloth for absolutely no reason. Leo stood before him, hands in pockets, his features a mix of feigned toughness and pure misery. Winn wanted to make light of the question, answer in easy platitudes tough guy style. *Because I hand-picked you, and I'm not stupid. Because you're a good man. Because you've earned my trust.*

All those things were true, but he knew this was not the time for off-handed clichés.

"Do you remember when I hired you? What I told you about screwing up?"

"That screwing up is something we never stop doing."

"It's true. Humans make mistakes. It's how we learn. That's not to say all screw ups are major, but I meant it when I said I wanted to know anytime anything went wrong, from forgetting to fill a water bucket to stealing a car, and that we'd work it out together. That we'd face consequences together."

"Yeah."

"So far, in the year you four have been with me, you've all lived up to that agreement. There have been so few screw ups, really. You told me when you forgot to give medicine to that filly back in Minnesota. You told me when you'd called in sick and actually gone out with some guys you'd met in Iowa. You promised me you hadn't taken a drag when they'd passed around the pot. And you took consequences like a man. The same is true for Sawyer, difficult as he is to read sometimes. And the girls are just as truthful. So, if you tell me you know nothing about what's going on today—you've earned the right to be believed."

The young man said nothing for seconds that dragged as slowly as the day. At last he pulled up a chair and sat, resting elbows on thighs and running his hands down his long, coiled hair.

"You're different," he said. "I never knew anyone like you before."

"Thank God." Winn set down his rag, lightening the mood with a wink and a smile.

"No, man, it's true. Nobody believed me before you. Ever. So I wanted to tell you, right to your face, that I for real don't know anything about the cutters or scissors. But I want to find the asshole who does know."

Winn reached out to put a hand on the boy's leg.

"I appreciate it, Leo. You're a good man, and I hand-picked you, so I've always trusted you." He smiled again as the platitudes found their proper time and place. "Just one thing. We have to do this calmly and by the book. We're all pissed off. But we show it only when appropriate, okay? I'll help you, if you'll help me."

"Like now? Sticking around for house arrest?"

Winn sighed, a rueful chuckle finishing off the breath. "Unless they charge one of us with something, we aren't under arrest. You guys can head out anytime you like. But the implication was that there'd be more questions for Sawyer and Mallory, so maybe we'd like to be around for them. I figure it doesn't hurt to appear as if I'm concerned for my missing stable hands."

"Well I ain't leaving either."

"I know." He nodded his thanks. "We just have to look as if we're doing this by choice."

Silence fell between them again, companionable, making them equals with their thoughts. When Renee stuck her head through the door, the atmosphere had eased.

"Hey, Dr. Sterling is back. She has someone with her."

Winn tamped down his pulse, which rose mutinously at the sound of her name. He stood and offered a hand to Leo.

"All right. Let's see what this is all about."

Tori arrived and offered a smile from beneath sheepishly lowered lids. For the first time since lunch that smile reached her eyes. The man she'd brought with her looked familiar. He'd been trackside that morning—late middle aged, medium height, trim but not muscled, salt and pepper hair, and an approachable demeanor.

"Hi," Tori said. "Are you all okay?"

"We're fine."

"Please don't be angry, but I did something without asking. I brought help."

"Oh?" His eyes grazed skeptically over the man again. There was another vague memory from that morning. This was the man who'd met her after the workout.

"This is my father, Hugh Sterling. Dad, this is Winn Crosby."

Taken aback, he grasped Sterling's outstretched hand and felt him squeeze with firm assurance.

"Mr. Crosby, nice to meet you."

"Call me Winn. Same here."

"Dad is an attorney," Tori said. "He's been in the business of horses and riders a long time, and he's gotten me through every bit of legal business I've ever had to deal with. I asked if he'd come talk to you. You don't have to meet with him, of course, but it might be good to have someone on your side when you answer the next batch of questions."

She'd done this for him? The fragile male pride part of his psyche wanted to be offended. As if she thought he couldn't fight his own battles. Or as if she thought he looked so guilty he needed professional help. But if he'd learned one thing in his climb from the basement of his life and in watching others start that climb themselves, it was that only a complete jackass turned down fortuitous help.

He cleared his throat. "I'm grateful, Tori. Mr. Sterling. I'm not sure what to tell you. I hope I'm not in a place where I need a lawyer."

"I hope not, too. And the informality is mutual. Call me Hugh."

"I'm so sorry I ran off without an explanation." Tori looked him fully in the eyes. "In all honesty I was so angry for you I didn't know what to say or how to help. So rather than say or do something that only made things worse, I followed a lead."

"More than one," Hugh added. "She went to the three other trainers who had tack damaged by someone or something."

"How did you find them?"

"Will Starkey was good to his word. He gave me the names. Unfortunately, one of them is none too fond of me. That's when I thought of calling Dad."

"None too fond…?" Winn's head spun a little as he tried to sort out the maze of information. "You *followed* the leads? You mean, you actually sought these guys out and talked to them?"

"I went as Sunspot's vet. Since the horse and Armand were directly affected by sabotage of whatever kind it was, I asked each trainer what happened and whether any horses were affected so I could start to figure out if this was about hurting animals or injuring people. Two of the three trainers were great. In fact, I told them I thought you'd like to talk with them at some point."

"Yeah, I guess I would." His head still reeled at the knowledge that Tori had gone on this hunting expedition on his behalf.

"The third trainer, Nick Forge, is a different story. He's one I think everyone should keep an eye on."

"What would everybody be looking for?" Winn scrubbed the back of his neck, unhappy that her digging had actually found something suspect.

"He's been in some trouble in the past," Hugh said. "Fined for a number of infractions including improper drug use. Suspended twice for the same. It's been a couple of years since the last suspension, but Tori was instrumental in getting him caught. Mr. Forge has no time or tolerance for her, and he made it clear today he had no information to share."

"So he could still have an axe to grind with her?"

"That's accurate," Hugh agreed.

"On the other hand," Tori said. "He's always been a pretty simple guy in terms of things he tries to get away with. I don't know if he's got the deviousness or even the inclination to set up a big scam that includes wrecking his own equipment to make himself look innocent."

"Sometimes it's the ones who don't seem smart you have to watch out for." Winn rubbed the deepening creases between his brows.

"Precisely why he's a person to watch." Hugh let his gaze swivel around the barn aisle. "If you're comfortable talking to me about what was found in your tack room, I'd be happy to see if I can help. Completely up to you."

Surprised, Winn allowed a grim smile. "You don't usually hear that from a lawyer. What happened to the earnest television pitch about how good you are at what you do?"

Hugh gave a loud scoff. "I'm too old for ambulance chasing. It's far better for me if you actually want my help. Better for you, too."

For the first time in very long day, a knot loosened in Winn's chest. There were few people for the new guy on the block to lean on for help. If Hugh Sterling was as legit as he sounded, maybe there was hope. Winn held out his hand.

"Then thank you. Welcome to the mess that is my world."

"Son, the racing world is messy by definition. All right. Tori tells me you're still looking for a couple of employees."

"Yes."

"Is it unusual for them to be hard to reach?"

"Not particularly. When they're off they're allowed to have lives. One of the two is my oldest, twenty-four, and the other is twenty-three."

"And in general you trust them?"

Unlike the police, Hugh's questioning held no skepticism or criticism. Calm and straightforward, he continued to invite confidence.

"I do. I get asked a lot how I can be so sure, and I've never had a good answer. I talk to them. They talk to me. We've come to a mutual respect."

Hugh contemplated the barn area again and nodded. "Fair enough. Would you show me the tack room where the supposed evidence was found?"

When they stood inside the twelve by twenty foot room, Winn pointed to a table in one corner stacked neatly with bins, plastic drawers, and sorting boxes that housed all his small bits of equipment, from screws and tools to duct tape and leather punches.

"They found the bag with a piece of stirrup leather and a Leatherman tool in it on that table," he said.

"Not hidden?" asked Hugh.

"No. In a spot near a corner and clearly visible. Today they found a small scissors and a heavy duty seam ripper tool in this cabinet." He opened the door of a six-foot metal wardrobe. All they had to do was open the door like I just did, and they were front and center."

Hugh tugged on his lower lip and studied the room, turning slowly in a circle.

"Looking at where the items were found, it's hard not to think something untoward is going on. It does seem unlikely one of your employees is responsible unless he or she isn't thinking too clearly. But if it was someone else, and the items were planted, they were put in extremely obvious places. Why?"

"That's the question I've been asking myself for the past eight hours."

"Let's sit for a few minutes and break this all down," Hugh said. "Maybe there's some kind of pattern. I want to know every unusual thing that's happened from the time the rein broke this morning."

At Winn's invitation, Leo and Renee bustled to get canvas chairs set in front of the tack stall for everyone and sat when Hugh assured them he wanted their input. With a critical eye Winn watched the seasoned lawyer interact with his kids and slowly relaxed. Hugh, as his daughter did, treated them with respect. Although he asked pointed questions, they were aimed at getting information rather than to search for guilt. Gratefully, Winn sat back and let the conversation flow without trying to direct it. The rare experience of letting his over-protectiveness take a rest left him wondering at the sudden power this man had over them all—and yet he couldn't see any reason not to trust him.

"It has definitely been a suspect day based on what you've told me so far," Hugh said after they'd spent half an hour going over the details. "You all have been here since mid-August and there haven't been any run-ins with other trainers or any strange incidents until today. Suddenly there's a broken rein on a Derby contender's bridle that was clearly the result of intentional damage.

That makes one of the things on my list to ask Derry O'Keefe or Fred who checked the tack ."

"Jockeys are meticulous about their tack," Winn agreed. "It is strange he wouldn't have noticed a loose rein."

Hugh nodded. "Exactly. As for the other trainers with damaged equipment, Tori says two had bridles cut, two had stitching on stirrup leathers ripped out, and one of those had a girth buckle compromised. Is that right?"

Tori nodded, her mouth a grim line as she listened to the recap.

"So we know the basic MO all around is the same. I think we need to talk to all the jockeys, not just the trainers. The grooms, too."

"We can do that," Leo said. "We see a lot of them in the cafeteria and they hang out at the gym sometimes."

"You'd be willing to do that?" Tori asked. "It could be uncomfortable, even a little dangerous, to talk to these guys if you're under suspicion."

Leo scowled. "We've made a few friends. There might be one or two that will believe us. Besides, I'm not going to hide now. That'll make us look worse."

"I'm sorry," she said. "I truly didn't mean I thought you should hide. More power to you, Leo."

She gave the boy a quiet smile that warmed Winn's heart. The longer he spent in her company, the more he knew his instincts about her had been right. How had he gotten lucky enough to connect with someone like her?

"If you'll see what they have to say, great," Hugh said. "As for the tools that could have been used to cause all this damage that were found in your tack room…" He rubbed his eyes and blew out a breath. "It happened after two searches—why wasn't everything found the first time? Where did the bags and boxes come from? And when?"

"It made me so mad that the police wouldn't admit the stuff had to be planted for that exact reason." Renee huffed out her anger, crossing her arms defiantly across her chest and kicking at the dirt with her boot toe. "If I were going to do something to hurt a horse or whatever, I wouldn't hide it in my own backyard. Jeez."

Winn smiled sympathetically and reached to give her shoulder a pat. "You'd think that would be obvious. I agree."

"The bad thing is, not all criminals are stupid," she replied. "This one apparently isn't."

"I think we need to wait to analyze the tack room issue after you've talked to, Sawyer and Mallory is it?" Leaning forward, his elbows on his thighs, Hugh smiled. "It truly doesn't do any good to guess or theorize until everyone has added his or her information. It's unlikely, but perhaps one of the others knows or saw something."

"Dad, I've been thinking." Tori bit thoughtfully on a thumbnail. "You have to add Blue Moon's colic to the mix, too. The horse was in perfect health; I saw him the night before specifically because this first workout was so important for Sunspot. And Blue Moon is entered in the same race Fallon and another of Armand's horses are running on Saturday. All these weird connections are plenty strange if you ask me."

"Sounds like we have quite a few questions for Fred," Winn said. "Do we know exactly what happened to Blue Moon and when?"

"Armand told me he was collicky," Hugh said. "But you're right. Fred would have talked to Moon's trainer and will have all the details. Fred is a trainer's trainer."

"He's a local legend," Winn said. "I've talked to him a fair number of times. I'd like to hear his take on all of this."

"I could go see if he's got a couple of minutes," Tori offered. "He's all about helping any way he can."

"Would you be willing to talk to him now?" Hugh asked Winn.

"Any time," he said, but his heart gave a stutter when Tori stood to fetch the veteran trainer.

The tiny group of six gathered in his barn area had created an illusion of safety. Insulated with people who were all on the same page, Winn could make himself believe even this mess would sort itself out. Hugh radiated positive energy, the three kids were tirelessly defensive of him and each other and, although he'd known her a ridiculously short time, Tori felt like the real glue holding them all together. She'd come to his rescue and his defense multiple times, she'd proposed solutions, and she looked at him as if she actually believed every word he said.

He didn't want her to leave now and bring back an interloper. The truth was, he didn't want the whole damn thing to be real. When Tori left and aimed a regret-tinged smile directly at him, reality closed in like pallbearers at a funeral.

If he needed proof Tori had special powers within the group, it came in the awkward silence that seeped in where moments before a sense of camaraderie had been growing. Hugh continued to study everything around him with the interest of an explorer who'd discovered a new cave. Leo and Renee stared at the floor. Jocelyn stood, mumbled that she was going to recheck a couple of saddles and disappeared back into the tack room. Winn tried to form questions for Fred in his mind but couldn't concentrate beyond wondering why nobody had found the cut in the reins.

A sense of powerlessness built as his optimism dissipated.

Footsteps from around the end of the barn, accompanied by familiar voices, finally dragged him out of his funk. Whipping his gaze to the end of the stall row, he waited, edgy with anticipation, and when Sawyer Hawkins, tall, blond, and confident with a habitual swagger that never changed, rounded the corner, Winn jumped from his chair. Mallory Carrick walked close enough beside him that their shoulders brushed, and she flexed her fingers in a way that appeared slightly nervous. She glanced quickly at Sawyer and then fixed her gaze ahead to catch Winn's eyes.

"Where have you two been?" He hadn't intended the accusatory tone, but nerves and relief mixed to sharpen his tongue.

"Uh, it's our day off." Sawyer lifted his brows and gave a pointed shrug. "What's with all the messages?"

"Dude you have no idea what's been going on here." Leo shot from his own chair as if someone had set a fire underneath him. "You should answer your damn phone."

"Whoa. Take it easy, man. We were at a movie and I left my phone in the car to charge."

"And I forgot mine." Mallory stared back. "Chill, Leo. What's going on?"

"It's kind of a mess." Renee joined the new conversation. "We're in a little bit of trouble."

"Jeez, what did you do?" Sawyer's features twisted in exasperation. "Did something happen to one of the horses this morning?"

"Sawyer." Winn stopped him with a word.

"Hey." Sawyer held up his hands. "I'm the one who turned on his phone to find ten crazy messages to get here as soon as possible. "What am I supposed to think?"

"That we need your help?" Winn suggested.

"Yeah, it wasn't so you could jump to some kind of conclusion." Leo curled his lip. "Maybe it was you who did something."

"What the…?" Sawyer sputtered.

"Don't get going, you two," Winn said. "We need a united front. Come on, we'll fill you in."

It took ten minutes to introduce Hugh to Sawyer and Mallory and tell them about the tack sabotage across the backside. The pair listened with wide eyes and no words until Winn told them about the bag and box found with the tools and broken saddle piece.

"Yeah. A weird, green lunch-type bag?" Sawyer asked, his brow furrowed but his eyes clear of any guile.

"Yes." Something deep in Winn's chest clenched in pain at the young man's easy admission. "Did you put it on the table in the tack room?"

"Yeah," he said again. "Some lady from the front office brought it late yesterday and said the post office dropped it by. It was in a box addressed to Churchill Downs and you, and the post office didn't know who should get it. Since I usually open the mail, I opened it. There was that weird bag, and another box. I didn't open those, but I put them in the box they came in and set it on the front of the table."

"The whole box?" Winn asked.

"Yeah."

"You didn't put the bag on the front of the table and the little box in the back?"

"They came together. Why would I separate them?" Sawyer's frown deepened.

For the first time, Winn's calm deserted him. Slamming his palm against a post in front of the tack room, he cursed vividly and dragged his fingers through his hair.

"This gets worse by the damn minute. Now we're not only under suspicion, but we have testimony that one of our own actually handled the items before this morning. It's going to be 'he said, she said' all the way to a suspension."

"Well, now, hang on." Hugh rubbed his chin. "You have testimony that someone else brought the items to your tack room. That's a lead that can be followed. It's not necessarily a bad thing."

"But where's the original box from the post office?" Winn asked. "There's no proof except my say-so and his own that Sawyer is telling the truth."

"I saw the box." Mallory spoke for the first time. "I wasn't here when it came, but I saw it when I was getting Fallon's tack ready last night. I didn't think that much about it. It looked like you'd ordered something, that's all."

"And nobody saw that box this morning?" Hugh looked from one groom to the other.

Jocelyn shook her head. "I was the first one here, but I didn't spend much time in the tack room. I grabbed the saddle and bridle and came out. That's when Renee got here. I didn't notice an open box. Did you?" she asked Renee.

"No, I didn't go into the tack room at all—it was my morning for stalls."

"None of this makes one single bit of sense." Winn blew a breath hard through his teeth and tilted his head back, searching for non-existent answers. Or even the slightest hint of wisdom. "It's like a knotted ball of yarn. Where the hell is the end of the string so I can start unraveling this mess?"

Hugh stood and took three steps so he could place a hand on Winn's shoulder.

"The post office is closed now, of course. But in the morning I'll stop by and see if I can corroborate Sawyer's story with…" he thought a moment. "I think Nancy works there tomorrow. I'll see if she remembers bringing the box to the front office. Then I'll check with Debbie there."

"How do you know them all?" Sawyer asked.

"Dad knows everyone in this place, backside, front office, and in between."

A spear of relief lanced through Winn's frustration when Tori appeared around the corner in time to answer Sawyer's question. Like a kid with a crush, he couldn't stop a grin that formed when she caught his eyes. The soft smile she offered in return brought calm back to his world.

"It's proof I've been around a bit too long, that's all." Hugh said, his eyes twinkling. "Did you find Fred?"

"He'll come by in about ten minutes. He's wrapping a horse's legs and said he'd be happy to talk to us. He wants this solved as much as we do."

"Good." Hugh nodded. "And I think it would be wise to let the police know Mr. Hawkins and Miss Carrick are back. One thing we don't want is to look like we're procrastinating in order to collude or create a story."

We? Surprise hit Winn for the millionth time that day. Since when did people circle their wagons with his? Only one person in his past had ever ridden to his rescue without hard scrabbling on his part to prove he was worthy. He'd learned all too well that earning trust took a very long time and a lot of calm non-confrontation. That part had been difficult for him, but once he'd figured out that mouthing off and arguing with authority only caused problems, he'd made it his credo. Head down, do your job, let the rising tide lift you along—if you were lucky. Yet here were two people with a lot of clout who'd embraced him and his motley bunch after mere minutes. What was he missing? Or maybe it was a simple case of the alarm going off soon and this would all disappear into the smoke of a dream.

He cleared his throat. "I'll call now. Hugh, listen. I hope you know I'm grateful for your advice. But didn't I hear you were retired and about to leave on an extended vacation?"

Hugh waved his hand.

"I have plenty of time to take a vacation. Believe me, my wife is perfectly happy to stay here even through the winter—she was sacrificing several pet projects to head off with me."

"Once I told him all the weird things going on, all the coincidences happening in one day, he was all in," Tori said. "The man can't resist a mystery."

She'd barely gotten the words out when the growing group in the barn aisle was stunned into speechlessness by a looming figure of a man. Well over six feet tall, his eyes a cold blue and his face as calm as the eye of a powerful hurricane, Nick Forge marched toward them. Winn had never met the trainer, but his presence was hard to miss. And his reputation as a hard ass was not a secret.

"A mystery?" the man said, his voice so quietly threatening it rang as if he'd used a bullhorn. "You're damn right it's a mystery. And you." He lasered in on Tori, making hot blood rush without warning to Winn's head. "You think you're the keeper of morals around here and you need to jump into every little issue and figure it out, don't you? Did you set the cops on me? Send them around to make me a suspect? What the hell do you think you are? Everyone's sanctimonious Sunday school teacher?"

When he took another step forward, bringing him to within six feet of Tori, Winn jumped.

"Back off, Forge," he said.

The next thing he knew, a rod of flesh-and-blood steel attached to a hand the size of a Humvee had swept him into the nearest post as easily as a swatter nailed a fly.

CHAPTER Eight

TORI HAD GROWN up with two older brothers who'd made play out of knocking each other silly, so she didn't cry out at the shock of seeing Winn hit the post and drop to the ground. She had no second thoughts, however, about launching herself at Nick Forge's arm and twisting it from the wrist until she brought it behind his back. She dealt with strong thoroughbred horses every day. A surprised trainer, despite his height and weight, was nothing.

"Are you insane?" She spat the words at him like venom and gave his backward-facing arm another yank.

She let him go when he allowed a quick grunt of pain. Dropping to the ground beside Winn, she placed a hand on his chest while he shook his head, eyes dazed mostly with surprise.

"I'm fine," he started to scramble up but she pushed him down. "Tori, I really am."

"Just make sure nothing cracked or got hit when you went down."

"The asshole took me by surprise, that's all. My shoulder hit the post and I lost balance." He protested but nonetheless quieted under her touch.

Angry shouting told her when the others descended on Forge and his protests began, but she refused to look up, concentrating instead on checking Winn's eyes and running her fingers along his shoulder to check for bruised spots. She would have been smarter to believe his insistence that he was fine. Touching him was like touching fire, or so it felt to her fingertips. He might not have been brawny the way Nick Forge was, but Tori doubted she'd be able to summon the strength to lift Winn's arm much less twist it behind his back. Funny the difference between adrenaline and attraction.

"Nothing hurts here?" She pressed one last spot.

"Na. The shoulder blade stings a little, but it was like knocking a funny bone—it'll go away. C'mon." His lowered voice caressed and wheedled as if he had to talk her into believing him. "Let me up now. This is hell on my male pride."

"I'll bet."

There wasn't anything funny about what had just happened, but they smiled anyway. Once they both straightened, Tori finally saw that the tall blond man she assumed was Sawyer Richards had pushed Forge up against a wall and was holding him there. The rest of the kids were haranguing the trainer with epithets and curses, and her father was allowing it for the moment. Clearly Nick Forge was putting up no resistance since none of Winn's young employees could have held him had he wanted to push them aside, but he did gaze back at them with arrogant amusement on his heavy-featured face. Seriously, the man looked far more like a steroidal gym rat than a horse trainer.

"All right, that's enough." Winn's tone brooked no argument, and he expertly guided his charges away from their quarry.

"He has no right to come around our barn punching people out." Leo was the last one to move back.

"True," Winn said. "But he made his own bed—don't you go sleeping in it."

"What kind of panty-waisted girl are you, Crosby?" Forge eased his shoulders as he stepped away from the wall. "I had no intention of knocking you down. You just needed to stay out of my way."

"I'd be careful about using the word 'girl' in that way, Nick." Winn eyed him with reproval. "It wasn't a man who got you into a hammerlock minutes ago."

Whether he did it consciously or not Winn couldn't say, but Forge rubbed his right wrist with his left hand.

"You're new around here," he said. "You maybe don't know the ways of the backside. But here we don't go around siccing cops on each other. We all have our methods and our lines in the sand, and you never know when you might need someone to stick up for you. Vets come and go, but if you want to make it as a trainer, I wouldn't get too cozy with someone today who could stab you in the back tomorrow."

"You do know there's an easier way, right?" Winn asked. "You play by the rules to begin with."

"Oh sure. And your band of ex-cons has done that?" Forge brushed at the legs of his pants as if he'd been the one to hit the dirt.

"In this business they have. And they've paid their dues for the times they didn't. Nobody here is hiding anything, man. We didn't tell anyone to check you out or question you."

"Your cozy little vet did."

"Because she wanted to compare notes and find out if we could come up with a suspect. If you weren't such an arrogant ass and sent her off without asking what she wanted, you'd know that."

At that, fury built again in Forge's eyes.

"You know damn well she suspects me, and now I can see why. She's signed on with you and your juvenile delinquents and wants to deflect attention. Well, *Doctor*." His mouth twisted in sarcasm. "The police questioned me all right, and I'm here to tell you they found nothing incriminating or even suspicious. So from now on, keep your theories to yourself and your damn nose out of my business."

Adrenaline surged through Tori's body, carrying anger with it. Something about the company, however, gave her the strength to tamp down the emotions and follow Winn's lead. If he hadn't lost his cool after being knocked to the ground, Tori could hang onto her own cool after a minor slight. With a deep breath she crossed her arms and struck the most casual pose she could muster.

"Mr. Forge, you're overstepping your boundaries here, and I think it's time for you to leave. The police followed up with everyone who had equipment damaged, not just you, and that wasn't my idea. If you don't believe that, it makes no difference to me."

"Oh I believe they talked to everybody. I also know they all but accused me. And where would they get the idea to do that except from you? I'm warning you, stay away from my business and my horses."

He left without looking back, and when he'd disappeared, calamity broke out. All four grooms fired questions at one time—some for Winn, some for Tori—until it sounded like Hitchcock's The Birds had descended on the barn aisle. Jocelyn sank into a chair her face crestfallen, her eyes bright and slightly scared as if she were thirteen rather than eighteen. Tori's dad leaned against a wall and waited. Finally Tori placed two fingers in her mouth, and a shrill siren of a whistle startled everyone into silence.

Winn half-grinned at her. "Impressive."

"Girls got to have skills," she replied.

"Okay, enough," Winn ordered his crew. "He's gone, and he's not likely to come back. He took a good, long look at Hugh and he knows we're lawyered up, as the saying goes. If Forge is the one behind all this, he won't come looking for more trouble. He'll likely do the opposite and try to disappear."

"You could have scared him off sooner, Dad," Tori said. "Why didn't you jump on him with threats when he knocked Winn down?"

Her dad nodded in understanding. "I thought about it. But it's for Winn to press charges, not me. That can still be done. Mr. Forge is also still our personal prime suspect and I wanted to see what he'd do and say. I'll talk with him again—but it was best to let this visit play itself out. I'm impressed, you all held your tempers well." He cocked his head and pointed at Sawyer. "Although you, Mr. Hawkins, might want to take a few deep breaths before you act. You, too, darling daughter."

"I suppose." She wished she felt even a touch of regret or embarrassment, but it had been highly satisfying to surprise the man.

"It was pretty cool," Sawyer said. "You'd make a good cop. I should know." His engaging smile won Tori over and she put out her hand.

"You must be Sawyer. I'm Tori, your new vet."

"Cool. I didn't know we needed one, but cool."

"And you must be Mallory." She addressed the bright blonde girl with the round, cheerful face who looked as if she could make the zombies on *Walking Dead* smile. "I'm really glad you're both back safely. I think your boss was a little worried."

Sawyer laughed. "Winn worry? What would make you say that? Just because he frets like my grandma used to about everything."

"Yeah, yeah very funny." Winn gave the boy a fake cuff on the top of his head. "Your grandma is salt of the earth if she took time to fret over you."

Once again Tori heard affection clearly through the teasing. Sawyer scoffed and stepped into the tack room, returning seconds later with a kit of grooming tools.

"Going to brush Daisy," he mumbled.

"You don't have to work. It's your day off," Winn said.

"I thought we had to wait for the cops. I'm not sitting around."

"Besides, I think he has a crush on that mare." Mallory gave him a flirty grin.

"And why not? She's prettier than most girls I know."

"Boys are so dumb." Mallory snorted at Renee and Jocelyn.

They all laughed, and Tori dragged an empty chair next to her father's and sat while Winn directed the four kids and got them busy.

"This is the strangest racing barn I've ever seen," she said. "His oldest groom is only twenty-four, his exercise rider is a teenager. They have a relationship like a bunch of kids living with a crusty uncle, and the atmosphere is half summer camp and half boot camp. I have no idea why I'm not running as far from this group as possible."

"I hear you, honey. I didn't want to like them either, but I do. Winn exudes sincerity."

"Are you absolutely sure you want to take this on? I don't know how serious it'll become."

"If Sawyer Hawkins's story checks out at the main office, these kids should be off the hook. There's not a lot of reason to suspect them if the items were delivered by someone else. I believe once the police talk to Sawyer and Mallory, they'll back off and investigate elsewhere."

"I hope so. They have a big race on Saturday. I'd like them to be able to enter it without a scandal hanging over their heads."

"And it will be your first race as Winn Crosby's vet."

"I guess."

"You sure *you're* okay being involved?"

"I have no idea why, but in a weird way they all seem too good to be true. I want to see what happens. There are only six weeks until the end of the racing year. It could be interesting." She took her dad's hand. "I am sorry about you postponing your trip, though."

"Don't be," he soothed. "We weren't exactly booked on an exotic tour. Arizona and New Mexico will still be there in a couple of weeks."

"Thanks, Daddy. You're the best. When y'all are on the case I'm sure everything'll be okay."

He laughed. "Honey, I'm a lawyer who happens to know about horse racing. I'm not Matlock."

"Who?"

"You babies know nothing about the classics. Half lawyer, half detective. Believe me; I'm not that."

"I don't know. I think you've solved a lot of cases with your own brand of investigation."

"Your faith in me is very uplifting, sweetheart."

She smiled as her phone rang. Surprised by the caller ID, she answered cheerfully. "Armand. Didn't expect to hear your voice. What can I do for you?"

"Are you still here. At the track?"

"Yes."

"Come quickly. Please. Sunspot is colicking."

"What? I looked at him in passing twenty minutes ago. What's he doing?"

"He's lying down. Kicking and biting his sides." Armand's voice held barely controlled hysteria. "You must come."

"I'll be there in three minutes. Where's Fred?"

"I don't know. He isn't in his room."

"Are any of your grooms there?"

"There's no one here at the moment."

"I'm on my way. If you can possibly get him on his feet, do it."

Armand's reply was unintelligible. Tori hung up anyway, loath to waste time calming Sunspot's reactionary owner on the phone.

"What's wrong?" Winn stood before her, fresh concern in his eyes.

"Can I borrow a couple of the kids? Sunspot is down in his stall colicking, and Armand is there alone. I need help getting the horse up."

"You don't have to ask. Sawyer is the biggest and strongest, Renee is good at calming horses. Go."

In the end nobody stayed behind, but Tori was too worried to care who followed her through the barns to Armand's stalls. Damn colic. Horses' digestive systems were such fragile things when it came right down to it for such large animals. They couldn't vomit so any impaction, weird feed changes, or twist in a gut could cause problems from mild to deadly. If Sunspot was down and unable to get up—it didn't point to mild. But what was worse was that she'd stupidly come to the track in Winn's car. She would have to scrounge for equipment and drugs if she needed them.

For the first time she chastised herself for letting emotions and feelings for Winn cloud her judgment. She wasn't seeing clients here today, but she never came unprepared. Cursing her stupidity under her breath she ran all the faster.

The colic didn't make sense. Sunspot had been chipper and chomping his hay half an hour before. What the devil was up with this day? It was as if Mercury, Venus and Mars were all in retrograde along with full moons on every planet.

Sunspot's stall door was open, and they found Armand on his knees, crooning words in German to the prostrate colt. The scene was so bizarre—the large man, always so proper except when he was excited, heaped in the shavings like he was filming a scene from *My Friend Flicka*.

"Armand?" Tori placed a hand on the portly man's shoulder.

He looked up. To her relief he wasn't weeping. That was something.

"Something is not right," he said, his accent heavier than usual. "He vas perfectly fine and he just lie down right in front of me. Now he is moaning and won't even try to get up."

"Okay. Let's have a look. I've brought some help. Where did Fred go?"

Winn and Sawyer stepped in and helped Armand to his feet.

"Fred was very strange as well," he said. "He was working in the tack room and suddenly said he felt very ill and was going home."

Tori's brow knotted. "That is weird. He was supposed to come and see us over at Winn's barn. Did he say anything about that?"

"No. He did not to me."

"Whatever. We can't worry about that now." Tori knelt beside the colt. She ran her hands along his neck and frowned. "He's soaked. What on earth? Sometimes horses sweat when they colic, but this is extreme. Armand, when did you notice him sweating like this?"

"When I came to check on him, right before he lay down, he seemed quite wet."

She felt beneath the big horse's jaw for a pulse. It was strong but rapid.

"Sawyer, Leo, I wasn't paying attention and I don't have my own truck here. I want y'all to try and get Sun on his feet. Any horse whispering will be appreciated." Her smile to the girls was hard to muster, but she got one in return from Renee. "If you get him moving, keep him moving. I'll be five minutes."

"What can I do?" Winn stood before her ready to sprint anywhere she sent him. Angry as she was with herself there was no time to panic.

"What's in your tack room first aid kit? Banamine?"

"Only paste."

She thought a moment. The pain reliever in paste form was slower to work than an IV injection, but if it was all she had… "Armand, will you give us permission to go into Fred's tack room? Do you know where he keeps his drugs and first aid supplies?"

"I do. Absolutely."

She and Winn entered the tidy tack room and opened the cabinet Armand indicated. Shuffling through items quickly, Tori found gloves, a stainless steel bucket and sponges, and an ancient stethoscope, but none of the analgesic she wanted.

"Okay, Mallory, run back and grab the Banamine."

"I have a thermometer," Winn said. "And a newer stethoscope."

"You do? Never mind. Grab them," Tori ordered. "Thank you, Mallory. Hurry."

She bit back her angry tears as she made to leave, only to be stopped by Winn. He took her by the upper arms and bent close.

"You had no reason to think you needed your truck. You were off for the afternoon."

"If I'm coming here, there's always a reason to bring my truck."

"He'll be okay. You've got this."

He couldn't know that; she was the doctor and *she* didn't know. But her heart thanked him for the words, and she tried to tell him so without giving away the mushy fear inside that made her feel completely unprofessional.

"Thank you. Let's try and make sure you're right."

Sunspot was up by the time she reached him, and Tori gratefully swallowed the lump of fear that had grown larger with each minute she'd stood in the tack room. She never reacted this way to a sick horse. Sick horses made up three quarters of her professional life, and she prided herself on a kind stall-side manner that complemented her analytical veterinary skill. But she'd lost all perspective with this animal. At this point she didn't want to trust anyone else with him, but that wasn't fair or responsible. To cling to arrogance at this point would be negligent and cruel.

"Winn, can you contact the guard house and see if any other vets are still signed in tonight?"

He pulled out his phone immediately and stepped away to make the call.

Thrusting nerves aside, she watched Renee lead the horse toward her. He looked bad, from the sweat-soaked copper coat and dullness in his eyes to the flared nostrils and reluctance of his gait.

"How difficult was it to get him up?" she asked.

"Both Leo and Sawyer put lead ropes on his halter, and we all did a lot of sweet talking, but it only took a couple of minutes," Renee said. "He really still wants to roll, and he's biting at his sides, but he's a brave boy."

Tori set her hand on the girl's shoulder. "You all did a great job. You can stop walking him for a minute."

She handed the bucket to Leo and asked him to fill it with warm water. Fitting the stethoscope into her ears, she listened to Sun's belly first on one side and then another. Old as the piece of equipment was, she still heard a scratchy whoosh of bowel sounds and relief flooded her.

"This is good," she said. "The plumbing is working, but I admit I didn't expect it based on his symptoms. When they're this painful I worry about a twisted gut. I'll do an internal exam and we'll give him the Banamine when Mallory gets it here. If we find another vet he can tube him. Let's see how he does with the Banamine."

"Jeez is everything all right? I heard there was something going on over here."

Tori's heart fell as Will Starkey closed in on them, nearly jogging.

"Hey, kid, now is *not* the time." Winn stepped in front of him and held up his hand. "You don't belong here, especially at this time of night on a non-race day."

"It's only seven o'clock, and I've been working on a story. What's going on with Sunspot?"

"This is a routine exam, not a story. I'm warning you to leave now."

"Come on." Will craned his neck and called to Tori. "Doc, I helped you out today. Haven't I at least earned a statement? Let me know what's going on."

"We're making sure the horse is healthy after his run this morning," she said, donning her professional face and dragging calm from somewhere deep within her. "Winn is right. This doesn't concern you, and any gossip-column type reporting would be speculation and get you in trouble. I know you're better than that."

"I'm wounded you even said the words 'gossip column' in front of me." His boyish grin outshone the curiosity in his eyes. "Doc, seriously, I'm interested in Sunspot as a fan as well as a reporter. I promise I don't want to do anything to hurt him. Is he really all right?"

"Sawyer." Winn hadn't taken his eyes off the young reporter, and he called his groom without looking.

"Yeah?"

"Stand here with this guy until he leaves. If he takes too long, walk with him. And I'm not talking about gangster movies, so keep your calm."

"Not a problem, boss."

"Just tell me the horse is all right and I'll leave," Will said.

"He's going to be fine," Tori said.

"Going to be?"

"For cripes sake, William," she called. "Stop overanalyzing. Come back tomorrow and I'll talk to you as much as you want."

"I'm holding you to that, Doc."

"All right, it's time to leave," Sawyer said, and took a step that brought him face-to-face with Will, who agreed peaceably.

Tori kept half an eye on Sawyer as he followed Will to end of the aisle, but they stopped short and the young reporter bent down.

"Hey, Doc, I think something got away from you."

He held up a syringe, its needle still attached but capped. Tori exchanged a frown with Winn, who retrieved it and brought it to her.

"What is that?" Armand asked.

"I have no idea," she said. "It isn't one of mine. It's empty but still wet inside, so it was recently used."

"You know what?" Winn said, his voice as dark as his angry features. "I'm getting damn tired of this day."

Tori stared at the syringe, completely at a loss. "Yeah," she said. "No lie."

CHAPTER Nine

WINN SENT HIS kids home by nine o'clock, and sank into a canvas chair beside Fallon's stall. Being near his horses calmed his thrumming nerves and let him begin the impossible process of sorting out the day.

"Bizarre" described it. So did "unbelievable." In fact, a hundred words swam through his brain, but none of them came close to encompassing the long day of exhausted worry. Only two words meant anything: Tori Sterling. Had it not been for her, this day would have been unbearable.

Sunspot would be all right. No other vets had been found to help, but Winn could still picture the quick problem-solving Tori had displayed working with the colt. She'd given him the pain reliever and, even though she didn't have the shoulder-length plastic gloves vets usually used to do an equine rectal exam, she'd taken the short gloves she did have and proceeded to put her entire arm in a place no person with a normal queasiness factor would ever consider. While figuring all that out and keeping Sunspot moving and monitored, she'd also handled the people helping her as well as Ringo the Reporter with command precision. Will Starkey would not be printing any story about what he'd seen after his dealings with Dr. Sterling.

Most vets would very probably have been equally resourceful; they all had to work under stressful conditions sometimes, but Tori had managed it with grace. The way she'd managed the entire day. She was now waiting with the horse until two grooms arrived to take the missing Fred's place. Above and beyond, he thought.

He'd come back to his barn when the police returned to take Sawyer and Mallory's stories. They and the steward had backed off temporarily, since Sawyer swore the items had come from somewhere else and that indicated none of the kids were involved. The problem was they were missing the box the items had been shipped in. Without a return address or name to place the blame elsewhere, the suspicion on Winn's staff couldn't fully be lifted, but all four kids swore they knew nothing and someone had to be using their arrest records against Will.

Now, in the quiet of the nighttime backside, Winn ran that idea over and over in his mind but couldn't come up with any reason he'd be a target. The best he could figure was that, as the newest trainer, he was simply an easy fall guy. Nobody knew him or his employees. Nobody had a personal investment in him or his operation. He'd come in very late in the year and would only be here a few months—nobody would miss him if he were forced to disappear early and not return. But why did they want him gone in the first place?

"It all sucks," he mumbled out loud, and stood to rub Fallon's ungainly head. "Right, boy? What about it?

Do you horses see all and talk about it amongst yourselves?"

"Would that they could, right?"

He started at the quiet voice and then allowed a small grin as heat crept up his neck. "Hey, Tori. All's okay?"

"Two of Armand's grooms are back. I'm about to take a trip all the way to Lexington. A colleague at Hagyard is waiting for me to deliver that empty syringe, and they'll get it out for testing. It could take a few days, so I want to get it into their hands now."

"That's great." Hagyard Equine Medical Institute was one of the top horse clinics in the country. They were a good resource, and a good ally for Tori. "So you're ready to leave? I'll take you."

Her smile was as tired as his felt. "Please don't take this personally, but I called Heidi. She picked up my truck and brought it here so I'd have equipment to take a blood sample from Sun. I'm bringing that in along with the syringe. I'd love to ride to Lexington with you, but it adds an extra hour for you, and you look settled in. Honestly, Winn, you've given me plenty of support today. So, I'm really here to thank you."

"I haven't done a single thing except embroil you in some sort of insane..." He shrugged. "Insane something. I have no idea what today was about."

Her hollow laugh rang with agreement. "I can't even think about tomorrow. Please, Lord, let this be a freakish anomaly. But you're wrong about one thing—you've helped so much. With everything from bringing my phone back, to talking me off of minor ledges, to treating a horse whose illness still makes no sense."

"You're welcome, but I have a list of things you've done for me today, too. I'd say we're even." He paused and then smiled with more confidence when she stepped to Fallon's other side and stroked his neck. "It feels like we've known each other longer than a day. 'Course when it's a day like today was I suppose that makes some sense. I have a poor track record with personal relationships but you made it easy to make a new friend. Professionally, and personally, too."

"I thought that was just me." She gazed at him across Fallon's forehead with a good-natured grin. "If I'm totally honest—for the first ten minutes I knew you, I thought you were arrogant and cold."

"Oh but I am." He returned her grin, but he wasn't totally joking. Reacting to her the way he had today was out of character for him.

"You're so far from either of those. I'm hoping to find your flaws, so this 'relationship' can go back to being colleague to colleague."

"Finding my many flaws is not difficult, Tori. The biggest is that I don't usually do things the way I should, and it makes life tougher for a lot of people."

"Not for those four kids you employ."

"I don't know; you'd be surprised. How many trainers trying to make it to the Kentucky Derby have zero seasoned horse people working for them? How many dump four kids with past problems into a brand new situation and expect them to live up to expectations? Life isn't easy for them, but I hope they're learning from it."

"All I had to do was see how they responded to questioning from the police to know they've learned a lot. You're a unique guy."

"When did you decide I was unique and not arrogant?"

"When you said you'd hired Jocelyn. I've known her a while. She's been ready to give up on this riding dream for a long time."

"I have tats and I used to have a pierced lip."

He almost laughed at the surprise in her eyes.

"I don't believe it. The man who rocks the sexiest newsboy cap on the track?" She obviously read his answering astonishment, because she wrinkled her nose and giggled. "Don't look so surprised—we've all noticed you."

"We?"

"The women around here. I assumed you knew and were pretty stuck on yourself. I've kicked myself multiple times today for believing stereotypes."

Swallowing a sputter, he gave Fallon a long last pat and stepped away. "Hell, you can bet I'll be wearing stall-mucking clothes and a hoodie on Saturday."

"Don't you dare! I just got a job with the hottest trainer at Churchill Downs. I want my moment of glory showing off."

He nearly choked again. "I am so not good at this. Enough with the praise."

"Sorry," she said. "That's very forward, I know. Like you said, I've started feeling as if I know you. So what I'm about to do is even more forward, and maybe inappropriate? But I'm doing it anyway."

The light brush of her lips against his cheek took him so completely by surprise that he barely felt the flutters of pleasure skipping down his spine.

"I can be trained to like inappropriate," he said. "I don't consider myself inappropriately pecked on the cheek, however."

"It's just a thank you. And if we manage to get through tomorrow morning without either of us having a crisis or a police confrontation, I'd love to stop by and finish the business talk from today. Meet all these guys, you know?" She swept her gaze along the row of ten horses.

"That'd be great" he said. "What if I were to add a non-business request? Would you consider dinner with me tomorrow night? Assuming all your crisis and law enforcement conditions are met."

Her eyes lit with pleasure. "I'd like that. Besides, you should be seen around Chandler County. After all, there's that little matter of the bachelor auction coming up."

He snorted, making several horses reply in kind. "Not on your life. I never said yes to your friend."

"You said you'd think about it."

"She *told* me to think about it; that's different. I don't need to."

"Suit yourself. You'll miss out on a great tradition. And..." The light in her eyes had grown from pleasure to downright adorable twinkling. "You never know who's been saving up to purchase exactly the right man."

"Isn't that kind of reverse sexism?" he asked, but his pulse tripped in fresh excitement at her implication.

"Not at all. Legitimate research goes into betting on a bachelor. It isn't all for shallow, eye candy purposes, you know." She winked. "I have to get going and get those samples to the clinic. See you tomorrow?"

"I'll be here."

She nodded contentedly and turned to leave.

"Tori? I forgot to thank you for bringing your father to meet us. I like him."

"I'm glad. I like him, too. And, I promise, he's really good."

She left him with a wave, and he sank back into his chair, less anxious but no less confused. He'd forgotten to ask if she knew how her dogs were doing. What did it say that after only a day he knew what her dogs were up to, what her house looked like, and had met half of her other pets as well as part of her family?

The hot schoolboy crush inside of him flared like a wildfire. It made no sense, but attraction never had. And because it had been so long since he'd paid serious attention to a woman, he didn't really want to force the giddy feelings away. They were pleasure-filled and exciting, if thoroughly unnerving. He'd proven years ago he couldn't handle an actual romantic relationship, but he guessed that didn't mean he'd never find another woman compelling.

The word gave him comfort. "Compelling" was much more mature sounding than "crush." It also explained how two people could bond in less than a day. With everything that had happened between them, how could they not find each other's lives compelling?

He finished his chores, and when everything was as secure as his slightly paranoid mind could make it, he took himself up to his room. For some reason, however, despite convincing himself he'd come to terms with his emotions, sleep did not come easily.

***

"He's fine, Tori? Yes?"

Tori straightened beside Sunspot and pulled her stethoscope free of her ears. With a sympathetic squeeze of Armand's arm she nodded."

"A thousand times, yes you did. And any vet could have done the same. I think he wasn't really as serious as he looked. It was a freak thing."

"Nein! No. Sunspot trusts you. I'm sure that has something to do with his recovery."

"That's kind of you to say. I love him, too, Armand. I don't want anything to happen now that he's come so far."

She left the stall and breathed a sigh of relief. So far the morning hadn't given her any nasty surprises, although it wasn't even eleven yet.

"His first race is in three weeks. Will he be ready?"

"I honestly think so. And you have one racing tomorrow, right?"

"Oh ja. Full Monty. But it is only to test him. He has been given the lowest odds of winning, so I'll be happy if he simply finishes. Fred thinks he will do better, but we will see. I don't vant him to be racing if he doesn't love it."

She smiled at him, truly fond of the way he cared about the animals no matter how eccentric he was. "You're a good owner," she said. "I'm glad you honestly want to find out if your horse likes his job."

"Of course!" His ebullience took over the worry he'd worn so openly. "I am so lucky to haf a job I like. I think my horses should be just as lucky."

Tori caught movement behind her and turned to see Fred shuffling down the aisle. His eyes squinted despite there being no sun, his skin held a wan cast.

"Oh my gosh," she called. "You don't look very well, Fred. Should you be here?"

A weak smile lifted the corners of his mouth. "I'm okay, Tori. I'm real sorry about last night. Bug came on like a sudden bomb. One minute I was fine, the next sick as the plague."

"You should still be resting."

"Nah. I'm really much better. I have too much to get ready for tomorrow. Trainers don't get to be sick on Fridays before race days."

"I don't know where that rule is written down." She studied him. His movements were normal and his voice seemed fine; he just looked pale and tired. She sighed. "You take it easy, okay? Doctor's orders."

He laughed. "I've hung around this game so long the horse docs treat me now?"

"Of course, you're half horse yourself."

"Thanks, Tori. You're good people. Do you still have questions that you didn't get a chance to answer last night?"

She thought a moment. Her father wasn't here this morning, he was tracking down the return address on the box Winn's kids had found the night before. As of twenty minutes ago, Winn had been out on the track with Fallon and three other horses. The police had asked all the questions they had for now of Armand...

"I mostly wanted to know about Blue Moon's illness. What, exactly, is keeping him from running?"

"His trainer said he was acting colicky," Fred said. "It looked pretty serious, but he ended up snapping out of it. Blue Moon's been scratched from the race tomorrow and entered in one three weeks from today. No chances."

"Did Dr. Marsh check him out?"

"I assume so."

Tori frowned. Fred would normally have been on top of any news about a horse supposed to run against his. He must have really gotten sick; the lingering effects were playing havoc with him.

"I'm glad to hear it's probably not serious. I have one more question. Who checked Sun's tack before the workout yesterday? Should he have noticed the cut in Derry's reins?"

Fred scratched his head. "Well Derry checked everything, I'm sure. He always does. I made sure the girth was right because we didn't want anything throwing off the horse's stride because of discomfort. I don't know, everything was done the way we always do it. That kind of a cut is hard to spot."

"I know. I'm looking for common threads, that's all."

"Maybe yesterday was nothing more than a coincidence all around." Fred patted her shoulder. "Some theories say coincidences are simply natural occurrences that have no choice but to happen simply because of the number of events that occur in the universe."

She laughed. "Since when did you become a student of metaphysical phenomena?"

"I have my hobbies. Look, today is going fine. I'm feeling better by the minute. I think we're past the bad day."

"Oh, Fred. I hope you're right."

"Mark my words. I'm here now, and I'll keep an eye on Sunspot. Go do your job and stop worrying."

She didn't believe for a moment the events of yesterday had been coincidence, but she let herself believe the savvy trainer had insight into today. With a nod she acquiesced.

"All right, fine. I'll trust you, but go easy. I hope you feel better."

"Like I said. Better already."

She saw two more horses, both of which were running in the race against Fallon and Full Monty, and when she finished she headed for Winn's barn, anticipation making her eager and hesitant at the same time. She'd slept deeply the night before, but that had led to really great fantasy dreams that hadn't yet dissipated. But there'd also been a nightmare—one where she'd only imagined all the unexpected attraction between her and Winn, and in reality he was the aloof and arrogant trainer she'd imagined him to be.

If that were true, she honestly believed it might break her heart.

You're an idiot.

Sure enough, her worries proved a hundred percent groundless when she found Winn whistling at Fallon's head while Sawyer and Jocelyn untacked the gelding with laughter and banter.

"You all seem happy this morning," Tory called, and relished the flip-flop of her stomach when Winn flashed a huge smile. She thought she'd memorized every detail of his face, but a pair of shallow dimples she'd not seen gave his handsome features an engaging new dimension.

"I am now," he said.

"Oooh, that was smooth. How did you know I could be bought so easily?"

"Oh no, I don't think that at all," he said. "I was only covering all my bases."

"I see. So, things are looking up?"

"Fallon worked like a winner this morning," Jocelyn said, even her normally somber face awash in smiles. "Since he worked yesterday I jogged him today and he felt amazing—pulling and unhappy he couldn't just go."

"He looks like a million bucks," Winn said. "I might even be getting excited for tomorrow."

"Fantastic!"

"He's not a strong favorite, but not bottom of the pack either. I have a good feeling about this gangly guy here. He might not be the prettiest one out there, but nobody thought Seabiscuit was pretty either."

"Aw, don't you listen, Fallon." Tori rubbed his forehead in a circular motion and the big gray lowered his head to lean into her touch. "You're gorgeous and talented, and you've got this."

"Aren't you supposed to be neutral?" Winn teased.

"Nah, I have my faves. I just don't usually say. This guy was Sunspot's guardian angel yesterday. I've put him right up at the top of my list."

"That's a high honor."

"It's just a fickle girl crushing on yet another horse." She kissed Fallon's muzzle and laughed when he snorted in her face. "Yeah, don't take me too seriously. Except the gorgeous, talented, winning part."

"Hey, Dr. Sterling!"

Mallory poked her head out of stall she was mucking, and Tori waved.

"Hey there. Leo and Renee are off today?"

"No, they're around, walking horses," Mallory replied. "We have Thursdays off, they have Tuesdays off."

"The rest of the time it's all hands," Winn said.

"Slave driver." Mallory returned to work.

"More like indentured servants," Sawyer added.

"I can always make it seven days!"

"Anything you want, boss." Mallory's muffled voice floated back.

They certainly made a unique team.

"Would you like to make the rounds and meet the horses now?" Winn asked.

"I'd love to. I want to learn about all their little quirks."

"Do you take this much time with all your clients?"

"I try. I know some vets have so many horses to care for they haven't got the time to know each one. But I have such a widespread practice that isn't all based here at the track, so I can treat them a little more personally."

"I appreciate that. So should everybody."

"I love the racing industry, but I'm not blind to its many problems. Anything I can do to make things safer, healthier, and more enjoyable for the animals I'll do. Most thoroughbreds love their jobs. I want to educate owners about how to make sure that stays true. It's not always easy."

They stopped at the first stall where a pretty bay mare munched happily.

"Here's Kimmy's Kiss, one of my two fillies. She's a three-year-old and has a win and two second place finishes this year. This one next to her is Daisy Chain.

She's coming three and finished second in her first race. She's my Kentucky Oaks prospect."

"Pretty little girls." Tori crooned to the fillies, stroking first Kimmy's sleek, liver chestnut neck and then the wide triangular star on Daisy's forehead.

They continued down the aisle. Leo and Renee returned from cooling their horses and immediately found their next tasks. Every animal appeared superbly conditioned and meticulously groomed. Clearly Winn was teaching his charges well.

"You have an impressive string, Winn. They look fantastic."

"They're pretty young, mostly untried as you heard. But Kimmy's doing well. And Fallon, Daisy, and Bob are my big players for next year."

"Bob the Builder." Tori giggled, as she had the first time she'd heard the big, black colt's name. "Not Midnight Rider or Black Gold or anything impressive."

"The owner has a five-year-old." Winn shrugged. "I don't name 'em, I only make 'em run."

"It's cute as can be. Okay then, I have my notes. I've met my new clients—hopefully never to become actual patients—and I'm excited. No Lasix for Fallon tomorrow, correct?"

"Correct."

"Then I'll come by and make sure all's well. It's an unusual day for me, I have five horses in that race tomorrow."

"Really?"

"Your Fallon, Master Blaster for Brett Mitchell, Pickle in the Middle and Catchastar for Ray Crowell, and Full Monty for Armand. It's pretty rare when I have even two."

"Impressive. I think Pickle and Master Blaster are early favorites."

"They are. One of Nick Forge's horses, Zipline, is running as well. Thankfully I'm not on his payroll tomorrow."

"I'm just glad you're on ours."

She didn't miss the "ours." The same way he'd included his whole crew the day before, he did again now, naturally, with no hesitation.

"I am, too, Winn. Thanks for the opportunity. And the trust."

They stood silently next to the tack room door, the scene of so much drama the day before. She sent a prayer of gratitude heavenward for the calm peace of this morning.

"What are your plans the rest of the afternoon?" Winn asked.

"I'm finished here. I'm going to talk to my dad, and he'll want to let you know if he's found any new information about that box that disappeared. I have seven piglets at my farm to vaccinate sometime today. And I have fall shots for a barn of five horses right after lunch. What about you?"

"It's errand-running day. I'm done here, too, and I have a good crew keeping an eye on things. I have a proposition for you."

She wiggled her brows and thickened a southern accent for him. "Why, good sir, I haven't been propositioned in a while."

"I'm very sorry to disappoint you, but I'm afraid I'm not talkin' about that kind of proposition. I just think we should take the afternoon off once your five horses are done. We deserve it after yesterday."

She mentally sorted through the list of tasks she'd created for her afternoon: fix the broken fence, take care of the pigs, ride her own sadly neglected horses, vacuum the lounge in her barn because cat hair basically filled the air like snow globe glitter whenever anyone opened the door. She rarely took afternoons off in the traditional sense of the word. Guilt assailed her for even contemplating abandoning her duties.

"I would love to," she said at last. "But honestly? I have a list a mile long of—"

"Hey, look, we all do. C'mon with me, and put the list off for one afternoon. At least part of it. Let's have lunch in Bourbonville. You've talked so much about The Brass Rail. I need to try this chicken they make."

Her mouth actually watered. The comfort bar food there was second-to-none. Ethan Hastings' chicken was universally accepted as the best anywhere. She hesitated only a minute, but Winn didn't push. He simply donned a hopeful-puppy expression that melted her heart the exact way a real dog would have.

"You're pathetic." She laughed. "Begging like a basset hound. Okay, fine. The Brass Rail. I can be done with the next call in an hour. How about we meet there at one-thirty?"

"I'm a very happy basset hound."

"Oh, my God, who are you and what have you done with Winn Crosby?" Renee popped up beside them and made a gagging face. "He doesn't ever talk like that."

Tori faced Winn with a feigned glare. "Is that right? Look here, bud, if you aren't Winn Crosby, I don't know you and I certainly don't want to meet you in a dark restaurant."

"Don't listen to her," he said. "She's mad I'm leaving her behind and in charge."

"It's my turn?" Renee's matter-of-fact question showed neither happiness nor distaste.

"Yeah, it is. You create the duty roster." At Tori's questioning glance he nodded toward Renee. "Everyone takes random turns running the show when I'm gone. They know we all pull our weight together around here, and during their lifetimes, they'll be required to take orders from all manner of people—from younger than they are, to good and bad managers. They have to learn to get along and make things work, and still get their jobs done."

"Amazing." She had no other words. Everything the man did surprised her—in the best possible way.

"So I am definitely me." He pointed a warning finger at Renee. "But don't get used to this side—you won't see it very often."

"We love you, Miss Hannigan." Clearly having choreographed their moment, the other three grooms walked up the aisle together chorusing the line from *Annie*. Winn curled his lip at them, then pulled a small spiral notebook out of his jeans pocket and slapped it onto the chair seat.

"Make your grocery list. Do not put beer on it. Do not put hard lemonade or hard anything else on it. Do not put a single pumpkin spice item on it. Other than that, your rotting teeth are your own concern."

The four young people jumped with glee, and Renee grabbed the notebook first. She scribbled for several minutes and passed it to Mallory, who passed it to Leo, who gave it finally to Sawyer. When they were finished it returned to Winn. He perused it and shrugged.

"One of you actually put grapes on here? Somebody else string cheese? Do I need to remind you those are healthy?"

"Sorry. Momentary loss of my mind," Leo said.

"Well, too late. It's on the list. Okay, guys, I'm off in about five minutes. Renee has the lead today. Finish the chores and then keep your eyes open. I have my phone."

"When will you be back?" Renee asked.

To Tori's surprise, Winn looked at *her* and raised a brow. "I don't know for sure. I'll call."

A low rumble of "woo-hoos," whistles, and cat calls followed his announcement. He ignored them and placed one hand gently at the small of Tori's back to urge her away.

"I must have been nuts the day I hired them." He leaned into the tack room and fetched a brown plaid newsboy cap. Tori's stomach gave a slow, pleasant roll as he settled it on his head, and she forced herself not to stare.

Day-um

"Ready?" he asked.

"Lead on." She cleared her head. "I admit, I haven't had a day off in a long time."

CHAPTER Ten

"OH MAN, THEY weren't kidding about this place." Winn groaned with pleasure and leaned back in his chair. The pile of stripped chicken bones on the plate in front of him explained why his belt now squeezed like an overinflated inner tube. He pressed his palms against his stomach. "Best roast chicken I've ever had."

"Yup. Don't even utter the letters KFC around here."

"But Ethan needs to make his portions smaller. On account of gluttons who can't stop at three pieces."

"I'm no better. I had cheese on my fries."

"And a salad. Proud of you."

He looked around the bar, crowded for lunchtime, taking in the ambience of scarred wood flooring, the enormous old bar with its polished oak top and shiny brass rail. It didn't look much like a spot for a gourmet chicken feast, but he couldn't argue with proof.

"This place is busy now, but it really heats up come evening," Tori said. "Pool and bourbon—the stuff of life to the working folk. The bourbon Ethan sells here is his own. He started and owns Wild Horses Distillery out on the northwest edge of town."

"This whole place, Chandler County. It's like its own country between two big cities, isn't it? Everyone is self-sufficient and creative, owns a business or makes what he needs."

"It might look that way," she said. "But we rely a lot on each other. And we live off the tourism surrounding the Kentucky Derby and the county birthday celebration that's coming up in two weeks. You can already see all the advertising and preparations. It's why Rachel was so pushy about the bachelor auction."

A quick, throat-clogging pulse spike made him swallow. "Let's don't start on that again."

"It's pretty fu-un." She waved her fork in the air, her voice rising in enticement. "Told you. You might meet someone."

"Somehow I feel as if I've met more people in the past day and a half than I've met in the whole time I've been here. I think I'm good."

"It's for a great cause."

"I'm doing my community service. Four times over."

"Is that how you look at your four charges? Community service?"

The question held no censure, but a touch of guilt still pricked at his mind as he heard his words. The investment he had in the kids, professionally and emotionally, couldn't be measured. He was prouder than he could say of them all. But he'd been so worried about his own feelings on the bachelor auction issue he'd misspoken.

"Sorry. That sounded callous. They're great, all of them. Anything they get from working for me benefits them, not some need I have to do good. I want you to believe that. But it benefits the community, too. Anytime lost kids find their ways, it's nothing but better for the world."

He couldn't read her eyes as she fixed them on him and chewed her lip as if deep in thought. She studied him for such a long moment he had to stop himself from squirming in his seat.

"What?" he asked finally. "Stop looking at me that way."

"Why?"

"Because I feel like I've grown an extra eyebrow or something."

"No, I meant why do you hire troubled kids? Nobody would choose to wind up under everyone's mistrusting scrutiny just because he's a nice guy. The racing business is way too hard and, face it, dangerous, to use it as a testing ground for employees who might not cut it."

He didn't do small talk about his past. His kids, and these four made the third set he'd hired in the past eight years from a series of halfway homes and work release programs that did good work, might not be charity or community cases, but they were definitely his pathway to absolution. At least they had been at first. Now, they were his life.

"What I told you earlier was the truth. I identify with them."

"But that doesn't tell me anything. Come on, you can trust me."

He sighed, wondering why that felt true. There were people he'd known for years who had no idea about his background and yet, for some reason, the short time he'd known her didn't matter. He didn't understand a single thing that was happening to his emotions.

"Now who's looking like a basset hound?" He paused. "No, more like an eager border collie. Like your Zoom. How are the dogs doing, by the way?"

She fisted her hands beneath her chin and leaned forward on her elbows, capturing him with unwavering eyes.

"They're doing okay, and nice try. I'm not that easily distracted, which is also like a border collie."

With a resigned shake of his head he leaned back and reached to run a forefinger around the handle of his coffee mug. He would much rather have had a shot of the famous bourbon.

"It's not a long story. My dad was the kind of guy nobody knew was a jerk. He wasn't abusive, but he pretty much ignored every duty a father should have. My mom passed away when I was eleven. My younger sister went to live with our aunt, but I stubbornly insisted I stay with my father. I was raised in our house, but it was pretty bare bones. Dad's main job was betting on horses at Hawthorne race track in Chicago. That's the less affluent of the two big tracks there, by the way. By the time I was twelve, I'd seen almost every seedy side of gambling and race fixing and horse doping there was. It's pretty amazing the places an eleven-year-old can hang out without being noticed. People said things they didn't think I was old enough to understand."

"You *saw* doping?"

"More accurately I heard them doping. See, the only place I truly felt like a normal kid who wasn't poor and ratty and had no friends because I barely stayed at school long enough to be legal, was when I was around horses. I heard about milkshaking, joint injections before races, blood doping, and I knew some of the people who asked their vets to do these things for them."

"That's why you asked me about my practices."

"Exactly. One day when I heard that a particular horse had died right after winning a race, I remembered he was horse that had been given several things I knew were illegal, or at least bad, and I finally told my dad. You know what he did? Told me I'd better not ever open my mouth about it again. When I said, "but…" he gave me the first and only fat lip I got from him. But worse than that, he stopped taking me to the track. I went to live with my aunt and my sister."

"My gosh!" She sat back. "Not that it was such a bad thing, I suppose. I'm guessing you could have gotten in big trouble had you blabbed about what you knew."

"I'm sure. But even so I was pissed. I lasted a couple of months with my aunt and uncle and then I ran away. I didn't go back for ten years."

"How old were you?"

"Fourteen."

"Where did you go?"

"I found all kinds of places to sleep the first two weeks—churches, gym locker rooms, closets at school. I made my first friends and they were exactly the kind of friends you'd think a homeless kid would make. I lied about my name, my age, my family and bounced around to three different foster families during the next year."

"Seriously? You were in the system?"

"I was, but not as me. I used the name Jake Olson. My uncle's name and my mother's maiden name. You'd think 'the system' would have dug a little deeper, but they didn't. I told them my parents were dead and I was an only child. They believed me."

"That's insane. Not you, but the whole idea that a system designed to protect kids really doesn't."

"Well, I was safe enough for a while. But I did start going to Arlington Park. I hung out enough that people started to know me, and I started doing stupid little odd jobs for trainers and grooms. Mucking a stall here and there, scrubbing buckets, once in a very great while I got to walk a horse. Those were the times that kept me going."

"And you worked your way up?"

"I started to, and I worked hard enough when I wasn't hanging out with some pretty shady so-called friends. I learned a lot of illegal skills along with the good ones that had to do with horses. It changed after I was finally arrested when two of those 'friends' and I broke into a warehouse to steal money from the office. We all tried to run when the police found us. I actually got away temporarily by leaving my buddy in the dust and breaking through a window. What I had no idea about was that this buddy had a gun. When he tried to buy us time with it so he could follow me, the police shot him. It wasn't a fatal shot, but he lost the use of one arm, and it was my fault. If I'd have simply stayed, faced the consequences and let them take us without a chase, the kid never would have drawn the weapon."

For several very long moments he couldn't tell what Tori was thinking. The rare times he'd told this whole story, he got to this point and the listener immediately began looking at him differently. Now he waited for "that look" to cross Tori's face. It never did.

"You don't know that. Maybe he'd have shot at you for leaving him. Self-preservation is a strong instinct."

Winn stared, almost in disbelief.

"That's not the reaction I usually get."

"Why? You were a kid."

"I was."

"And you got caught. You said."

"By the cop waiting outside. And, the upshot is, they dug out my real identity, found my aunt, who really didn't want responsibility for me. They tried to find my dad, but he was long gone. So, when I went to a halfway-type house, the only person I could think to call was one of the older trainers I'd worked for at Arlington. Sean McLeod. He had zero reason in the world to help me, but he did. He saved my life. He was a badass disciplinarian, but he was fair and smart and a hell of a good horseman."

"Is he still around?"

"No. He died maybe four years ago. I could never repay him."

"Except by passing on what he did for you."

"That's it."

"It's quite a story," she said quietly. "I think I have even more admiration for you than I did before."

"Please don't. This all happened because of luck and the grace of God. I'm nobody to be admired. I do what I do and try not to get anyone or anything hurt ever again."

"Oh, Winn, you're such a tough-but-nice guy. You'd never hurt anyone."

"I keep to my business to make sure that's true."

A rush of relief that had risen within him as he'd told the story dissipated now that the telling was done. He was far from proud of his youth. He didn't like at all that he'd needed the charity of somebody else's good heart to help him be a respectable person. He was thankful, of course. But he didn't like telling people he hadn't been able to manage respectability on his own, or that he'd run from responsibility like his own father had when someone else's life had been on the line.

Embarrassment was supposed to be anathema to Real Men, but Winn found his past highly embarrassing.

"You shouldn't be keeping yourself so private, you know. You should be shouting your ethics to the world. God knows, the racing industry needs voices like yours. Voices calling for changes."

"Hell, no. I also want to make a living."

"I haven't known you for even two full days, Winn Crosby. But I call bullshit."

He sat back at her use of the word. She hadn't let so much as a mild curse word fall from her lips since meeting her. He'd noticed because the backside was as cuss-laden as a sailor's galley.

"Bullshit?"

"You don't care about money. Enough to live on, okay. But you're here because you love the sport, you love the horses, and you love those kids. Period."

"I want a Derby win."

"Sure, but if you never get one, it won't ruin your life."

He had to admit that was true. He was as competitive as the next guy, but if a win never happened legitimately with a perfectly and legally trained horse, that was fine. It was the journey.

He almost gagged on his own sappy thoughts.

"Okay, so now you know my sad story and have me psychoanalyzed. You haven't run screaming, so maybe let's leave it there."

He didn't mean to sound annoyed. He hoped he didn't. Her interest was sincere and guileless; he'd voluntarily told his tale; he had no reason to be unhappy with her. And yet he now sat fully exposed in front of her. There was a lot she could do with all this information in the future.

"I'm sorry." She surprised him—for the hundredth time since they'd met. "I shouldn't have pressed for your story. I can see you don't like to tell it."

He only shrugged.

"Don't be mad." She offered a genuine warm smile. "I meant it when I said you could trust me. It's not my story to tell, so I never will."

Damn. She could also read his mind.

Slowly, his embarrassment and worry faded. He closed his eyes in thanks and reached for her hands. With a squeeze he gathered them into his palms.

"I believe you. I guess it's good to know the truth about someone who hires you. That's all the truth I have."

"Hey," she said, and flipped her hands within his so they clasped fingers and her touch sent a hot spark through his stomach, and lower. "It's not like truth from you surprises me. You're one of the most honest guys I've ever met. Look, I'm glad to know why you do what you do. It makes you real and relatable. We all have pasts."

"I think yours was a lot less shady than mine."

She shrugged. "I grew up the child of a lawyer. I've seen the seedy side of racing, too. I didn't have to run from it, true, but my dad defended some things I wasn't in total agreement with. I had my bout of running away from home—although it was to my best friend's and it was only for a summer."

"Your angry young woman moment?"

"Absolutely. Still, it helped me see that my own family was in a lot better shape than some. And my dad's morals weren't hideous. We all need to learn about life somehow."

Winn released her hand and lifted his coffee mug. "To learning about life."

She raised her glass of diet soda. "Prost. Now, let's say we ditch the serious conversation for some pigs? You can come along and check out your best friend."

"Best friend?"

"Axel the giant wuss. He fell in love with you yesterday, remember?"

"Ah, the dog with good taste."

"That's the one."

She signaled their waitress.

"Please let me get this." Winn touched her hand again. "I asked you to come. You listened to my story. And, in the end, I'm glad you did. Not a payback, but a thanks to a new friend."

She laughed. "Such nice manners you learned from that old trainer of yours. Hey, I might be able to fold back a guy's arm given the right amount of adrenaline, but I'm not so dumb as to turn down a lovely lunch date. It's nice of you."

"Finally. A woman who knows how to take a compliment without getting offended that I'm being a chauvinist."

"You've already proven you're not a chauvinist. Or one of those strident alpha guys. You're okay, Crosby."

"Uh, thanks. I guess I'll take okay if strident is the other choice."

"That's definitely my motto." She gave him a flirty shrug. "Take what you can get."

"Wow. My ego is soaring."

Her playful little shrug shouldn't have fanned the fire starting inside him, and the lashes she batted after a mischievous wink were not, he knew, intended to be sexy—but, lord, they were.

"C'mon, Okay Man. Ride with me to the farm. I can bring you back later since I have some grocery shopping to do anyhow. Might as well take only one vehicle."

"Let's see. I'm not an alpha male, I'm pretty okay, and now I'm letting the lady drive. Guess that's the capper on my masculinity."

"Oh I wouldn't let anyone tell you that. Didn't I tell you once you rock a hot newsboy cap?"

She grabbed his hat off the table and plopped it on his head, tugging on the brim with a satisfied nod and a strange glazing of her eyes. He grinned, perfectly happy to let her steer the teasing this way. The picture of her jumping in like a TV cop to twist Nick Forge's arm nearly out of its socket had never left his mind and it, too, was sexy as hell. He'd left out the part of his story where he'd done plenty of punching in his youth. He could hold his own, but he'd very contently let her drive him around.

For the second time in as many days he rode up the long, pitted gravel driveway, past the pretty painted sign reading "Sanctuary Pond Farm."

"The name sure fits," he said.

"It's serendipity, honestly. The farm was 'the old Martin place' when I was growing up. It wasn't until it went up for sale and I looked at it, only because the acreage was right not because I really wanted it, that some plat map showed a small lake labeled as Sanctuary Pond. I literally bought the place for the name. I'm still not sure it was a smart financial decision, but it's home."

"Why do you say it wasn't smart?"

"Heaven have mercy, I found more to do when I moved in than a stripe counter on a zebra plantation. I had no idea. I've been here five years and work my butt off, but it won't be done by the time I'm ninety-two."

He laughed at her wonderful southern speak. "Isn't that sort of the definition of a farm?"

"So I've learned, especially after seeing the range of properties I visit as a vet. Even the wealthy farms require constant upkeep, and believe me, this sure as horse manure ain't one of the wealthy places."

"Well, it looks great. Welcoming. I told you that before, and it's still the same."

"Thanks, I'm glad. Hard to call your farm 'Sanctuary' if it looks like the sanctuary is for the family from *Deliverance*. Which it did the first year."

He took in the neat, brown fencing that had lined both sides of the driveway and now broke off in two directions creating the end of a large pasture to the left and a border fence leading to Tori's house on the right. Woods surrounded the house and trailed off behind it. In a large, slightly overgrown garden plot near the house's front corner, several bright orange orbs in the tangle of browning foliage told him she'd grown her own pumpkins.

"Big garden."

"My mom helps with that," she said. "I love it, but you can see it's gotten a little out of hand now that it's fall. I'll have to figure out how it'll all get picked and tilled now that she'll be leaving for the winter."

Tori turned away from her renovated farmhouse with its soft, inviting yellow color and white and black trim, and headed down a spur road to the barn. The old building wasn't as shiny and updated as the house. Its gray siding was worn and one loft door was missing, but it still stood sturdy and strong.

"We'll check on Zoom in a few minutes. Let's get the pigs done, and I'll introduce you to the barn's residents."

She'd told him she had a lot of animals, but nothing prepared Winn for the variety of critters housed in the barn and the paddocks around it. Three cats greeted them in the lounge, two orange tabbies and a huge Maine Coon—the one she'd mentioned the day before with only three legs.

"Larry, Curly, and Moe?" he asked.

"Fritz, Mango, and this is Danae," she said as the giant, fluffy gray cat crawled into her lap.

"Of course. Those were my second guesses."

She introduced him to Minnie and Maxie, two rabbits who shared half a stall that had been converted to a hutch, and to Matilda and Woolworth—"Really?" he asked when she told him the name—two sheep, one with a missing ear and the other with a clubbed foot and a permanent limp.

There were seven horses in the pasture, she told him, along with a mammoth-eared donkey named Ashley and a miniature burro named Stewart. But by far the most unusual pair in the barn was a white-tailed fawn starting to grow out of its spots, and a fourth cat, this one a tough-looking gray tiger with one closed eye and a stumpy tail.

"Stella and Mike," she announced. "The fawn has been here a little over two weeks, orphaned when hunters got her mom, like the old Bambi story. She was skittish and undernourished but Mike, who wasn't readily accepted into the cat tribe anyhow, adopted her. She started eating and letting us pet her and check her out. She'll go to an actual wildlife rehab facility soon because I don't want her too domesticated. It would be good to re-introduce her to the wild eventually."

By the time he got to the promised litter of piglets, Winn conceded that Tori Sterling had the most eclectic farm since Old MacDonald.

"So, it's weird, just like I said it was, isn't it?" she asked, as they leaned over a stall door watching the pile of classic pink piglets awaken to the sound of human voices and start tumbling over each other in response.

"Yes. Weird because each of those piggies has a collar. And each collar is a different color. Tori, they're pigs."

She stuck out her bottom lip in a defensive little pout, and he kind of wanted to give it a kiss. "How else am I going to remember their names until they get bigger? Except the runt, there. She's easy."

"They have names, too?" He felt laughter starting to threaten, but he honestly didn't know whether or not she'd be offended if he let it loose. "Seriously. I say again. They're pigs."

"Liesl, Friedrich, Louisa, Kurt, Brigitta, Marta, and Gretl."

He stared at her. The woman was slightly crazy after all. He wished he didn't find it so damn attractive.

"You know. The Sound of Music kids. There were five females and two males in the litter. It seemed perfect."

"I really have to tell you. When I got up this morning, I never for one moment dared hope I'd get the chance to meet the Family von Oink. They sing, too, right?"

She lifted her brows. "Just wait until you hear them sing. You can hold them for me while they demonstrate."

She wasn't kidding. Half an hour later he'd heard every single von Oink baby squeal in notes a coloratura soprano would envy. He'd managed to avoid being pooped on, but he definitely smelled like pig and knew exactly where hold one so it couldn't move for its shot. He'd also decided that if pigs stayed babies he'd get one for himself. They were cuter than some breeds of puppies.

"Baptism by fire, Okay Man," Tori said, when they'd shut the door on the freshly vaccinated piglets and headed out of the barn. "Thank you. So much. That wasn't what you signed on for when you asked for the afternoon off, I'm sure."

"I really doubt I could have come up with a more romantic date if I'd thought about it for a month."

"Oh, you wanted romantic?" She laughed, and heat crawled up his neck. *That* wasn't remotely what he'd intended to say. "Shoot, we could have gathered some manure samples for parasite testing, or given a gecko an enema. I've done that, by the way."

"Jeez, Tori. Do you have to make fun of my idea of romance?"

Their laughter mingled, and when she purposely bumped him with her shoulder and hip, it sent warmth cascading through his entire body.

"A vet's life is far from glamorous ninety percent of the time, and this kind of thing is what's lost me a whole lot of dates in the past that really could have been romantic. You didn't have to help. So…thank you."

"It was my pleasure." She looked at him so skeptically he laughed again. "Really. A new experience. But now it's your turn to tell me why? You asked why I rescue the kids. Why do you rescue animals?"

"My story isn't nearly as altruistic as yours. Honestly? I've always loved animals. And when you become a vet, you see way, way too many animals that aren't loved, and you want to save them all because they can't save themselves. I'm a sucker for that."

They reached the car and she faced him, suddenly serious. "The problem is, I don't treat this like a hobby. This is my life and these animals are as important to me as, well your kids are to you, as others' children are to them. Most people don't understand that."

By "most people" he got the distinct impression she meant men. For the first time he wondered how badly she'd been burned.

"I'm sorry," he said. "I understand. My own people don't get me, either."

"Do you have people still? Your father? Your sister?"

"They're both in Chicago. I see them now and again. My sister is cool. My dad is the same neglectful asshole he always has been. And since I won't give him any 'insider information,' as he calls it, I'm not a favored son. Never mind that I have no information to give him even if I could. But at least he's sober and he's never killed anyone, so I guess I'm lucky."

"That's kind of a low bar, isn't it?"

"It's the highest one he can reach."

She sighed. "We sure do know how to bring a mood down, don't we? Come on. Let's go check the dogs. Then I'll bring you to the actual pond, and you'll see why I bought this place despite its problems."

"No more talk of fathers?"

"Deal."

As if answering a cosmic summons, her phone rang as soon as she'd spoken. Winn waited while she pulled the cell out of her back pocket and checked the caller ID. Laughter spilled from her, and she held up a finger.

"You won't believe this," she said, and answered the call. "Hi, Dad!"

CHAPTER
Eleven

TORI HUNG UP from her father and met the concern in Winn's eyes. She smiled in sympathy and shook her head to ward off his fears.

"It's all okay. He tried calling you and didn't get an answer so he called me."

Winn grabbed his own phone out of his pocket and scowled. "Aw hell. I turned the ringer down at lunch and meant to turn it up again in the car. Sure enough, a missed call."

"No worries. All he wanted to tell you was that he thinks he has a lead on getting a name for the owner of the P.O. Box where the mystery package came from. Since it's private information he has to get a court order so the post office will release it. That might take a few days since we're coming up on the weekend. Just a status update—no bad news."

He lifted his cap and ran a hand through his thick sable hair. With a sheepish grin he set the cap back in place and adjusted it. She could have watched him make the series of motions a hundred times and sighed in appreciation with every repetition.

"I guess yesterday still has me jumpy. Sorry."

"I feel the same way. But, hey, we're past it, right? Come on. Dogs await."

Even though he was no longer frightened and injured, Axel bounded into Winn when he entered the house as if he were a long-lost best friend. This time, however, he rose to his full two-legged height and placed elephant-sized paws on Winn's shoulders.

"Whoa, buddy. Hello there." Winn ruffled his neck fur and accepted dog kisses before Tori could correct the dog and pull him down.

"I'm so sorry. He shouldn't jump like that."

"It's all right. I couldn't get my hands or knees up fast enough to stop him."

She kept the dog off of Winn with some effort and led man and beast into the clinic where Zoom still sat morosely in her kennel and cone. To Tori's delight, the little border collie stood when she saw them and gave several sharp, excited barks.

"You're putting weight on that foot!" she crowed.

Eagerly she let her dog out of the kennel and had her sit. Barely obediently, she allowed her to snip the tape on her bandage and unwrap the gauze. She felt the paw, and Zoom pulled slightly with a whimper.

"Warm," she said, relief rushing to her head, strong as Wild Horses bourbon. "It's still swollen, and the cut from the tight wire is still oozing, but the circulation is back. We might have saved that paw after all."

"That's awesome," Winn said. "Congrats, Doc."

"Nah, Zoom had a lot to do with it. She wanted to get better, didn't you, sweetheart? Oh what a good girl!"

She removed the e-collar. Zoom responded by slathering her cheeks with dog kisses and bouncing like a battery-operated toy even though she didn't yet land with full force on the injured leg. Tori bandaged the wire cut but left the paw free and the collar off.

"Okay! How about I give you a tour of the house and Zoom can come along? We'll see how she does."

"Sure."

Tori loved her house. The remodeling she had planned was far from complete, but she'd filled the spaces she had finished with all the comfy things she loved. She'd never cared about buying all new and modern furnishings, but she'd splurged on cushiony living room furniture and pretty rugs in her favorite blues and purples. Each room had its own rich color scheme, but with help from her talented mother, everything flowed—from creams to yellows to pale blues. It wasn't a crowded house, but it was filled with pictures, portraits, and books she loved.

Not that she had all that much time to sit quietly and enjoy it. Or keep it perfectly tidy. It was barely tidy enough for a tour. Still she enjoyed Winn's compliments as much as if he was congratulating her for something actually important. In truth, it was nice, for a change, to share pieces of her life and herself with someone special.

Was he someone special? She couldn't possibly know that after two days. All she did know was that she hadn't enjoyed someone else's company this much in a long time.

Her pleasure doubled when Winn stopped to peer into Shaq's terrarium and actually spoke through the glass to the sleeping snake. His greeting of "Hi, darlin'," gained him far more than brownie points—it made her wonder if the man was for real.

They left Zoom in her kennel for the walk to the pond so the bandaging would stay dry, and Tori led the way through her back yard and into the woods. She breathed deeply the musty scent of damp earth and fallen leaves. The fall colors were coming to an end, but some maples and oaks still held tight to their pops of color and gave the sunlight plenty to bounce off of. Patches of bright light splotched their path.

"It's nice here," Winn said. "So different from the postcards of Kentucky bluegrass pastures and miles of fencing."

"I know. The backwoods feel is great. We aren't into the eastern hills yet, but we get some of the benefits here. I like fall."

"It is nice. Not as cold as Chicago," he said. "The weather has been surprising."

"We're having a warm autumn. It'll get colder and rainier."

They broke out of the woods and Winn gave a low, sweet whistle. "Wow," he said. "This is it?"

"Sanctuary Pond. Yes. Nice spot, right?"

"More than nice, Tori. I'd have bought the property for this, too."

"So you can see the charm? Past all the work there is left to do?"

The one-acre pond lay nestled in a field of Kelly-green grass, salted with scatterings of bright white rocks and clumps of end-of-season black-eyed Susans. The sun shone on a dizzying blue water surface, reflecting surrounding pine and maple trees and beckoning them to the edge of the water. On the far side, four of her horses grazed. If Winn wanted a postcard, here was her offering.

"In my opinion, there's nothing left to do if you have this to come to every day."

"You're right, but I don't get down here nearly often enough anymore. I used to spend hours here with the dogs and a good book. I've been too successful building up my practice, and there's never time to waste anymore."

"That would not be wasted time."

To her surprise, Winn took her hand and tugged her closer to him. He popped his brows upward in a quick question, and she answered by firmly adjusting her hold in his. They strolled to the naturally wild banks of the pond and followed the pasture grass around toward the horses, who lifted their heads and watched from beneath a lone oak tree.

"You've got a good place here," Winn said.

"I think so."

"Thanks for taking this time with me today. I know it was asking a lot."

Yeah, she thought, he was *definitely* too good to be true. With his reputation for aloofness there was no way he could stay this considerate. She'd been away from men and entanglements for so long now that this man's handsome face and sincere-sounding compliments had turned her head. She didn't mind the novelty for now, but once they both got over this, he'd go back to being his real self and she'd go back to having no time for an afternoon like this.

An afternoon where the spice of aftershave mixed with the sweetness of water and fall leaves carried to her on the hint of a breeze.

Where shivers shot up her arm just from the squeeze of his hand.

Where the silence filled with an anticipation that came far too soon after she'd met this man.

They stopped at a boulder-sized rock jutting from a swell in the ground. Winn sat and pulled Tori to sit beside him.

"It's been a long time since I found a place that made me feel more at home than a race track. I'm not sure I understand it, but this place is well named."

"You *do* feel it." She thrilled with the knowledge. "Sometimes I think this is the only place I love better than my job, too. It's got some kind of pull. As if there's a peace spell over the pond."

"Yeah, I feel it."

Silence fell again, and heat from Winn's body pressing against her side worked its way deep into her body, lighting fires along the way that melted all her wariness into excitement. It pooled low and warm in places that hadn't cared about feeling heat in a long time.

"Don't let anyone ever tell you what you do here isn't incredibly important," he said at last. "If they don't understand, they don't need to take up space in your life."

Her mouth opened in shock at the words. She hadn't said anything about her past with Dale. Nor anyone else. Yet here he was, touching that nerve that had been raw for so long she'd learned to ignore the sting.

"Why would you think—?"

With gentle fingers he touched her cheek and swiveled her face toward his. "Tori." His voice was a low rumble, almost part of the breeze. "Somebody at some point made you too good at apologizing for what you do. You joke that it's crazy, weird, something nobody gets. I laughed along, but not anymore. You don't need to make fun of this. You're a pretty amazing woman." His smile was close, his eyes near enough to spellbind her. "You can save a wild deer *and* put a hammerlock on a six-foot man. Don't you apologize for anything."

The softness of the kiss that followed took her breath away. His lips invited her to accept his, and she angled her head willingly, loving the pleasure. His fingers played at the back of her head, delving into her hair, urging her closer, locking their mouths in sweet exploration. When his lips parted, desire shot through her like needles, so intense she couldn't remember ever reacting to a kiss that way. She met his tongue and tasted, diving into the heat, letting it push the sharpness of her desire into her core.

It didn't scare her until she heard the softest moan and realized it was hers.

The fog of pleasure evaporated and she gasped in dismay. Breaking away she pushed at his chest and he released her immediately then jumped to his feet.

"Tori, I'm sorry. I—"

"No! No it's not that. This was mutual. Very mutual. I...I don't understand. I don't do this."

"Ever?" A slight twinkle returned to his eyes.

"I—" She tried to frown, but her head still spun. "Of course 'ever.' But it's too quick. Winn. Isn't it?"

"A day and three-quarters? Yeah, by most measures I suppose it is. But if it really was mutual, then couldn't it mean we found a different measuring stick?"

"No. Yes...No! I don't know. You're right. I'm defensive about all of this because not once in the past has a guy truly understood. Three of them plus a fiancé who, by the way, were all around quite a bit longer than you've been, have chucked this once they learned I wasn't going to give up the animals for them. They honestly believed I would. I don't want to do... no, I *won't* do that to myself again."

"I get it. Tori, I don't *do* this either. I've had my spectacular failure, too, and I don't have time for a relationship. In fact, I'd be a sucky relationship partner. I don't know why we kissed now except that it felt about as right as anything I've done lately."

She groaned at the words. "Don't say that."

"Why? It's the truth."

"Because I was thinking the same thing and I don't want to justify it."

"You have to justify a kiss? Wasn't it simply an experiment? And a successful one at that?" His smile reached all the way to the summer-sky blue in his eyes.

She stared at the ground, her insides a quivering jumble. "Yes. Pretty successful."

"Come here." He pulled her to a stand and peered at her until she met his eyes. "Can I repeat the experiment? It could be we'd get an entirely different result, and all our worries are for nothing."

She started to shake her head, to guard her heart like she'd claimed she wanted, but without her permission her heart made its own decision, and she lifted onto her toes. They kissed again, without urgency, without tongue, but with bone-melting exploration and intimacy. When he pulled away, he brushed the hair from her face and gave a fatalistic shrug.

"Sorry. Same result."

"Yeah. Dang it." Her attempt to hide her smile failed.

"Look. Nobody can claim to have the results of any experiment with only two samples. If we find we need to prove this theory of successful attraction, we'll have to have a lot more data."

He was definitely succeeding in un-complicating their whole situation with his humor. Her heart still thudded in nervous uncertainty, but it was clearly enjoying the sensation enough to urge her head to follow.

"You have a point."

"Here's how I see it," Winn continued. "The first attempt was a random occurrence—mutually discovered. The second attempt I directed. For the next one, if there is a next one, you should set the parameters. And since you told me this place has some sort of unusual atmosphere—a peace spell, was it?" She nodded, holding back a giggle at his ongoing Mr.

Science character. "Then maybe the experiment needs to be attempted in a different location…"

"Oh I see. You're thinking the site could be affecting the outcomes. When we return to real life, results may vary."

He did laugh this time and pulled her into a warm embrace. Her heart sighed; she rested her head against his chest, suddenly quite all right with the idea of never leaving the pond at all.

"That's exactly right." His voice resonated beneath her ear, deep and blissfully mesmerizing. "Maybe we don't have to worry. Maybe it's just the pond."

She stopped thinking it was "just the pond" as they wandered their way back through the woods and toward the house. They didn't touch, but they talked, and even though the kisses weren't mentioned again, and the silly experiment metaphor fell away into conversation about thirty animals on a one-person farm, and learning how to bet the trifecta at age ten, the bulk of Tori's brain power seemed bent on reliving the moments at Sanctuary.

It wasn't even the first, much more physical kiss that filled her thoughts but the sweet, soft, intimate touch of the second that sent waves of pleasure through her. And the farther they walked from the pond, the stronger the waves got.

Winn halted in the backyard, one of the many spots on the farm that hadn't been touched in terms of renovation. She kept three birdfeeders, and once in a while she mowed the grass, but otherwise trees, wildflowers, and sprouted bird seed made up the landscape. Still, he looked around and nodded appreciatively.

"You're amazing to have created all this yourself."

"Thanks, but nobody ever does anything alone. My parents are amazingly supportive. Heidi works her butt off for me."

"Hey, where is she?"

"She worked this morning, but I try to give her Friday afternoons off. One of my brothers lives in Lexington. He's a musician and jack-of-all trades, including being my part time lawn care dude. So, you see, I can't claim the credit by myself."

"You're kind and modest."

"More like honest and forthright."

"That, too. I like it, though. They're good qualities. People know where they stand with you."

"I could have said 'opinionated and blunt,' you know. Some people don't like those qualities."

"See? You're too hard on yourself. Let me continue telling you to stop it over dinner."

"We could eat here."

"You said you can't cook."

"I said I don't like to cook, not that I can't. I'm willing to do it for a good cause."

"A good cause am I?"

Her phone rang from her pocket and she reached for it, smiling. "In a scientific sense, a very good cause." She studied the caller's number and frowned. "It's Will Starkey. What on earth could he want?"

"Do you have to talk to him?"

"No, but I'm curious, aren't you?" She answered the phone, locking her eyes on Winn's. "Hello, this is Tori."

"Doctor Sterling? Will Starkey. Sorry to bother you but I thought you'd want to know there's another case of colic at the track. A horse you usually take care of, but Doc Marsh is handling it."

"Which horse?"

"One named Master Blaster?"

"No! Will, I appreciate the information, but why are *you* calling me?"

"I asked if anyone had talked to you, and I thought they were making an awful lot of excuses. I asked where you were. Nobody knew and nobody seemed to want to find out either. I'm not sure why, but I thought it was as if they didn't want you to know. Figured I'd see what you thought."

"What the heck? Ringo, my friend, I owe you one. I'm glad someone's seeing him, because I'm a solid half hour or forty minutes away, but I definitely should have gotten at least a call since the horse is supposed to race tomorrow."

Behind her Tori heard Winn's phone ring followed by a *sotto voce* answer she couldn't make out.

"I didn't think you had to come or anything," Will said. "I'm just trying to figure out what's going on around here."

"You think something is strange today?"

"It's been strange for a while now. From the time..." He trailed off, an unfamiliar hesitation in his tone.

"What?" she urged.

"I'm a reporter, Doc, I'm supposed to deal only in facts, so I don't want to pretend I know anything."

"William. C'mon. You've been digging for a story the entire past week. Since I lived a headline-worthy one all day yesterday, I'm looking for any answers I can get. I'll even talk to a reporter. Now tell me what you think."

She waited out his final hesitant second.

"Fine. I *think* things started to go wonky around here when Sunspot returned to stay at the track for the fall. In the week since he arrived, trainers who normally have no problem talking to me have started to clam up. A few people who've never mentioned the Kentucky

Derby are talking about how they might enter a few of the qualifying races. Now tack is being targeted, and all four trainers who've sustained damage are those who might be considered legitimate Derby contenders."

Tori's mind raced through the observations he'd listed, but she couldn't get them to ring true. Things that obvious would be noticeable to everyone, and nobody was talking about such stand-out issues.

"You put this theory together yourself?"

"It's not a theory, just notes. I was sent out here by Rachel to do a comeback kid story on Sunspot because Anderson didn't want to waste his time on it. I went around to get everyone's take and all the angles, you know? But one non-answer led to another, and yesterday, when I found that empty syringe after Sunspot's colic episode, I didn't have any proof that it meant a single thing, but it seemed strange. I know I'm a newb, Doc, but it's feeling like things are mounting up in a really weird way."

The new churning in Tori's stomach was far less pleasant than the butterfly excitement from earlier by the pond with Winn. The situation at the track probably meant nothing. And Master Blaster was being cared for by an experienced vet. On the other hand, one of her horses had an issue, and now she needed to know if the circumstances were suspicious.

"All right. Seriously, William, thanks for letting me know. I'm coming, and I'll be there in forty minutes. Would you do me a favor? Don't tell anyone you called me. Don't tell them I'm on my way."

"No problem, Doc. It'll be interesting to see their faces when you show up all of a sudden. We could learn something."

The kid had a quick brain if, as was likely, a little overactive. And he had done her another big favor. She owed him one.

"Let's hope not. I'm planning on this all being innocent."

"Whatever you say, Doc."

Winn stood across the driveway, his phone still against his ear. Tori's heart fell. Dinner with him was so much more appealing than cutting this lovely afternoon short. For the first time she could remember, something tugged at her equally as hard as the desire to run and check on a horse. She didn't really want to tell him, but Will's theories weren't easily dismissed now that he'd suggested them to her. She could only pray with all her might that this was no more than the kid's pathological eagerness to find a big story.

Waiting for Winn to hang up, she shoved her hands in and out of her pockets, shuffled in place, and practiced words in her mind that would make an excuse for returning to Louisville sound anything but obsessive. When he finally stuffed his phone away, she'd worked herself into an apologetic mess, which worried her. She never apologized for her work.

"Everything okay?" she asked.

"I don't know." His eyes were as troubled as she was. "How about with you?"

"I don't know either. Who called?"

"Mallory. She's concerned about Fallon. Says he's slightly agitated and has a mildly elevated temperature. Not a fever—a hundred and one point two; but that's higher than his normal by a degree. She also said another horse entered in the race tomorrow colicked."

"That's what Will called about." A sudden deep fear sent her heart into triple speed. "He actually said he thinks Master Blaster's trainer wanted to keep me purposely out of the loop."

"Now that you say that, Mallory told me someone came looking for you, except they asked in a really odd way. She said it was more like making sure you weren't there."

"Okay, I'm officially spooked *and* livid. I don't know what the crap is going on, but I have to find out. And then there's Fallon. If something's going on with this race tomorrow, I'm really afraid of him being targeted, too."

"It's not that big a race."

"It didn't start that way. I'm trying to think what's making it important. The only thing that comes to mind is something Will said—that all this week, more and more unknown trainers are starting to talk about the Derby and entering lower level horses."

"Trainers like me?"

"I don't know if you have anything to do with it. And Fallon might be completely fine. He might be anxious and picking up on anticipation in the grooms. I'm sure your guys are nervous for him."

"Maybe."

She sighed and reached for his forearm, looking for comfort from his physical strength as much as to plead her case.

"I'm so sorry," she said. "I don't want to cancel our afternoon off, but—"

"You don't need to say a thing." He pulled her in for a hug, his own nervousness evident once she could feel his heart beating through his jacket. "We're going back to the track. I wouldn't have it any other way."

"I'm still sorry."

"Oh believe me, Dr. Sterling. I am, too." He kissed the top of her head. "I hate putting experiments on hold."

CHAPTER Twelve

SHE INSISTED ON checking Fallon before finding Master Blaster, and Winn was humbled that she'd put his horse first even though she'd been invested in the other for much longer.

"Why would you even think such a thing?" she'd asked. "It's not about me, it's about the horses. Blaster has a vet with him. It's more important that we know Fallon is okay."

She stood up now after listening to the gelding's gut sounds and declaring them perfect. His temp was back to normal, and he was calm after finishing his feed.

"I think he's fine, Winn," Tori said. "I honestly think it was nothing. You said he never seemed painful? You never saw him sweat?" She asked Mallory.

"No. He rolled twice, but they all do that sometimes. He was dancing in his stall and that's not like him."

"You did a great job observing him," Tori said. "You can't take anything for granted the night before a race. I think if he stays like this and nothing changes overnight or tomorrow morning, he's fine to run."

"I have no problem scratching if he's not a hundred percent." Winn's words held no regret or uncertainty.

"I know. But he's a hundred percent." Her face lit with a smile that held needed reassurance. "I told you I could see you aren't in this for greed."

"Money yes, greed no. I've spent my time with greed. It gets you nowhere."

"Hear that?" Mallory called to Renee and Leo. "Life lesson moment. Pay attention."

"Thanks, coach!" Leo called from the tack room.

"You'll be sorry if you're not taking this seriously. There'll be a quiz tomorrow," Winn called back and blew out a long, relieved breath. It was damn good to be joking. The drive to the track had been tense.

"Hey, Doc, you're here."

Winn turned to the young reporter who was suddenly much less annoying. He approached in his usual running walk, wearing his familiar kid-with-a-new-puppy expression, but Tori smiled.

"You're still here?"

"I wasn't going to miss it when you pop up over at Master Blaster's stall."

"Nothing's going to happen," Tori replied firmly.

Will only shrugged. "You don't have a sick horse here, too, do you?"

"No, honestly not," she said. "We're a little paranoid because colic seems to be going around. But this guy's fine. Are they still working on Blaster?"

"They are. They don't know I've been watching from a distance. He seems to be worse off than Sunspot was last night, but I don't know for sure. They're walking him a lot."

"Then I guess it's time his regular vet made an appearance."

"I'd like to go with you." Winn touched her arm.

It was mostly an excuse to touch her at all. Even in the midst of more potential crises he couldn't shake the memories from an hour before. He hadn't lied. He'd avoided relationships like the proverbial plague for the past few years, but she'd broken though his defenses like a herd of horses through a weak fence. He didn't want to lose the closeness they'd stumbled upon at the pond. Maybe he'd joked about experiments and magic spells, but beneath the façade of fun, he'd been serious about his feelings.

"Okay," she said simply. "The moral support would be nice."

Moral support he could do.

He walked beside her through the maze of shed rows to Brett Mitchell's barn. Sawyer followed, along with Will half a barn length behind him. Winn knew Mitchell better than any other trainer on the backside although he wouldn't have called them friends. Aside from Sunspot, Brett Mitchell had the highest profile horses here, yet he was down-to-earth and personable enough.

The size of the crew in front of Master Blaster's stall surprised Winn. He counted eight people: Brett, Doc Marsh, four grooms with tack polishing rags in hands and, most surprising of all, Fred Gault standing beside a young woman in her late twenties or early thirties. Master Blaster, a big-boned bay with a vivid white blaze, stood still at the moment while Marsh held a stethoscope to the horse's belly.

"Hello, everyone!" Tori called. "I heard my guy was having some trouble. How's it going?"

It turned out Will Starkey had not overestimated the shockwave that hit the group when they saw Tori standing mere feet from them. Winn had never seen grown men blanch so quickly or go speechless so completely.

"Tori!" Brett Mitchell was the first to gain his voice. "They told us you were out of touch for the day. I'm so glad you're here."

His words held the brightness of forced sincerity.

"I had left the track, but I can always be reached by leaving a message with my service," she replied, her voice casual, non-accusatory. "Kevin, how's he doing?"

The older vet straightened, his lined face serious, his salt-and-pepper brows furrowed as if he didn't quite comprehend why she was there. "Gut sounds are starting to come back after two hours of pretty severe cramping. He was one hurting horse."

"Any other symptoms?" Tori pulled her stethoscope from a jacket pocket and unwrapped it.

"Profuse sweating. Elevated temperature. Flank biting, rolling. No bowel torsions."

"Would you mind if I took a listen?" she asked. "I had a similar case last night. It might be helpful to compare."

Marsh held out his hand in invitation and Tori placed a hand gently on the colt's neck.

"Hello, baby," she murmured. "You look awfully tired."

While she bent, Winn studied the others. He couldn't miss the look of consternation that passed between Marsh and Mitchell, but the grooms, three Hispanic men and one black girl, simply watched in interest. None of them looked particularly concerned. Finally there was Fred, and Winn chose him to approach.

"Hey, man. Surprised to see you here."

"Naw," he replied. "I'm here for the same reason Tori is. It was so damn scary last night, I want to know if this is anything like what happened to us."

That made perfect sense. Fred was well known for following up on the smallest of details when it came to his horses. He would be doing all he could to protect Sunspot.

"Sun is okay today?"

"He looks great, yeah. He's mad because he can't follow his barn mates out to the track."

Winn laughed. "I have a couple like that. Babies that are here to learn and seem to be quick studies, so they want to work."

Tori stood. "Things are pretty sluggish," she said. "He seems calm, though."

"Much calmer than he was," Marsh replied. "He's improving slowly. I'm guessing it's an impaction that's slowly breaking up. Maybe we'll get lucky and that'll be that."

"Such odd symptoms." Tori shook her head. "Thanks, Kevin. Looks like he was in good hands."

She left Marsh looking slightly surprised, as if he'd expected her to take over. Nobody but Fred had even acknowledged Winn's presence, but their heads swiveled as if they were a collective entity, watching Tori head for him now. They couldn't see the curtain of fury in her eyes, but he could.

"You are a model of restraint," he said, keeping his voice low.

"Anything else would have been counterproductive, and unprofessional." She plastered on a smile for Fred. "Sorry. Déjà vu much? What do you think? Same thing?"

"I don't know. He seems worse than Sun was. It's scary." He reached to give her a warm hug. "So they didn't call you, huh?"

"Nope." She raised and lowered her brows for emphasis. "And I plan to have a chat with Brett about that. Did you notice he'll barely look me in the eye? What's that about?"

"He knows you're pissed off," Winn said simply.

"I am. I couldn't care less about Kevin Marsh being called; that's exactly what should have been done. I wasn't around, and the horse needed immediate care. I should have been sent a message, however. I need to know everything that's going on with a colt before a race. If anything goes wrong, I'm the vet of record. I deserve a heads up."

She released a long sigh and looked at Winn, her eyes clearer. "Sorry. I'm angry and I'm worried. I don't like this double whammy of weird colic. It reminds me of something I can't quite put my finger on. I have a little research to do tonight."

"You're a good vet," Winn said. "If there's something to figure out, you'll do it."

"Well done on the moral support, Mr. Crosby." She stroked his upper arm. "I feel better already. Fred, I'd like to look in on Sun. Would that be okay?"

He shrugged. "Sure. It's four-thirty. He's probably just coming in from getting walked. Tori?" Fred stepped back to stand beside the younger woman who'd been utterly silent. "I'd like you to meet my daughter, Cynthia. She arrived this morning from New York. I'm sure you've heard me bragging about her." He smiled.

Cynthia Gault stepped forward; her snow white turtleneck sweater and khaki wool slacks looked as if they belonged right on Millionaire's Row with Kentucky's elite.

"I sure have." Tori held out her hand. "Nice to meet you, Cynthia. What brings y'all to Kentucky?"

"I work as a financial planner in New York City, and I act as Dad's CFO. Twice a year I catch up with him, and we go over his business. It was my turn to come here since it's getting cold in New York, and I do cold very poorly."

The woman spoke with diction sharp as a Manhattan lawyer's and smooth as Kentucky bourbon. She was also as beautiful as her father was weathered, with straight, blunt-cut brown hair and dazzling eyes that looked right through a person. Something imperceptible as she offered a hand to Winn unnerved him, and he kept their shake short and impersonal.

Tori asked Dr. Marsh to call her if there were any changes and told Brett Mitchell in a deceptively pleasant voice that she'd talk to him in the morning assuming nothing changed. He, too, nodded with obvious relief. After that she led the way from Master Blaster's stall without looking back.

Innocuous small talk accompanied them back to Fred's barn, and it was only after they arrived to find Sun's stall still empty that Sawyer leaned in and whispered his first words to Winn.

"Where's that reporter dude?"

Winn looked around and frowned. "I don't know. I haven't seen him since we left our barn. What do you make of him?"

"No clue. At first I thought he was just an asshole looking for any kind of story. But I think he really wants to get things right. And he's actually helped out a little."

"I agree. Well, you have a good sense of people. Keep an eye on this one." He nodded toward Cynthia.

"She's pretty chill."

Winn snorted. "Right?"

They waited perhaps three minutes before Sunspot, led by one of Armand's longtime grooms, came around the corner. Tori immediately gasped, and Fred stared at her.

"Stop!" she called to the groom. "Stop walking now!"

"What?" Fred asked.

"He's three-legged lame. On the injured leg."

How she'd seen that in four seconds Winn didn't know, but his heart raced for her. For a horse to show lameness at the walk was bad.

"What the hell?" Fred asked again.

Tori sprinted halfway to the horse, slowing only so she wouldn't startle him. Fred trotted right behind her, Winn followed with Cynthia and Sawyer on his heels.

"Didn't you notice him limping?" Tori grilled the groom, who shook his head, eyes wide. He knew exactly what was at stake. "Damn it."

She swore for the second time, squatted, and ran her hand down Sunspot's leg, feeling the cannon bone and then gently squeezing the flexor tendons down the back.

"No swelling. No heat," she murmured to Fred. She stood. "Okay, walk him a few steps."

This time even Sawyer saw the alarming limp. "Jeez," he said.

"Oh no." Winn's heart sank further.

"Hang on." Tori held up her hand.

She bent again and lifted Sun's foot. "Crap! Look at this. The shoe is completely sprung. But this isn't naturally pulling off. Somebody started to pull this by hand and purposely bent it."

Winn caught a look at the lightweight aluminum racing shoe. The left side had pulled loose from the hoof and was bent lengthwise from toe to heel.

"Those racing plates are pretty soft," Fred said. "It's possible it caught on something."

"It would have had to be something pretty strong, and he would have twisted something in his leg to bend it that way," Tori replied. "If the end had bent up or the nails pulled out and bent around I'd have said yes. But this was deliberate."

Immediately Fred's face hardened. "I don't believe

that, Tori. Who would have reason to do something so ridiculous? What purpose would it serve?"

"Someone who wants to reinjure that leg? Someone who wants to keep a talented colt out of the big races? I don't think his colic was a random happening either."

"Oh, come on." Cynthia spoke up. "I've been around my dad's horses all my life. Colic happens all the time."

"It does." Tori said nothing else even though Cynthia tensed waiting for more of a response.

"Fred, grab a shoe puller."

Once the trainer had retrieved the long-handled pliers-like tool, Tori got the broken shoe off in seconds and had the groom walk Sun again. The horse still limped very slightly but Tori let out a huge breath.

"He looks better," Fred said.

"Much. The unevenness now is due to the one bare foot, I'm pretty sure. He might have a sore muscle or two tomorrow, depending on how long the shoe was like that, but I don't think he injured anything."

"Thank God," Fred said. "I'll make sure his stall has extra bedding."

"Oh no, he's not staying here."

Winn had never heard Tori's voice as commanding as it was now.

"He has to stay here." Fred stared at her.

"He's coming to my place. Today."

"Armand won't…"

"I'll call him. Armand will do what I suggest. Look, Fred, you have so much to do in the next week. Tomorrow's race. Four more before next weekend, and then Sunspot runs two weekends after that. We can't take any chances. Somebody is after him."

"You know I love you, Tori, but I think you're overreacting. We can't continue training if Sunspot leaves. I'll make sure he's got round the clock eyes on him."

"He'll have eyes on him all right." She set her jaw. "At my barn. I'm only a few miles from Murphy Equestrian, and they have a great training track. We'll take him there. You and I can coordinate. I'm sure Derry will come and work with him in Chandlerville. I also happen to know a great exercise rider. She'll do you and Derry proud." She met Winn's eyes. "You can spare Jocelyn a few hours a week?"

"Absolutely." He grinned, loving more and more this decisiveness in her personality; such an attractive counterpoint to the sweet vulnerability he'd seen earlier. "Whatever you need."

"I don't have time for a horse to be thirty miles away." Fred sighed, clearly aggrieved.

"Fred." She stood before him, smiling kindly. "This isn't a slam against you or the care you can give him. It's about thwarting whoever wants to hurt him. There's something very weird going on around here, and even though none of it makes sense or seems connected, I want to do something proactive. This is better than having something happen, right?"

Fred patted her arm, glanced at his daughter who shrugged, and then smiled, resigned.

"You're right, Tori. Of course you're right. The horse is too valuable, and he's come too far. I know you're invested in him, too."

"I am." Tori kissed him on his lined cheek. "I'll call Armand now, and I'll get Heidi to go grab my trailer. Meanwhile, let's wrap Sun's legs to give him some support and get the farrier over here to replace the shoe immediately."

"All right." Fred nodded.

"Winn. Which of your four kids would be the least heartbroken to miss Fallon's race tomorrow?" She smiled. "Would someone be willing to babysit Sun? I'd like to hire a personal guardian for the next couple of days if you're willing to spare someone."

"I'll do it." Sawyer offered without hesitation. "I'm sure Mallory will, too. Renee is Fallon's main caregiver; the horse loves her. She should be here for his race tomorrow."

"You can rotate if you want to," Tori said. "And if Winn needs you, Heidi can fill in."

"I think you should take one of my guys," Fred said. "Vincente knows the horse and his routine."

Tori cupped her hand on his arm, just above his elbow. "Fred, listen to me. I don't believe for a moment your staff had a single thing to do with this. But honestly? The only person I trust around him right now is you. And since you can't possibly leave and stay full time at my place, I want to control who has access to Sun for a while."

"And you trust Crosby's kids? Tori, some of them have records. How do you know they aren't behind this?"

Winn looked at her in amusement. How was she going to answer this one? he wondered.

"Two ways. One, I've gotten to know them, and I've seen how they care about horses. Two, they don't have the expertise to pull off some of the things that are going on. They also have no motive whatsoever."

She'd already shown multiple times that she'd accepted his unorthodox work family, so why Tori's vote of confidence this time still had the power to shock he had no idea. He relished the deep warmth her words gave him and sent Sawyer a thumbs up.

"Winn isn't behind any of this, Fred. Help me out. Keep your eyes open and let's solve this—if there's anything to solve."

"Dad's whole business depends on horses like Sunspot." For the first time Cynthia's smooth voice held an imperious edge. "He'll be vigilant, you can rest assured."

Winn's annoyance bubbled under the surface on Tori's behalf, but once again she staved off his anger with her unarguable calm.

"Believe me, I hope your dad is absolutely right and I'm being ridiculously paranoid. Nothing would make me happier than to look a fool over this."

Cynthia clearly had no retort, so she shrugged. "Do what you think best, Dad."

"I don't like it," Fred said, "but I'm afraid you're probably right to err on the side of caution."

"I don't like it either, but in this business, caution is always the best." Tori sighed. "You won't regret it. Okay. Sawyer, will you stay here until the farrier comes and give me a call? I want to look at the hoof angles with him before he fits the new shoe."

"Sure thing, Doc."

"I'll be back after I talk to Armand and check Fallon one more time."

She watched Sunspot walk into his stall and, apparently satisfied that he was all right for the moment, turned, grasping Winn's arm as she walked away.

"Sorry," she said when they were out of hearing distance.

"What for?"

"For taking charge of Sawyer and assuming it was okay. I'm not his employer."

"Jeez, Tori, no worries. You told him in a tangible way nobody outside of my group ever does that you trust him implicitly. He's a good young horseman even though he's still rough around the edges. But did you notice that not a single sarcastic remark came from his mouth? Believe me, you have my blessing."

"I know Fred isn't happy with me for this, but I have to be honest with you. Anyone who was in that group around Master Blaster's stall makes me uneasy, Fred included. Even he looked at me like I was the Ghost of Christmas Future. I think he was there for exactly the reason he said he was there, but still..."

"He was there." Winn finished. "Well, I hope to God you are the ghost of the future. Someone needs to see what's coming."

"I see nothing. I wish I did. None of this makes any sense, and there's nothing that binds busted up tack, two colic cases and a broken horseshoe together."

"Except both horses are under your care and all the evidence points to me and my kids."

"But you and I just met. We aren't connected before yesterday."

"I know." Confusion swept through him—a familiar feeling. "That's why I have no theory."

"But you feel it, too? The weirdness of coincidence? I'm not being crazy?"

He chuckled. "You might be crazy. I'd like to take the time and find that out for myself. You are definitely, however, a very good vet. I would follow your advice without question, crazy or not."

"Well then. Ain't I just more special than yesterday's leftovers in the pig trough?"

He laughed out right. She didn't let her southern side show all that often. When she did, it was silly, and sexy as hell. He put his arm around her shoulders.

"Have I told you I like leftovers?" She snorted and bumped him with her hip. "C'mon, Dr. Sterling. I'll help you move a horse."

CHAPTER
Thirteen

T ORI YAWNED, PARTLY from fatigue and partly to encourage the regiment of butterflies encamped in her stomach for the past eighteen hours to finally leave. She stood with the crowd looking over the Downs' famous paddock and saddling stalls where Renee held Fallon's bridle and Derry listened to Winn's final instructions. She loved watching him—an insight she'd gained throughout this morning while he'd efficiently choreographed his barn into race readiness.

He was fit and toned, not like the trainers she knew who definitely didn't keep themselves in the same shape as their horses, and it certainly made him easy on the eyes. The real attraction, however, was the way he worked with no wasted effort, like a circus performer who knew one extra movement could cause an act to fall apart. This morning she'd also watched him ride for the first time, heading off to the track with Jocelyn as they strategized a new exercise for one of the colts. He rode as beautifully as he walked.

Now he stood with his hand on Derry's shoulder and nodded as the jockey asked his last questions. Winn smiled, gave Derry's back a pat of encouragement and laced his fingers together to give him a leg up. Once his jockey was astride, Winn gave Fallon a last pat and left them, trotting toward Tori with a slightly pale smile in place.

"My job's done," he said. "Up to Derry and Fallon now."

"And you'll honestly be happy if he simply avoids coming in last?" Tori laughed as he took her arm and propelled her away from the paddock.

"I'll be relieved. Secretly, of course I want the win. I'd be thrilled to show. But that isn't going to happen his first time out against a strong field. I would have preferred a race of all maidens, but that was too far in the future. He needs the experience and I need to see him compete. So…Derry's instructions are to keep him safe, keep him mid-pack and guide him into running his own race. He's got talent, I know that, but we'll see."

"Wanna place a bet on him?"

"Oh no. No, ma'am. I never bet on my own horses. Bad juju."

She covered her mouth and grimaced. "I'm not allowed to bet, but is it bad juju if I had William place a bet on him for us?"

"You did?"

"Sorry."

"No, no, I think my superstition only extends to me. What did he bet?"

"Oh big bucks." She laughed. "Two dollars to win."

He covered his eyes with his hand and screwed up his face to keep from laughing. "You're insane."

They made their way to the seating area and settled behind two women the right age split to be mother and daughter. The pair avidly read off the names of the seven horses in Fallon's race, the third of the afternoon. Tori chuckled at the women's debate. Names and silk colors seemed to be their betting criteria. She loved it.

"So Sunspot was okay this morning?" Winn asked.

He rolled and unrolled his racing program constantly and drummed his thigh periodically like a jazz percussionist. The toe of his left foot kept the same rapid beat.

"He was great. I think he likes the sheep. He was all about craning his neck into their stall to see what they were having for breakfast. It's good to have Sawyer there. He walked him out and Sun looks perfect. I think we really dodged a bullet. Hey. Are you always this nervous?"

"I have been every single time I've run a horse at Churchill Downs."

"So, once!"

"Do not mock me."

"I wouldn't dare." She rubbed his arm soothingly. "You have a very tough job."

"I love training them. I hate racing them."

"I get it."

He was adorable when he was in a panic.

In the row ahead of the mother and daughter, Tori watched three men find seats. Immediately they unfolded several sets of racing forms, sheets and newspapers. In juxtaposition to the women, they discussed merits of trainers, jockeys, race records, and times.

"Want a great distraction?" She whispered to Winn and pointed surreptitiously. "The two ends of the parimutual spectrum. Pure fun versus statistical analysis.

"Look at this, Julie," the woman said. "Since the names aren't speaking to us, here's a jockey wearing red and purple with a little yellow. My three favorite colors."

"Fallon," the daughter named Julie read. "Is that the one? Decide, Mom. We don't have much time."

Tori poked at Winn with an excited giggle. "Look at you, getting the fun vote."

"Ma'am?" One of the men in front of Julie turned, slight condescension puckering his features. "I would be happy to help you make a more informed choice than silk colors. There is an art to betting—would you like me to explain the racing form?"

"Oh we're only here for the fun." Julie's mom smiled happily. "We have our own system. But thank you for offering."

The man pressed his lips together to mask a patronizing smile, and when Julie left to place her last-minute bet, all three men shook their heads and chortled together. Tori curled her lip at their backs.

"Know-it-alls. Takes the fun out of it."

"Oh yeah." Winn's skin had a slight green tinge. "This is so much fun."

Julie returned, told her mother they each had five dollars on Fallon to win and two to show. Then she asked the men who they'd bet on.

"The winner," one said. "Pickleinthemiddle."

"Such a silly name for a race horse," Julie replied. "Who wants a horse stuck in the middle?"

At that the men laughed out loud and waved their hands in dismissal.

"I agree with the ladies," Winn whispered.

Ten minutes later the seven horses were amassed behind the starting gate and Tori nearly had to sit on Winn's hands to keep him from shredding his program. She checked the odds and wasn't surprised. Pickle was going off the favorite at three to two, Catchastar was second at five to one. Nick's horse Zipline was in the middle, Fallon was going off at ten to one, Full Monty was near the bottom at twenty-five to one. It was exactly as expected.

"He's going in," Winn said, as Fallon politely entered the starting gate, Derry's red-and-purple silks front with their red-and-yellow diamond-patterned sleeves making him easy to spot. Seconds later the wait ended with the bell as the gates sprang open. "All right, boy. Let's do it."

Suddenly much calmer, Winn turned back from spectator to trainer. Tori heard him analyzing under his breath as Fallon settled into the middle of the pack with Catchastar and Pickle in the lead, and Full Monty bringing up the rear.

It was a mid-distance race of six-and-a-half furlongs, just over three-fourths of a mile, and the first quarter was slow. Winn muttered "good, good," and Tori's heart pounded in her chest along with the hoofbeats. The horses reached the three-eighths pole and the pace picked up. By halfway through, they were speeding and Fallon passed first one horse and then another to find third place.

"Holy shit." Winn stared. "Check out our boy."

"Not only that!" Tori waved wildly. "Check out Monty!"

Unbelievably, Armand's high-odds gelding was charging from behind, getting roars from the spectators as he crept up on Fallon and seemed to push the gray into a new gear. Then it was Zipline's turn to make a move in the backstretch, and as the field rounded for home Fallon passed Pickle with Full Monty sticking behind and closing a one-length gap.

Three horses, Catchastar, Fallon, and Full Monty thundered toward the finish, and Winn was on his feet, his shouts lost in the roar around them. Tori couldn't even hear herself until Monty gave yet another surge and drew head-to-head with Fallon. Derry hunched further over the big gray's neck, pumping with his legs, but keeping his whip still.

"Go! Go, Fallon! You can do it, baby!" Tori shouted at the top of her lungs with the rest of the crowd.

She wasn't really supposed to take sides when it came to her clients, but how could she not want this baby racer to win his first outing? Winn slapped his rolled program against his palm and Tori jumped up and down like an idiot fan at a rock concert. Suddenly, Catchastar faded and Zipline pushed into third place. With only yards to go, Fallon, too, dug in. He swept past the finish post first by a head.

"Oh my gosh, Winn, he did it! He won! *You* won!"

For one instant Winn looked frozen, as if he'd been blinded by an explosion. The next second Tori was in his arms, lifted a full two feet off the ground.

"That," he said, his forehead against hers, "is my Derby horse."

He kissed her and she pressed in to take every sweet bit of his offering. It was no more than celebratory adrenaline, she promised herself. But the heat of their touch liquefied her bones and sent tremors to her core. The kiss didn't last long, but the tremors continued while they held each other for a long, exciting moment to let reality sink in.

She began to laugh when Julie leaned forward to show her ticket to the men. All three of them threw their papers and tickets to the ground.

"Un-fucking-believable," one of them grumbled, nearly stomping from the row, his buddies behind him.

"Come back for Wilma's Tips anytime," Julie called. "Mom's made an art of being an unbelievable winner."

Tori unwrapped herself from Winn's embrace and

pulled the winning ticket Will had purchased for her out of her pocket. Tapping Wilma on the shoulder she held it out.

"I bet on the colors, too," she said, and winked. "But I kinda know the horse's owner, so I don't need this. Please—take it, if only to stick it to those guys."

"My gosh! Why thank you. But you really know the owner?"

Winn snatched her hand and pulled her toward the aisle before she could fully answer. "Winner's circle," he said, laughing, and Tori pointed at him as she followed.

"Congratulations," she said to the women. "I like your system."

The pair waved and Winn pulled Tori into the crowd heading for the rail.

The celebration lasted for the next two hours. Champagne flowed in front of Fallon's stall once all the requisite drug samples were taken and weigh-ins were completed. Armand, in his maroon plus fours, maroon, purple and yellow argyle socks, and a gray tweed coat was equally elated with his surprise second-place finish, and offered up his favorite Augustiner Dunkel beer to toast both Winn's and Fred's extraordinary successes. Fallon was walked and bathed and wrapped, and fussed over as if he'd already won the Derby. Tori was certain Renee took a minimum of a thousand pictures.

Her euphoria and relief over the win made up for every bit of stress from the past two days. Whatever was or had been going on took a pale second place to the sheer joy of watching Winn greet fellow trainers, owners and grooms who passed by to say congratulations. The rest of the world might have had no idea that a young gray horse was being celebrated for winning its first race, but that didn't matter. Fallon had given Crosby Racing reason to hope they might have a champion—and the small racing community at Churchill Downs' fall season knew. That was good enough for now.

Once the furor died and Winn, Renee, Leo and Jocelyn could get back to evening chores, the whole atmosphere around the barn had changed. Tori came and went as clients needed her before other races, and each time she returned, everyone smiled. Winn picked up a muck fork and dug in to help cleaning stalls. Renee spoke multiple times with Sawyer and Mallory, who promised everything was great at Sanctuary Pond, too. Tori promised to bring pizza home after the last race. It was that utopia Nick Forge entered and without saying a word froze in place.

"Congratulations," he said, ignoring everyone's narrow-eyed stares. "Heard you had a good celebration over here earlier."

"Nick." Winn stepped forward before Tori could open her mouth. Probably a good thing. "Your horse did well, too. Quite a comeback for all of us."

"Bingo," Nick said drily. "That's exactly why I came by. Have you spent any time wondering about this race?"

Tori released a frustrated sigh. The man was a walking irritant.

"What do you want?" she asked. "Three good horses beat a favorite. What's to wonder about?"

"Ah, Dr. Sterling. Apparently you haven't heard the rumors starting to rise outside the bubble of Holier-Than-Thou stables here. "It seems people think you two have some sort of plot going."

"Plot?" Winn's features darkened. "What the hell does that mean? There's no damn plot."

Nick held up a hand. "Easy, Crosby. We might not do things the same way or even like each other very much, but I'm not here to accuse you. I'm giving you a heads up."

"Why would you do that?" Tori asked.

"Because we both want to win races when our horses win them on their own, not because other people's horses are kept from winning."

"That's what he's accused of doing?" Tori asked.

"That's what both of you will be accused of doing if talk is as cheap as they say. Think about it. A favorite horse that you were treating is scratched less than a day before the race. Another favorite that you treat faded in the stretch so that two *more* of your clients' horses, who were long odds at best, can take first and second?"

"Are you saying I'm the one the rumor mill is chopping up?" Tori stared, her stomach starting to roil in anger and honest fear.

"Add to it the fact that Crosby Racing makes it a point to hire people with known criminal records. That makes you," he looked at Winn, "the perfect scape goat for anything that goes wrong."

Winn pinched the bridge of his nose and scrubbed across his forehead as if trying to chase away the pain. Finally he spoke.

"Aside from the fact that this is so ridiculous I can barely find words, why are you really here? You should be dancing in the aisles over Tori being in hot water."

"Look. We have our differences, like I said. And I was plenty mad when you came after me those coupla times—especially because you were fresh out of vet school and thought you knew every damn thing. I figured you'd mellow out and learn that things aren't always pristine and angel-perfect in this world, and you'd fall in line. Well if there's anything I've learned in the past five years it's that you'll lose a client before you'll do anything that could have a whiff of scandal."

Winn didn't smile, but he put an arm around Tori's shoulders. "I've known her for less time than that and I know it. It's true."

"If there's something going on around here, it's big time shit, but it ain't you, Tori. You don't have it in you to be capable of 'big time shit.' I think you're a little naïve and a lot sanctimonious, but you're honest, and I don't mind telling people so."

She had no idea how to respond. Nick Forge had managed to insult her and compliment her in one breath. He'd also exonerated her—the very last person she'd ever had though would do such a thing.

"Thank you, Nick. I'm not sure why you're willing to stand up for me, but it means a lot."

He dismissed her thanks. "It's selfish. Everyone back here knows you and I have an ongoing feud. Who do you think will get added to the list of suspects if anything else goes wrong with any of our horses?"

"You know, I could do big time shit if I wanted." Tori offered a peacemaking smile.

Nick snorted. "Hell. Your heart and your brain would plain quit on you if you tried anything. As for you, Crosby, I don't know you at all, but you already have a reputation, too. St. Winton, did you know they call you that?"

"I did not." Winn actually laughed. "That's funnier than hell."

"You're the charity worker, turning all your little bad guys into good guys. It might be funny, but for all I know you have the best front of all. Maybe your guys are good actors and actually are involved with something seedy. But I don't think so. When you've been around as long as I have, you can spot underhanded stuff pretty quickly. Your guys sit around the restaurant and they talk, but they don't talk about anything of importance. They don't go anywhere they shouldn't. They fuckin' like you. So that doesn't add up to big time shit either."

Tori folded her arms across her chest and studied the two men, in their weird faceoff. Despite knowing she was now part of this storm in a way she'd worked her entire career to avoid, she felt oddly detached, as if she were watching it happen to someone else. The night breeze blew the scent of horses and shavings, pungent liniment and saddle soap through the air. In the distance she could hear the track announcer. She loved this place, almost as much as she often hated it. But all she'd ever wanted was to make it better—safer for the animals, cleaner and more legitimate for the people. How could she do that if everything she worked for could disappear at someone else's whim?

"Then there's you," Winn said. "You've been suspended for doping and for several other drug infractions. Am I supposed to believe that you're here, to warn me about a witch hunt, out of the goodness of your heart?"

"No. Out of self-preservation. You're right. I've seen a lot of doping. That's what made me suspicious of this race. The way Fred Gault's horse put on that burst of speed from the back? That wasn't normal. I've watched that horse run many times. He has no Secretariat-like come-from-behind ability. He's a mid-packer and no more. You know what causes that effect when given to a horse? If you don't, ask an expert. Me."

"Cobalt."

Nick's eyes taunted in amusement. "Ah, the ethical vet does know her dark arts. Got it in one."

Tori's brain raced with the idea. Giving undetectable cobalt to horses had been a huge fad while she'd been in vet school. It gave horses a burst of speed in the last half of races. It could also kill them outright before they finished a race—but some trainers tried it anyway. They now had unreliable tests for the substance, and it wasn't so prevalent. She hadn't run into it much, but she had done research on it early in her career.

"How can you prove this?" Winn asked.

"Sometimes it shows up in drug tests. Mostly you have to catch someone giving it." Tori frowned at Nick. "I get it. Since you've used it, if it shows up in a horse, you'll be the first one they come after again."

He shrugged and nodded.

"And you aren't using it now, or you *wouldn't* have come to me."

For the first time Nick's belligerent façade softened slightly. He blew out a breath. "Necessity makes strange bedfellows, Dr. Sterling. But, that is the truth. I need your help."

"Sounds like we need each other's help. You have better eyes and ears on the ground than we do," she replied.

"Maybe." His smile was humorless.

"Strange bedfellows is right." Winn held out his hand. "I guess thanks are in order."

Nick took a moment to accept, but after a brief consideration he put his hand in Winn's. "We're a long way from being bosom friends. But I'll keep my eyes and ears open if you'll do the same."

"Of course."

Tori offered her hand as well and Nick took it with less hesitation this time.

"I still wouldn't hire you as my vet," he said.

"I still wouldn't take the job."

He started to leave and looked back. "Good win today. If we go with my premise that you aren't using anything funny in your water, then your horse beat those who did."

"And you took third. Also impressive."

Nick curled his lip. "It could have been better."

And there went the Nick Forge Tori knew, she

thought as he disappeared, his leather jacket slouched over his shoulders, and the hem of his jeans ruched over dust-covered cowboy boots. Slightly surly, unapologetic…with a closet decent streak?

"I have no idea what to do now," Winn said. "That was bizarre and disturbing."

"We ignore it. Try and fight it and we'll get nailed harder. We haven't done anything either of us."

"I'm used to this," he said. "Ever since getting into this business, I've been called every pansy-assed name in the book. It's you I'm sorry about."

"You think I'm not used to it? Goody-Two-Shoes, the Church Lady Vet, Holier Than Thou? Nothing new there. Granted, I've never been accused of participating in a doping scandal."

"We aren't accused yet. It's just talk."

"Yeah—" Her phone buzzed an interruption, and she checked the number, breathing a sigh of happy relief at the name. "It's my father. Hi, Dad!"

"Hey, sweetheart. I'm so sorry I missed the race today. I hear Winn's horse did well."

"Very well. Broke his maiden first time out. Winn is pretty stoked."

"That's wonderful. Listen, the reason I missed today was because I was doing a little tracking down. I think I have some information on the P.O. Box that package was delivered from. Where are you?"

"At the track. Is the news helpful?"

"I'm not sure. I have some questions. Will you be there long?"

"I'm heading home in about an hour, and I've promised the kids pizza. Do you want to join me…" She looked at Winn and mouthed the word "you?" He nodded. "Join us there?"

"Perfect. I'll bring some celebratory libation."

"Go ahead, sound all sophisticated, when all you

mean is some of your favorite blend."

"Maybe."

"Well we haven't toasted with bourbon yet, so you're on. I'll be home by nine-thirty."

"See you then."

"Dinner with your father?" Winn asked.

"If pizza constitutes 'dinner.' He has info on the P.O. Box, but he has questions. Can I say—as much intense fun as it is to be part of your team now, I could do without all these roller coaster ups and downs."

"Yeah. Ever since we met…" He glanced around to see that nobody was watching and gave her a quick, soft kiss. Like all the others, it chased away her fears in an instant. "Do you think we need to break up this partnership before the coaster actually goes off the rails?"

"We would if we were smart. It has to be us, don't you think?"

He kissed her again. "It does. Or…it could be that we got together just in time, and things could have been far worse."

"Lord 'a mercy, do not say that. Besides, it's only been three days. We aren't really together."

"Only scientifically speaking."

"Oh. Right. Then I guess maybe this experiment should probably continue. We don't want to take chances."

He grinned, stepped back and tilted his head to study her. "You're definitely the smartest and the prettiest partner I've ever had, on any experiment scientific or other. I'm glad you don't want to break up the new team quite yet."

"Through pizza at least."

The fun she had with him was nearly powerful enough to let her push aside Nick's message and warnings. Winn was right. They'd done absolutely nothing wrong, so they simply had to wait this out and keep their heads down.

"Okay, I just need to go fill out some final paperwork," he said.

"And I have one more horse running in the next race, so I'll go check in with his trainer one last time. Meet you back here in half an hour."

It wound up taking her forty minutes to make her rounds, but she returned with her spirits still high. So far nobody acted as if they'd heard negative rumors about her or the race. She rounded the last corner, took one look at the crowd outside Winn's tack room, and deflated inside as if someone had blown a poisonous dart into her heart. How could she not have known things were too good to be true?

Sandwiched between a police officer and Rob Parsons, the track steward she recognized all too well, stood Winn, Leo, and Renee, and for the first time since she'd met them, all three faces were filled with genuine panic.

CHAPTER Fourteen

"I HAVE A warrant, Mr. Crosby," Parsons said. "If you have nothing to hide as you claim, then I won't execute it and it won't go on the record. I'll do this with your permission."

Winn nearly bulldozed into the man's space to knock him flat. Anger filled him but only partially. After Nick Forge's warnings, his fear was real.

"You have a warrant to enter my tack room for the third time? Tell me what you're going to find. I don't believe for a second you don't have a specific goal."

"This is not all that unusual, Mr. Crosby." Parsons was fast becoming an annoying, bureaucratic prick. "After a race where there's a clear upset, we often field enquiries. This is a formality."

"That required a search warrant. This is bullshit."

He'd seen Tori arrive, but when she made it to his side and touched his arm his emotions warred between gratitude and embarrassment. How many times could she believe he was innocent of the accusations piling up against him? He offered her only a grimace and looked away.

"I'm calling my dad," she said.

He shook his head. "There's no time, and they have a search warrant. He can't stop them. But if I give permission at least it won't look like I'm hiding anything."

"You can refuse on principle."

"Believe me, I'd like to. I'm not sure I have the moral wiggle room to pull it off."

"Oh, Winn." The sorrow and sympathy in her voice only made him feel worse.

"Go then," he said to the officer, steeling his voice to hold in the fury.

Once the officer and Parsons had stepped out of sight, he took in his three kids who stood with granite spines and pale cheeks.

"I'm sorry," he said simply.

"What are they looking for this time?" Tori asked.

"I don't know. But I'll bet Fallon's entire winnings that we're about to find out."

"They aren't going to find—"

Officer Hogan stepped out of the tack room, his palm opened displaying two black bundles the size of electronic key fobs. Winn peered at the objects, and he spun away as bile rose in his throat. Tori's breath caught.

"Do you recognize these, Mr. Crosby?"

For a moment he literally couldn't say a word. He watched Tori's brow crease at his failure to deny the implied question within the question. Finally he cleared his throat. "I know *what* they are, of course. I have no idea whose they are or what they're doing in my tack room."

After the denial his knees threatened to buckle. Nick had talked about big shit. This was not shit; this was an armed bomb ready to explode.

"What are they?" Leo asked.

He and Renee looked at him beseechingly, clearly lost. Jocelyn's eyes, however, flooded with fear.

"Buzzers." Winn's voice finally found itself, thick and so angry he could hear his own tension giving away how much trouble he was in.

"Huh?" Renee stared.

It was to their credit that that they didn't know. Jocelyn, however, had hung around enough exercise riders that she did. Not that Winn suspected for one minute she'd ever even held one in her hands.

"Buzzers," Winn repeated. "Joints. Machines. Not all that many years ago, trainers and jockeys were often known to carry them during races. They're used to shock a running horse in order to give him a burst of speed at the end of a race. They're completely illegal, but even today some jocks are adept at hiding them and getting them into a race. They're an abomination."

"And yet, you have them with your equipment."

Hogan held the devices out to the group. These looked homemade, the shape of two double-A batteries wrapped securely in electricians' tape, with a simple switch and two metal points protruding from one end. Hogan closed them into his palm with a menacing snap.

Winn lifted his head and clung to calm only by clenching his fists so hard his nails dug into his palms. "I just won, as you said, a surprising race. Why would I be so stupid as to put these anywhere you could find them in one minute flat?"

"Maybe it felt like the perfect place seeing as we'd already searched your tack room twice."

"I have too much experience to do something like that. In addition, these kids and I *are* already under suspicion." He glanced at Jocelyn whose face held the disbelief of a child who'd had her world battered by a sudden hurricane. Eighteen was too young for this. "You really do see me as brainless if you think I'd give you more ammunition. If we had actually used these…things, I'd have thrown them so far away they'd never have been found. Here's what's going on. I'm the new guy, my staff members have records that makes us perfect targets."

"For what reason?" Parsons asked.

"I wish to God I knew."

"You know full well what the penalty for finding these machines is, Mr. Crosby."

"Oh, come on." Winn's stomach rolled with sickness again. "You have no proof those are mine, and I'll say it again, they aren't. Who suggested you'd find them here?"

"You *know* I'm not going to tell you that." Parsons' condescending tone nearly earned him a real punch. This time it was Tori's hand on his arm that stopped him.

"Dad's on his way, Winn. Don't lose it yet."

"Where are your other two employees?" Officer Hogan asked.

"They've been away since yesterday, watching over a horse at another facility."

"Can any others corroborate that?"

"Of course they can," he growled. "Dr. Sterling and her assistant. Mr. Hawkins and Miss Carrick are at her farm."

"It's true," Tori said. "I'll vouch for them."

Parsons let silence, heavy and ominous, settle around them for a faked thoughtful moment before lowering his edict.

"Mr. Crosby, I'm sorry. Normally we'd call a board of inquiry first, but with three suspicious incidents in two days,I have no choice but to temporarily suspend your license pending the full investigation."

"Are you fucking *kidding* me?"

His anger finally won. With one swift powerful kick he slammed a canvas chair into the barn wall. Renee and Jocelyn jumped back. Tori grabbed him by the waist and pulled him to her.

"Don't, Winn. Come on. You're totally justified, but this won't help."

He shook in her arms. Her familiar horse-and-roses scent filled his nostrils, but although it stopped him from kicking anything else, it didn't calm him. He wanted to yell at her, too, but the power of her hold cut through the red haze enough to give him back the tiniest bit of control.

"She's correct," Parsons said. "You don't want to do anything to jeopardize your case."

"My case?" He ground out the words. "You mean the case where I'm guilty until proven innocent? Where are your brains? Does this really make sense to you?"

"Winn…" Tori's voice warned him to back off.

"Around here we have to take a different tack, Mr. Crosby. When lives both human and animal are at stake, possession of these buzzers constitutes ownership of them, until and unless you can prove otherwise. As I said, there will be an investigation. But I must ask you to have your personal effects removed by tomorrow morning. Your horses and grooms can stay as long as you designate an interim licensed trainer to take over for you. Any races you've entered can be run, assuming the same, but you yourself may not take part or have a money stake in any of them. Any questions? If not, we'll be in touch when we've set up the board of inquiry."

"Do I have any questions? You bet your ass I have questions."

"His lawyer is on his way as we speak." Tori broke in and stepped between Winn and Parsons. "I assume, Rob, that you'll be around if he does have things he wishes clarified? May we send him to you?"

"I'd welcome the chance to talk with him." The self-righteous bastard *smiled* at her.

"Thank you. We really look forward to clearing up this misunderstanding."

"I hope that's the case, Dr. Sterling. I appreciate your help."

At that, at last, Winn dragged himself out of the red zone. His anger at Tori melted as she smoothed the waters he'd churned up. The sense of unbelievable injustice still flamed in his gut, but he kept his eyes on his new champion and forced himself to take a physical step back. When Parsons and Officer Hogan left, he righted the chair he'd abused and sank into it, as close to tears as he'd been in twenty-five years.

Nobody said a word at first, while he covered his face and tried in vain to form a plan. Hell, he could barely find a coherent thought. The first person to speak was Jocelyn, and her quiet words stunned him.

"Mr. Crosby. You've given me instructions on how to ride eight of your horses now. Every horse has a different training program, but one thing has been the same. 'Teach him how to love this job.' That's what you tell me. No whips. No badgering. No forcing. Just encouragement. You would never use a buzzer. I'll tell anybody how kindly you train your horses."

He lifted his head and very nearly lost his composure. All three of his misfit staff members were watching him with no judgment, just faces filled with anger and sympathy. Behind them Tori nodded, smiling at Jocelyn with tears in *her* eyes.

"I can't come close to telling you how much that means," he said, his voice thick. "I'm sorry I lost my temper after all the lectures I've given you about the importance of keeping yours. No excuses."

"No excuses?" Leo nearly snarled. "Those assholes are looking for someone to blame. We've known that all along. This is wrong. I don't blame you for being pissed."

"More than pissed," Renee added. "Too bad we can't sue them."

Winn laughed without humor. "Yeah. Unfortunately, they're right. Unless I can prove how those damn things got in our equipment, they were found here and we're responsible. I'm responsible. And," he took a slow breath, loath to say the next words, "since none of you is a licensed trainer, we're going to have to lay the horses up until this is settled."

"No!" Leo smacked the side of the barn. "There are four races this week—a big day next Saturday. We've waited for this."

"Leo. I know." Winn's heart broke for the kids. They were more excited than he was for every race. This was all shiny and new for them—a goal they'd been working toward all summer. "I'll figure this out as fast as I can. I promise."

"It's not fair." Renee was the first to openly cry. "We didn't do anything. Who put those horrible things here?"

Winn shook his head sorrowfully.

"This might sound crazy." Tori spoke for the first time. "But desperate times, right? I think we should take a chance on Will Starkey."

"The press? Aw hell, Tori…"

"No, think about it. He's been like a little bloodhound the past three days, but did you see a thing in the paper that came out yesterday? No. Nothing specific—just general news about vandalism at the track. He's sitting on the details to get the real scoop. I think that shows he might be fair. And maybe he's been skulking around in the right shadows lately to maybe learn something that can help us."

Winn covered his face again and every ounce of fight drained from him.

"What the hell," he said. "I've been suspended; that news will already be spreading. Ringo or Jimmy Olsen, or plain Will, whatever it is you call the kid, can't do any more damage. If you can find him..."

"And I'll talk to Fred. I'll bet he'd be willing to oversee your next week's racing schedule."

"Damn. Whatever. Thank you." Winn had no more words, and no more energy to find them.

"Hello, everyone. I guess I'm not going to ask how you're doing. It's pretty obvious."

Hugh Sterling's voice had the same welcome and calming effect as his daughter's.

"Dad! Thank you for coming! I'm so glad you're here." Tori gave her father a huge hug, and he caught Winn's eyes over her shoulder.

"I was happy to come. Winn? I'll do all I can."

Winn stood. "I have to admit—it's awfully damn good to see you."

"Things are a mess, son, I know, so let's have a chat and figure out how to clean it up."

CHAPTER Fifteen

"H ERE'S TO COMMISERATING in the great Commonwealth of Kentucky." Sawyer lifted a highball glass filled with ice and two fingers of Wild Horse bourbon. "Where they make bourbon, the best doping agent in the world."

Tori lifted her glass, happy enough not to comment on the inappropriateness of his remark. What was supposed to have been champagne and celebration, along with news from her father about the sender of the mystery box, had turned into depression-binging on deep-dish pizza and too much beer and bourbon. Nobody was on-the-floor bombed, but everyone definitely felt less pain than they had two hours earlier. Even her dad had indulged in his standard party-fare of two bourbons.

They had no solution to Winn's problem, but her father had outlined his plans for an investigation, and managed to pull Winn temporarily out of his funk—a funk Tori totally understood. Her heart broke for him. She'd been in the racing world long enough to know that he was in deep trouble if his suspension was upheld. No, it wouldn't be forever—but it would be long enough that his clients wouldn't wait for him and his reputation would take a huge hit.

She looked around her living room, filled tonight with people supporting each other, and dogs doing what they did best—giving unconditional affection without a single care for what was going on in the human world. Giant Axel sat with his adoring head on Winn's lap, Zoom had found a friend in Renee, and Things One and Two made the rounds of everyone.

Despite the fact that this wasn't the most uplifting reason to have guests, Tori basked in playing hostess. She took so little time for socializing anymore; it was nice to have voices and laughter in her space. When had work taken over so much of her life she'd stopped inviting friends over? Just because she avoided romantic relationships didn't mean she couldn't have company. And now... she gazed at Winn, her heart jigging at the sight of him toasting with the others, smiling despite the worry in his eyes. Now maybe there was a chance the romance was changing, too.

If necessity was the mother invention, disaster was looking to be the father of relationships. She certainly had a family of new ones. And the only way she could think of to help them at the moment was to treat them like family.

She clanked her glass with a fork and forced the toasting to a stop. When she had everyone's attention she cleared her throat and hoped she sounded more clear-headed than she felt.

"I want you all to know that you're welcome to stick around here and finish the pizza, beer, and bourbon as long as you want to. I do have a rule, however. Nobody who's had more than two drinks drives home. I once patched up a horse involved in a drunk driving accident, so—that means y'all have two choices. Find a couch, chair, floor or extra bed here, or talk to my sweet mama, Emma, who's offered to chauffeur anyone who has to get home tonight."

"Woo hoo, Doc!" Sawyer raised a glass again.

"And there's no question it's the couch in the barn lounge for you, kid," Tori laughed.

"I'll bunk with the sheep. I like the sheep." Sawyer garnered an entire chorus of rude calls and comments for that, but he only grinned and, with speech one step from being blurred, he added, "no worries. My name's not remotely Scottish."

Coughing with laughter, Mallory slapped him on the back. "It's okay, Dr. Sterling. Sawyer might not be in any shape to keep watch, but I'll keep an eye on Sunspot overnight."

"Aw, thanks Mallory. Horse and man will both be in good hands, am I right?"

Mallory blushed but didn't disagree. Tori still wondered if Winn knew about this budding love affair.

"And!" Winn spoke up. "My rules about drinking are still fully in place. I've suspended them for one night because of corporate catastrophe."

Leo, Renee, Sawyer, and Mallory all exchanged amused looks and took a collective breath.

"Yes, Miss Hannigan. Thank you, Miss Hannigan," they chanted in unison.

"You're all disrespectful ingrates." Winn tilted his glass toward them.

"And there's no catastrophe," Tori said quickly. "An unfair setback. Fred will help out at the track, Dad will talk to Derry and meet with the racing commissioners on Monday. We now know the incriminating package came from New York and someone named M. Bonner. We're taking steps. So, we can't sit around feeling sorry for ourselves."

"Sure we can," Renee said. "Look at how good we are at it."

"Like Winn said, this is a one night only pity party. Next weekend, in addition to some big races for you guys, it's the Chandler County birthday bash. Starting at the end of the week, there are big doings. The Halloween Ball is on Friday, there's a carnival and fair at Murphy Equestrian, a whole lot of partying Saturday night…" She raised her brows at Winn. "The bachelor auction."

"You have my answer on that."

"We'll talk. Anyhow, I'm in charge of the annual petting zoo, and I am always looking for volunteers to help me."

"Ooh, I can!" Mallory raised her hand as if she were in school.

Tori smiled. "I thought maybe you'd fallen in love with the rabbits and pigs, and I could sucker you into volunteering."

"Devious." Mallory rubbed her hands together. "Count me in."

"Thank you. I can find things for us all to do. And I'll be at the track, too, so I'll put Winn to work around here with Sawyer."

"That's supposed to cheer me up?" Winn asked.

"Not at all. It's supposed to keep you so busy you won't care if you're cheered up."

"Oh, in that case I feel so much better."

"As intended!" She offered him a flirty smile. "Look. Chandler County is proud of its horse savvy and up-to-the minute knowledge, and by mid-week a lot of people will know every detail about the goings-on at Churchill Downs. It's more important than ever to make a friendly impression around town and show everyone things are normal and we support each other. So party on everyone! Tomorrow the work starts."

Well after midnight she bunked Sawyer in the barn lounge and Mallory temporarily in the living room, knowing full well they'd end up together. Leo got a ride back to the track with her mother and father so he could sleep in Winn's room over the barn. Renee stayed in the guest room. Winn chose the pull-out bed on the porch.

"I'll sleep with Shaq," he'd said.

"There's a couch in my office," Tori offered. "You really don't have to sleep in the same room as the snake."

"I like pretty girls."

They were the last ones still awake, and Tori sat on the arm of the sleeper sofa, watching Winn dig through the small duffel bag he'd brought from the track. Pawing slowly as if he had no ideas what he searched for, he looked like a man who needed a month of sleep. He'd been offered a room at her parents' but he'd elected to stay in Tori's guest room for the week, and his decision thrilled her. She had no expectations for their budding relationship, but if he was willing to stay here it could only mean they were in the same place—absolutely not running from whatever was happening. With all her heart, Tori wished they could be happier about this experiment.

"Are you really all right?" she asked.

He looked up, his eyes sad, his mouth twitching into a small smile. "No. But I have you sitting here asking me, so that helps. A lot. Have I thanked you for taking over and herding this group of pathetic cats?"

"I'm a vet. We deal with herds. I'm really sorry, Winn. This sucks big time. I won't make light of it and insult you."

"I keep telling myself it will all get sorted out. I didn't do anything. But I haven't been around here long enough to have many allies or even know where to go to get information. People at tracks don't tell other folks their secrets. Nick is the closest to a confidant we've got and I still can't figure out his motivations. Or what he really wants."

"I don't know either. I've chosen not to worry about him. Let's concentrate on the things and people we do have control over. Let Dad get the legal stuff rolling, and we'll put it aside for a day or two."

"The thought of not going to the track…" He shook his head. "Of letting someone else deal with the kids."

"They're bright, smart young adults who only want to please you. They won't let anyone change that. I'll bring you updates and take pictures." She grinned. "And I really do have things you can help me with for the birthday bash. How are you at fixing rabbit hutches? Or creating a portable piggy hut?"

"I can wield a hammer and saw. Why?"

"Part of that petting zoo. I have to set that up by next Wednesday. And two more things."

"Sheesh, and they call *me* Miss Hannigan."

She ignored him by pulling him to sit on the mattress beside the arm where she sat. "My parents always go to the Halloween ball, and they invited us."

"Oh hell no. I'll do the bachelor auction before I'll dress up in a costume."

"Really?" She met the glare he fixed on her with delight. "Can I quote you on that?"

"What is your fixation on that damn auction?"

"I'll tell you. But in the interest of fair disclosure, the Halloween ball isn't a costume party. Well, not really. It's a hoity toity party for the Chandler County elite. Mom and Dad were going to miss it this year because of travel plans, but since those have changed…"

"Well good, because I definitely can't go if it's for the elite."

"But I'm related to the elite—and you are by osmosis if you come with me. Here's the thing. All the owners around here will be present. People who are very often between trainers or looking for fresh perspectives. You could benefit."

"Not while all this shit is going on."

"Especially now that it is. I can introduce you to Barron Steele. He's a good man, tough, and smart. He doesn't listen to gossip, and he doesn't care about rumor mills. He's got excellent horse sense and lots of friends."

"Doesn't sound like my type."

"You want to compete here in Kentucky horse country; you've told me so. These are the people who need to know you."

"I'll think about it."

"And the auction…"

"Come *on*, Tori."

"I'm serious about this, too. I have a nice little mad-money savings account that I'd like to use on finding me a really cool guy. One that will make all the other girls drool their bourbon onto their fancy dresses when we walk by. Not that I'm a big mover or shaker, but I don't have an awful reputation. If I'm willing to bid until I get you, it might make people think twice about judging you."

"You're forgetting completely that it could go the other way. Make people think twice about your 'not awful' reputation."

"I'm willing to take the chance."

"You are a force, Tori Sterling. I give up. I put this week into your hands, but know this. I make no promises about how I'll behave in polite company."

"I'm not worried. You've behaved perfectly well, to this point."

The atmosphere shifted from teasing to supercharged in the time it took for her eyes to lock on his. Before she even knew what she was going to do, a spark of desire pooled low in her abdomen, and all she wanted was a taste of him. A sip—like the fine bourbon no true Kentuckian could live without. She slipped onto the bed beside him and drew a quivering breath, trying to slow the sudden rise in her pulse.

"Do you know you've kissed me twice since you told me I got to choose the next trial setting?"

"Twice? I'm sorry. Does this mean our experiment has been invalidated?"

He brushed a hand softly along the hair at the side of her head and smoothed it back to her pony tail. With a gentle tug he pulled off the band and fluffed her freed hair through his fingers. Shivers erupted across her shoulders.

"I don't think we have to be that hard-nosed about the rules," she whispered. "But we do need to make sure we keep detailed notes on this attempt."

With silken ease she slid her arms around his neck and tilted her head to kiss him. "Yeah, here's to good notes," he whispered against her mouth, and another sliver of pleasure drove through her stomach. She led the dance, slipping her tongue in to meet his, pulling back, tasting his lips and relishing the goosebumps he caused by nibbling on hers.

He tasted of mint and delicious heat, and they played with the sensations, wet and intimate, and frictionless except for the pressures they chose to share. With increasing need, Tori ran her hands up the back of his head, burrowing into the heavy softness of his hair, pulling him tighter and squirming to face him so she could straddle his lap.

They groaned simultaneously as their bodies meshed, and he grasped her bottom to pull that closer, too. Heat ignited through her torso and burned through her limbs. Without forethought, she moved against the hard length of him, thrilled at his timeless reaction to her. Her own body reacted exactly the same way, hard and hot, and a little shocked but electrified with excitement.

It had been so long.

He lay back slowly, taking her along without pressure but tense with urgency. She followed willingly, knowing in the back of her head that this was all still a grand experiment, that they could stop and it would be all right. That of all the bad things they'd been through in the past three days, this was the one thing that would be perfect.

Winn rolled her over and lay atop her, holding his weight on his forearms, pushing her hair from her face and kneading her temples with the pads of the thumbs. More gooseflesh rose when he found the skin behind one ear with his teeth and worried it gently. Then he roamed her face with his kisses, leaving her breathless and powerless to reciprocate. With a happy moan she tilted her head back and let him kiss down her throat and onto her polo shirt, across the fabric and up the swell of her breast until he closed over the tip, kissing through shirt and bra.

"Oh!" Aroused and delighted, she sucked in her breath. "That shouldn't feel nearly so good."

"And why would you think that?"

"I...don't know!" She laughed at the erotic tickle of his hot breath filtering through the fabric. "Clothing? Happening too super-fast."

"When everything goes according to your hypothesis in an experiment, clothing is definitely not an issue."

"I would agree, but here's the problem. I can't remember anymore what, exactly, the hypothesis is we're trying to prove."

His laugh broke the heavy tension, and he kissed her once again on the lips, lingering to slip their tongues together several times in playful French.

"Wasn't it something about whether this whole kissing activity felt like the right thing to do, or whether it was simply the atmosphere at the pond?"

He propped himself on one elbow and stared down at her. She traced the full masculine angle of his upper lip.

"It wasn't the pond. And it feels right."

"Oh it does. And, sadly now, it feels right to slow it down before it doesn't feel right. Does that make me a jerk? Don't think for a second I wouldn't love to finish this."

"No, you're not a jerk, you're a wonder. I'm not ready for more yet. I don't think you are either—especially not now. But, can I tell you? It's a wonderful surprise, suddenly wanting to learn to trust someone again. I've avoided that for a long time."

"Who hurt you?"

"Nobody intentionally. I was engaged, but he decided at the last minute that it had to be him or the animals. To me it was proof I couldn't have really loved him, since I wasn't willing to give everything up for him."

"He shouldn't have asked."

She shrugged. "He had a right to his comfort level, too. It was lucky we found out before the wedding. I wish he hadn't waited until the invitations had been sent to figure that comfort level out…"

Winn winced. "Ouch. Tori. I'm sorry."

"It was four years ago. I'm not pining, believe me, but I have learned that this is who I am, just as much as my height and the fact that I don't like cooking or eggplant or mushrooms is who I am. I told you several men have been scared off by my obsession. So…I'm wary." With a sudden flame in her cheeks, she realized how ridiculous that sounded based on her reactions to him. "Not that I've shown any of that to you. Here I am at second base after a mere three days."

"Well let's make this officially too fast. Sleep with me tonight."

"And by that you mean…"

"Sleep. I'm not looking forward to tossing and turning. I think maybe you could help with that. So my motives are one hundred percent selfish."

"I'm not sure it would look good if we were found like this in the morning."

"You have an alarm on your phone? Set it and leave early."

"You have all the answers, don't you?"

"I have no answers. Not for anything except maybe the antidote for insomnia. I think the cure is to keep holding you."

"I have to admit. I've never heard this line before."

"Never used it before."

She reached for two blankets on the end of the bed, handed him a pillow and straightened everything out.

"Okay, Mr. Crosby. Make room."

CHAPTER Sixteen

SHE SLEPT WITH him the next three nights. Amazing nights, where deep, exploratory kisses were enough before they drifted off in each other's arms, and he slept so deeply he missed any passing dreams. During the days, while he waited for the boom to lower on his life and career as a trainer, he discovered an entirely different life—one where he learned Tori had told the truth about not liking to cook, so he fell in love with making her breakfast at six in the morning before she left to feed the animals and head for work. This life had him learning how to care for piglets and donkeys and ball snakes. It had him repairing hinges on a rabbit hutch door and designing a tent-like structure for piglets about to spend four days at a petting zoo.

It had him directing his kids in a completely new capacity and fearing he'd lose at least one of them to career party planning. Leo chafed at being stuck on the farm. He hated the day Sawyer took a turn at the track, and he groused about painting the refurbished hutch and checking over yards of fencing that would enclose the petting zoo critters. The only task he took on gladly was watching over Sunspot when they let him into his paddock. That, he told Winn, was the way racehorses should live—being allowed to stretch their legs at will even while they were in training rather than strictly standing in a stall. The boy was developing an exceptional feel for horses, starting to surpass even Sawyer, Winn realized.

Mallory, on the other hand, basked in the variety of jobs she found to do at Tori's. She groomed all the animals, played with them, repaired popped nails and cracked boards in their stalls. She weeded flower beds and discovered the overgrown vegetable garden with a glee that rivaled a junkie stumbling on a stash of heroine. Once she had the weeds dispatched, she discovered a treasure trove of fall veggies ready for picking: zucchini, acorn squash, four good-sized pumpkins, and a row of red potatoes that hadn't yet been dug.

Renee and Sawyer were flexible and went without complaint to wherever they were needed, although Sawyer always managed to be wherever Mallory was. By day three it was clear Leo and Renee preferred watching over things at the track, and when Mallory lobbied for Leo to stop switching and stay at Churchill Downs so everyone could be done with his constant whining, Winn laughingly let him have the job. He was good with the horses. He knew every routine, and even seemed to get along best with Fred. Once things were settled, Winn wasn't worry-free but he could, at least, trust his operation was holding its own.

On Tuesday afternoon, with the rabbit hutch finished and a sturdy A-frame shelter ready for use, Winn made arrangements with Fred to bring Sunspot to Murphy Equestrian Center, the huge training and therapy facility in Bourbonville. He went in search of Mallory who, to his shock, wasn't with Sawyer, and found her in Tori's kitchen, mixing bowls out, baking ingredients spread across one counter and a cookbook open to a zucchini bread recipe.

"The world as I know it is ending!" He gazed at the recipe, and then at Mallory. "My best mucker is going domestic goddess?"

"Tori said this was an easy recipe to start with, since it's been so long since I've baked anything."

"Hey, I'm not sure Tori is the right one to be giving cooking advice." He laughed, wishing Tori were there herself to take the teasing and throw it back at him.

"Don't worry. She told me that if she could make this, so could I. But I used to bake with my grandma, when she was still alive and we still had a sort of a family. Hey! Did you know there's a baking contest at the fair? And something called a cake walk? It's like musical chairs but you land on a number when music stops and if you're on the right number you win a cake!"

Winn grinned at her excitement and marveled at the fact that a twenty-four-year-old these days didn't know what an old-fashioned cake walk was.

"So the zucchini bread…?"

"If it works, I'll make some for the baking contest. And I'll try baking a cake, too, for the cake walk. I haven't been to a fair since I was really little. I can't wait."

"It's a goofy, small town celebration, Mal. Don't expect state fair quality."

"I know. But Tori says they do a really great job, and it's pretty fun. I guess they're already setting things up. They even have a dunk tank!"

He eyed her suspiciously. "So?"

"You and Sawyer are going to be dunkees. It's for a really good cause—the therapy program at Murphy."

"I am not going to be dunked! Tori already has me signed up for charity events I do not want to attend. Don't you start."

"Too late! You already have a time and everything. Saturday at 10:30 a.m. Sawyer is right before you. You'll have plenty of time to get dried off and spiffed up for the auction."

She winked, and Winn glared at her. "You shouldn't even know about that. I'm still your employer."

"Yes. And you won't fire me. I'm your best stall mucker."

He was rapidly losing control over these kids. All this farm freedom had gone to their heads like horses who'd escaped into the wild.

"Yeah, you keep thinking that. I'm inclined to forget about why I came looking for you in the first place."

"Tell me!" Mallory set the measuring cup she held onto the table.

"Sawyer and I are taking Sunspot over to Murphy Equestrian. Fred, Derry, and Armand are meeting us there. If all goes well, Fred will increase the workouts, and he'll run a week from Saturday. I thought maybe you'd want to come. But I can see…"

"I haven't started yet! Of course I'll come! I'll finish this when we get back."

Winn smiled, relieved he hadn't completely lost her to the charm of the kitchen.

"Come on then. I want to watch a horse run. I'm going through withdrawal."

"It sucks." Her sympathy was genuine. "When is the board of inquiry going to decide something?"

"Hugh said last night the first hearing is tentatively set for next Monday. I don't know what we'll have to present by then, but he's working on locating this Bonner person in New York."

"He'll find something."

"Counting on it. Okay, kid, let's go."

Murphy Equestrian Therapy Center was twice as big as Winn had imagined. Set on a series of gently rolling hills, with traditional white fencing instead of the brown that now characterized most Kentucky horse farms, Murphy epitomized efficiency, beauty, and attention to detail. Pastures flanked either side of the drive up to the main house. Signposts directed them to the office, training barns, therapy and rehabilitation areas, and an on-site cafeteria. They followed a sign pointing left to the training track, and Sawyer whistled through his teeth.

"How the other half lives."

"There is a lot of money in these parts," Winn agreed. "Someday, my friends, someday."

"Look, they *are* already setting up for the fair." Mallory pointed to a row of booths half-built along the pathway and read off the signs. "Mechanical horse race, Win-a-Unicorn, caricatures, Old-time photos, funnel cakes, a stand for Hot Browns—those are the best sandwiches in the world!"

Sawyer laughed at her. "How old are you?"

"Ten again!" She giggled. "And I don't care. "Winn, I'd give anything for this whole track mess to go away. But since I can't, I'm glad I get a chance to be here. Thanks."

"Glad I could help," he replied drily.

They were the first to arrive at the track—a tidy five-eighths-mile oval, just big enough to give a trainer room to work. By the time they'd unloaded Sun, however, Fred's tan F350 pulled in beside the trailer, and Armand burst from the truck, clucking like a German mother at the sight of his horse.

"He looks vonderful!"

"We're taking good care of him," Winn promised.

Fred stepped out of the driver's side, his face stern and unhappy. Then, to Winn's shock, Tori and Jocelyn emerged from the crew cab. Tori smiled, but it was forced and tight—a match to Fred's. Jocelyn, on the other hand, looked like her serious face could break into song and dance at any moment. She and Armand were a freakishly happy matched pair.

"I didn't expect you," he said when Tori came to his side. "I guess I should have."

"I'm not about to let him exercise without watching him. I'm still protecting my reputation."

He surreptitiously gave the top of her head a peck. "I call bullshit. You don't care about anything but the horse."

"Don't tell Fred. I had to convince him I have a medical need to be here."

"And Jocelyn?"

She sighed. "They suspended Derry this morning. He can't prove you didn't give him a machine to use on Fallon. He's in the same boat you are."

"Aw hell, that's not right."

She touched his arm in warning. "Don't say a word. This is a powder keg and Fred is a step from blowing it all up. Don't light a match to the explosive; keep your cool. Derry is fine and is singing your praises. It's not entirely a bad thing."

"I don't know, Tori. This is all a bad thing. When I start taking others down with me…"

"You aren't taking anyone down, least of all yourself. Have some patience. We'll get to the bottom of this."

He sighed and gave her a quick hug. "Some crazy stars aligned the day we finally met. Thank you."

She waved her hand in dismissal, but her smile, this time, was genuine.

By the time Jocelyn had fully calmed her excited disbelief over the chance to gallop Sunspot, and Fred was talking through instructions for the workout with her, they had a small crowd, similar to Sun's comeback at the track days earlier. The center's owner, Bernie Murphy, had arrived to welcome them, two instructors on breaks leaned against the railing, and an older custodian had cut the engine of his lawnmower and stood watching as well, chatting with Sawyer.

Winn stood beside Tori who calmed the perpetually hyperactive Armand. Fred let Jocelyn go and took up a spot beside Winn, much calmer than he'd been upon his arrival.

"You doing okay, son?" he asked.

"I'm hating every moment of this whole thing, thanks. I admit to being a little glad Sun isn't at Churchill. I told my groom earlier—at least I get to see something go."

"Yeah. I'm sorry. Some shit going down over there isn't there? I understand how you feel—I've been there. Most of us get caught for some dumb thing and spend our time in the penalty box. It passes."

He wanted to shout, again, that he hadn't done a damn thing, but he let it slide. This wasn't Fred's problem, and the older man was right about one thing. One way or another, this would pass.

"In my case, I do wish the horse *was* at the track. I can keep an eye on him there. But when it comes to this horse, Armand listens only to Tori."

"She brought him back from an almost certain career-ending injury. Can you blame him?"

"I don't. He's a valuable horse."

"She a good vet."

"Technically, medically, one of the best. A little idealistic perhaps. When reality bites her one day, and it will as it does all of us, she'll know the world isn't all unicorns and perfect outcomes, and she'll add some more tools and realism to her skill set. Then she'll have so much business she won't know what to do."

Winn frowned to himself. He didn't much like the insinuation that following the rules made Tori a less competent doctor, but it struck him what she meant when she'd said she faced this every day. It was the very reason she didn't have as many clients at the racetrack as the older vets. She wouldn't compromise. Winn kept his mouth shut.

Jocelyn started with backtracking, taking Sun clockwise around the track for a lap at a slow jog. Tori murmured positives to Armand. Fred watched with unblinking eyes, frowning again. When Jocelyn brought Sun to a walk she turned him the right direction.

"A five furlong fast gallop, or as close as she can manage," Fred said. "I'd rather not have an exercise rider do this, but it's a small track, and all my jocks were booked." He pulled out a timer. Jocelyn galloped toward the starting marker and let the horse go.

Winn stared in awe. The horse was honest-to-God one of the most beautiful runners he'd ever seen.

At a quarter mile Fred shook his head. "No, no. Tori watch him. Something's not right. He's slow, damn it. That stride is uneven."

Tori trained binoculars on the flying colt. "Fred, he looks great. Honest."

"I'm telling you. I know that horse. He's not ready for this."

"Are you sure, Fred?" Armand's nervous words fluttered past Tori who continued watching."

"How long have we known each other?" Fred asked. "When do I not tell you what I'm sure of?"

"Tori?"

"I'm watching him, Armand. I've spent a very long time with him as well, and I've diagnosed a lot of lameness in galloping horses. He's perfect. Fred, you'll have to describe what you're seeing, because I see nothing wrong."

Fred sealed his lips into a firm line and watched with clenched fists as Sun rounded the final turn and Jocelyn brought him home, letting him coast gradually to a trot and a walk before turning and jogging back to the group. Winn, too, had watched thousands of horses run and considered himself pretty good at spotting trouble. Most trainers did. But he'd seen nothing.

"How did he feel, Jocelyn?" Tori asked.

"Great! Oh my God, he's amazing. So responsive. So eager! I would be willing to ride him anytime, Mr. Gault."

"You didn't feel anything off?" Fred held the horse while Jocelyn hopped down. "In that back stretch he looked short on the left side."

"No. I thought he felt great. He made it so easy to stay straight. Like sitting on a motorcycle!"

"I don't like it," Fred said. "I don't think he's ready to race, Armand. You can do what you wish, but I won't train a lame horse. In my opinion we need to back him off, do some very slow work and see where he's at in a month."

"A month?" Armand's face fell. "But we won't get much if any racing in here if we do that."

"You can move him to Florida for the winter. Gulfstream or Hialeah. Lots of opportunity and a horse that's actually ready."

"Fred, that's a little overly conservative, in my opinion." Tori frowned in concern.

"Well we have two opinions."

"I'll check him over thoroughly, and we'll rest him for the next two days. Let's see what you think on Thursday."

"Friday."

"Fine."

Fred walked away and Tori fixed her eyes on Armand's. "You know how much I love this horse. I would never for any reason let you run him if I thought he wasn't ready."

"I know. I trust you, Tori. You brought him back when so many others said he vould not race again. But you are sure they weren't right? Perhaps we both vant this too much?"

"It's a fair question. But, no, they weren't right. He's fit and he's strong. You don't have to give up on your dreams. I'll talk to Fred. A lot of bad things have been happening lately. He's worried."

"You think that's it?"

"I do."

Armand patted her arm slowly and walked away. Without his quirky racetrack plus fours and his exuberant voice, he looked as sad as Rudolph the Red-Nosed Reindeer with the fake nose his father had made him wear.

"What the hell is that all about?" Winn asked.

"I honestly don't know. I can only hope it's exactly what I said, and Fred's just having panic attacks. I can't blame him. Meanwhile I have something to show you. I have no idea whether it means a thing, but take a look while I check Sun from top to bottom so I can tell Fred he's fine."

She handed him a piece of notebook paper folded into quarters. He opened it and read a list of twenty races run over the past three days. A winner was listed for each—name, starting odds, finishing pay-out, trainer. He recognized a few names. All were middle-pack runners with middle-standings trainers. His was among them.

"What's this?"

"Races in which heavy favorites were beaten by mediocre horses. The phenomenon isn't unusual, but the frequency is. It doesn't prove a single thing, but to me it's very suspicious. If what Nick Forge said is true, we have an underground scandal going on. Jocelyn is the one who thought to look at this. Will did the legwork for us. This is his list."

"I talked to two other exercise riders yesterday at lunch," Jocelyn said. "It was weird what they were saying. The horses they were exercising were nothing special. We can kind of tell when we have a horse that really loves to go, that wants to keep going faster. But these horses were sluggish. They didn't have that will to win we love to feel. And yet, both of their horses won their races. Afterward the jockeys said it was like they got a burst of energy at the three-quarter mark. That sounded like what you told us Mr. Forge said, so I asked Tori."

"Brilliant girl." Tori gave her shoulders a squeeze. "You're the trainer, Winn. What does it sound like to you?"

"Surprise horses win sometimes." He shrugged. "If only the favorites came in first, there'd be no point in people betting. But...I agree this is a long list for only a few days."

"So what do we do?" Jocelyn asked.

"We keep watching, keep writing these things down, and we listen for any clue we can get," Winn said.

"Exactly." Tori sighed. "I wish there was more, but I can tell you from personal experience that overt digging will do nothing but get you in trouble. So...we wait."

CHAPTER Seventeen

"I CAN HONESTLY say I've never worn one of these in my entire thirty-six years of life."

Winn held the tuxedo on its hanger extended in front of him as if it were a dead rat. Tori laughed and took it, laying the borrowed formalwear across the guest room bed. He really was attractive when he was stressed.

"We don't have to stay long, I promise. A couple of hours and we can come home. You can stand by Mom and me the entire time, hold a drink and smile. Let the world come to you."

"Nobody will come to me."

"Never say never. I'm going to change now. You do the same and don't pull any funny stuff like escaping out the window. I'll meet you downstairs in half an hour."

She left the room and heard him mutter something under his breath.

"Doesn't matter what you said, the answer is no!"

"I asked if you wanted pink or red roses."

"You did not."

"I said the window sounds like a great idea. Worth the wrath of a woman scorned."

"Okay. Then don't expect me to bid on you tomorrow night."

"Someone will. Don't worry."

She padded down the hall to her room, laughing. It was so much fun having him in the house. He was funny and sarcastic, bossy with his kids and worried, but through it all he was caring. For a guy with a tough past, he'd made himself into good man. Even if he whined like a child about putting on a tuxedo.

She closed her door and pulled her dress out of the closet. She'd bought it for this event two years ago and decided that time not to wear it. She'd gone with her parents and no date, and the dress, a teal chiffon strapless gown with a spray of rhinestones at the side waist and a split skirt, had seemed far too showy. As if she was looking to be noticed. Tonight it was perfect. Not only did she want to be seen with Winn, she needed every person to know how proud she was to be introducing him to Chandlerville society.

She slipped off her jeans and T-shirt, stepped into the shower to rinse off the scent of track, horses, and the potions of her trade, and was out in minutes. She wasn't a society person herself, but tonight's appearance was a mission in disguise. And danged if she wasn't looking forward to it the tiniest bit.

She took a little extra time with her make-up, sculpting a touch of sophistication onto the face everyone described as sweet and cute rather than beautiful. She curled and fluffed her hair with an electric brush and left it long, pinning it to the side with a rhinestone clip. She spritzed on her favorite inexpensive scent and finally stepped into the dress. It still fit like it had been custom designed yesterday, its pleated bodice covering the right amount of skin, the beautiful rhinestones spreading from her waist to just beneath the bustline, and the chiffon draping over the satiny crepe skirt slit slightly past the midpoint of her thigh.

Donning a pair of silver, open-toe sling-back pumps with a chunky sole she took a last look in her mirror and nodded. This would do.

He was waiting in the living room, sitting on the sofa with Axel between his knees, scrubbing the big dog's head with his knuckles. The crazy mutt had his eyes closed and was moaning like a lover.

"Oh my gosh," she said. "You own that dog now, you know. I'll never be good enough."

He glanced up, and started to retort, but whatever he'd intended to say died on his lips. He pushed Axel's head gently away and stood, ignoring the canine protests.

"My brain has never been so full of cliché lines in my entire life," he said. "I got nothin' original. You are…beautiful."

He looked so honestly gobsmacked Tori found words despite her own stunned reaction to him.

"Clichés become clichés because sometimes they're the only perfect things to say. Thank you. And you…"

"Just say 'beautiful' and make me feel less lame."

"Oh no, no. Let's try heartthrob meets James Bond. I'm afraid we'll get mobbed when we arrive at the ball."

"Now, see?" He threw up his hands. "You had to outshine me even with words, didn't you?"

He did look pretty magnificent in the tux she'd borrowed from her father's collection of three. It was classic black with satin lapels and black buttons down the white shirt front. He'd even done a passable job on the real bow tie. His blue eyes shone brighter because of the black. She wanted to swim in them all night. Never leave the house.

"I thought you'd never worn a tux. How did you know how to tie the bowtie?"

"I Googled it."

"Are you serious?"

"You can find literally anything on the Internet. Don't forget it."

She lifted her hands and straightened the bow slightly, smoothing out one wrinkle and adjusting an end. "I don't need the Internet to explain what I really wish I was doing with you. I think I could get this tie off without instruction."

"You're evil," he whispered. "Plain mean. You remember, Cinderella, We only have the coach for two hours. You said so."

"Then let's go," she whispered. "Two hours isn't all that long."

Winn slid into the Halloween Ball like a cool splash of water into a rich glass of bourbon, creating a murmur of pleasant surprise, a richness to his surroundings and making the whole night much more palatable for Tori. Her mother kissed her hello, gorgeous in a simple lime green floor-length sheath that was as different from her normal casual dress as Tori's gown was from hers.

"Look at us," she said. "Cleaning up for show. That dress is stunning, sweetie. Thanks for coming to keep us company. And this must be Winn. I can't believe it's been almost a week since I started hearing about you and I haven't met you yet."

"Mrs. Sterling…"

"Emma," she said. "I feel like we're family. Hugh is very invested in you, so I am as well."

"I can't tell you how sorry I am that your travel plans were ruined."

"Ruined? Good lord, we can travel whenever we like now. Let's get you out of this jam first and then we'll make our getaway. Don't feel bad for a moment."

"That's very nice of you. Thank you."

Tori hugged her mother again. "Thanks," she whispered. "He's nervous about being here. Thinks he'll be ostracized or ignored. That was a nice welcome."

"My pleasure."

"I'm going to introduce him to Barron Steele and some of the other farm owners around here. A quick round and I'll bring him back to safety. People just need to know his name. I'm so impressed with the way he works his horses. Others will be, too, once they get to know him."

"Good luck, son." Her father shook Winn's hand. "She's throwing you into the deep end."

"I've absolutely given up worrying about it. This is your daughter's party; I'm here to sink or swim."

She ran her hand soothingly up and down the back of his jacket. "You won't sink. I gotcha."

The rounds were far more successful than she'd dared hope. With the good bourbon and excellent wine flowing, and people present for no other reason than to see and be seen, nobody wanted to bring up track politics or gossip. Relatively few had heard Winn's story at all. Certainly business was always discussed, but it was done quietly one-on-one, so Tori took advantage of everybody's good will and better moods and introduced Winn to breeders, to owners, to other trainers, and her friends.

She savored their head turns and their eyes filled with eager questions about the two of them that nobody dared ask outright. Winn charmed them all, and she made a serious mental note to nail him for lying about his social skills. The man could schmooze. Yet he came off as the neighbor everyone had known for years.

The closest Winn came to a discussion of his suspension was with Barron Steele, who, when Tori finally found him without a crowd around him, simply shook hands and said, "I hear Hugh Sterling has your back over the trouble at the Downs. Sounds like things are in a mess."

"Nobody is quite sure what's going on," Winn said.

"Sabotage and sick horses. And now perhaps some doping?"

"Can I ask where you heard that?"

Barron pointed across the room. To Tori's shock, Rachel Blakely stood casually beside Anderson Matthews and Will Starkey. They scanned the room but not a pad, pen, or smartphone was in view.

"I know Rachel pretty well," Barron said. "She doesn't have many details, but she knows what she's got ready to print. Sounds like you're in the middle of a breaking story."

"Just my luck." Tori saw Winn grimace slightly as Rachel caught sight of him and waved, her smile amping up in greeting.

"Tori's father is the best. If he believes in you, you'll be fine. Come around some time and take a look at our prospects. Always happy to talk to trainers."

"I appreciate it. Good to meet you, Barron."

"Same here. Good luck."

He moved off, aiming a "heads-up" nod behind them. Tori turned and nearly ran into Rachel's arms.

"Hello, Tori. Why, Mr. Crosby in the flesh. I hoped I'd see you here."

"I was about to say the same thing." Another voice drew their attention, and they turned to stare as Cynthia

Gault in a resplendent, red cocktail-length dress glided up and wrapped her hands lightly around Winn's upper arm. "I was hoping to find you here, since I can't at the track anymore."

Tori wrinkled her brow in distaste. What a callous thing to say. And what was with the woman's touchy touchy?

"Cynthia! Hi, I didn't know you were back in town." Rachel leaned in for a one-armed hug and cheek kiss. "It's great to see you."

"Rachel! How goes the newspaper biz?"

"Good. Great. I have a new reporter and that gives me twice the news gathering power. But things like this event are just meringue on the pie. I get to hang out and maybe interview informally my most eligible bachelor. But I see you've met."

"Of course. He's been helping my dad and vice versa at the track. We're very grateful he's come our way from Chicago. Eligible bachelor, you say. So you two aren't together?" She aimed the question at Tori.

"We came together." Tori said. "We'll be leaving together, too, so I guess that means, yes, we're together."

Cynthia ignored the sarcasm. "But not tomorrow during the auction? Hmmm. I might have to find me a little mad money and come spend it."

At Cynthia's use of the same phrase Tori had used to describe her auction money, she bristled to the bottom of her toes. The motive behind such over-friendliness completely escaped her since their first meeting hadn't ended on the most cordial of tones when she'd disagreed with Tori about moving Sunspot.

"You *should* come," Rachel said. "It's for a great cause and we have a lot of bachelors this year. We'll do very well, I think. How long are you in town?"

"Until next week. It's time to go over Dad's books again, and it's so much easier to come here than try and do things electronically."

"I'm glad you do. Let's have lunch before you leave."

"Absolutely." Cynthia leaned even closer to Winn. "It sounds like I might get to see you tomorrow, too."

Tori wasn't sure how Winn did it even though she stood right next to him, but he deftly extracted his arm from Cynthia's hold and put his arm around Tori. Every movement was casual and fluid, and Cynthia didn't seem to notice he'd brushed off the advance.

"Sounds like it," he said. "Is your father here tonight?"

"He was, but he went back to the barn. With two barns full of horses to check on he didn't want to stay late. So, I came looking for someone I knew to keep me company. And here you two were, with Rachel as, what did you say, Rach? Meringue on the pie? Oh, I'd forgotten how much fun this whole birthday bash celebration can be. So many fun little things and people I haven't seen in ages."

"I feel the same way," Rachel said. "I have more fun this time of year than in May during the Derby. This is far more rewarding, especially when we get a little bit of new blood to help out. Winn, I am so happy you agreed to help with the auction."

"You have to thank Tori here for that. To be honest, you beautiful ladies scare me to death, and I tried to run as far away as I could."

Tori joined in the annoying female laughter so she wouldn't stand out as a crab, but all she really wanted was for Cynthia to leave and Rachel to start reporting on something.

"There's method to my madness." She smiled to hide her annoyance. "Y'all have been so understanding and kind to Winn, but I'd like everyone to see he's a stand-up guy with lots of support."

"He'll certainly garner lots of support. That I'm sure of." Cynthia winked at Rachel.

"Cynthia, dear, there you are!"

Tori sighed with relief when Martha Freeburg, the elderly wife of a long-retired county commissioner, approached and put a trembling arm around Cynthia's shoulders. The woman had been ancient when Tori had been a girl, and now she looked like she might actually be on her last legs. But she spoke with authority and held out her hand.

"Do, you remember I told you last week when we met at the store that I had something for you if I could find it?"

"I do, Mrs. Freeburg."

"I found it, honey. Look."

She opened her hand. In her palm lay a chain attached to a large oval locket. The face of it was bright blue and gold cloisonné with an ornate letter "B" in the center.

"It's beautiful," Cynthia said. "Too beautiful to give away."

"Nonsense. It's been lying in a bureau drawer for fifty years. It's lovely, and it was designed by a prominent artist of the day, but it holds no meaning for anyone in my family. You, however, have always collected letter 'B' things because of your mother. When I saw you, I thought of this. If you'd like it, you may have it."

"What's that about?" Winn whispered to her for the first time.

"No idea."

"Why 'B'?" Rachel asked the question for them. "It's gorgeous, but your initials are C and G."

"My mother's maiden name was Bonner. She collected 'B' things and I inherited the collection when she died."

She continued with her story, but Tori heard no more. Winn grasped her arm and tugged her out of range.

"Bonner." His eyes were wide.

"The box," Tori added. "There is no such thing as coincidence, right?"

"We need to find your dad."

Tori had always known her father couldn't resist a good mystery. He may have been a lawyer, but he was also an adept investigator, and whenever there were facts to be learned, Tori's mom teased that he fancied himself a poor man's Columbo. After chatting several more polite minutes with Winn's newest fan club members, and making as calm a good-bye as she could given the adrenaline pumping through her system, Tori and Winn found her father, chatting with a former partner.

"I'm so sorry, Dad. Can I interrupt for two seconds?"

"Sure." He stepped toward her and she put her lips to his ear.

"I think we found Bonner."

Twenty minutes later she and Winn had fabricated a mini crisis with the dogs at the farm and made their apologetic exit. Ten minutes after arriving home, her parents joined them. The hot anticipation from before the ball about what would happen once two hours had passed, vanished in the wake of the newest discovery. The four of them made a ridiculous sight trooping into the barn in their glitz and glamor to check on Sunspot, but when they found the horse was fine nobody cared about dust on their skirt hems. Nobody commented either on the stray piece of hay in Mallory's hair, or the mismatched buttons on Sawyer's shirt. The potential meaning of finding Bonner's origins tied to Cynthia and, by association, Fred made anything else insignificant.

"This can*not* have anything to do with Fred Gault," Tori insisted, rubbing Sunspot's forehead. "He's salt of the earth. He has to have mentored every horseperson in Kentucky at one time or another."

"I agree," her father said, "but what sense does it make that his daughter would be doing something on her own?"

"Something to do with his finances?" Tori asked.

"This is a high-risk occupation," Winn said. "My owners pay me set training fees and percentages of winnings, but if the horses don't perform, they get taken away, and new owners don't want to sign on with a losing trainer. Money can get to be a huge issue. But this is Fred. He's got job security for life."

"How old is he?" Winn asked.

"Seventy-two," Tori replied. "I remember they had a big seventieth party for him summer before last. It was quite the bash. Everyone loves Fred. Why would he need to do anything illegal at his age?"

"Before we can accuse him of anything at all, we have to establish with one hundred percent certainty that Cynthia's connection to Bonner equals a connection to the package. I can have my colleague in New York dig some more, but he said the post office employees were starting to shut down over his questioning. I'm not sure how effective he'll be."

Tori felt Winn's eyes on her and she met his gaze. In the same moment they both nodded.

"Will," she said. "He's been in heaven passing tidbits of gossip the past three days. He hasn't found anything terribly useful so far, but I know he'd jump at the chance to sleuth out something bigger."

"Remember, though, he's loyal to the paper and to Rachel Blakely," her father said. "And from what you told me, she's pretty good friends with Cynthia. I don't know if you should chance the editor of the paper finding out about this."

"I know, but who else is there? If I start calling New York, the connection will soon be obvious. Same with you, Dad. Same with Winn. My little William wants desperately to be the new Bob Woodward. He thinks it's great to go covert and then spring his findings when he has them. I really think he could come up with a cover story for getting info from New York."

"You know him better than I do." Her father shrugged. "Whatever you think. Can you talk to him tomorrow?"

"I'll find him. But one other thing is nagging at me."

"What, sweetie?" her mother asked.

"We tried really hard not to react or leave abruptly when Cynthia mentioned the name Bonner. She shouldn't have any reason to think we'd be familiar with it, but I don't know. If she's involved in something and *is* the one who sent that box of evidence, she might be watching us. What if this is a family effort and she tells Fred we left after she got that locket?"

"Oh, I don't think…" her mother said.

"But Fred's watching all of Winn's horses." Tori's heart had barely begun slowing down after the rush home. Now it pounded out of rhythm again.

"What can we do?" Sawyer asked. He'd been silent but stood by, now openly holding Mallory's hand.

"If I can split you two up temporarily, you can help." Winn lightened the mood with a wink that turned

Mallory's cheeks a pretty pink and elicited a self-conscious laugh from Sawyer.

"Sorry," he said. "We've spent a lot of time together and…"

"It's okay," Winn said. "I'm not *that* employer. You both work hard and your personal life is your own. But I would like you to go back to the track tonight. Leo and Renee are perfectly capable, but you're much more of a physical presence. Plus, you can fill them in and help watch for anything at all out of the ordinary."

"It's a good idea," Mallory said. "I'll stay here with Sun."

"This is all an overabundance of caution." Tori bit her lip nervously. "I have no reason to think anything will happen here. Or at the track for that matter. But we can't take chances until we're sure Fred has nothing to do with all of this."

"I have one more radical idea," Winn said and pulled out his phone. "Forgive me for this, Tori. Hugh. But I think an old enemy needs to become an ally."

For a moment she didn't know what he was talking about. Then he pulled up a number and showed her the screen. Her surprise only lasted a second and then it made perfect sense.

"We have to trust someone," she said. "Go for it."

He tapped the call button and waited. In the quiet of the barn they all heard the voice answer. "H'yello. Forge."

"Nick? This is Winn Crosby. Do you have a minute?"

CHAPTER
Eighteen

ONE MORE. YOU can get through one more.

If this *one more* event didn't kill him. Or send him to the emergency room with hypothermia and pneumonia. Winn stood off stage at Jairo's, a local blues and jazz supper club with what had turned out to be the best perk of the night—great appetizers. Now, as his stomach bubbled with nerves, he wished he hadn't eaten anything. He'd never been sold on Tori's "great idea" of putting him in front of a crowd and auctioning him off like a yearling at Keeneland. He didn't really care if people in Chandler County got to know him. Certainly he wanted to grow his reputation, but he doubted this was the best PR for a trainer.

Still, there was a big, enthusiastic crowd, and even though he would be cold until the fourth of July from his dunking in the carnival tank this morning—which Mallory had conveniently failed to tell him was an *ice* water dunk tank, hence garnering a higher price per throw—he had seen bidding for his fellow bachelors this evening go as high as seven hundred dollars. He supposed getting forced into the arctic drink by petite little Jocelyn and letting Tori waste her money on buying him for charity was worth a little stage fright and pneumonia.

He just wasn't a stand-in-front-of-the-crowd kind of guy. Sawyer should have been the Crosby Racing representative.

The gavel sounded on the man in front of him. A local electrician's apprentice, with a fairly long beard and an eagle tattoo, grinned as he stepped off the stage to meet the woman who'd bid four hundred fifty-seven dollars for him. Winn's nervous heart rate threatened to choke him.

Other than his polar plunge, the day had been surprisingly fun. He'd let the kids split their shifts so they all could come to the fair. Mallory had manned the petting zoo with so much ownership, Tori hadn't had to spend a minute within the enclosure.

He also hadn't eaten so much junk food in years, but everything from the Hot Brown at lunch with its ham and gooey cheese on slabs of homemade bread, to hand-dipped ice cream covered in fudge and chopped pecans, had tasted as fine as five-star cuisine. If Leo wasn't sick as a dog tomorrow, Winn would be amazed. He'd actually entered the pie-eating contest last minute and come in a respectable fifth out of fifteen.

They also had three cakes among them from participating at least twenty times in Mallory's cake walk. Her own offering had been won by a ten-year-old girl whose fluffy pink party dress had matched the frosting on the three-layer cake.

The day had been a total success. Even multiple calls to the barn and two reports from Nick Forge, their unexpectedly willing partner, proved all was quiet there.

So why did the night have to end on this mortifying note?

"And now, the bachelor we've all been waiting for." Rachel's endlessly cheery voice shook Winn into focus. "Many of you have already met him. You all know he's one of thoroughbred racing's rising stars with winning records across the country and already at Churchill Downs. He's new to Kentucky and we're out to make him one of Chandler County's own. Ladies get those wallets out for Winton Crosby. One look and you'll know exactly why they call him Winn!"

The cheer as he ascended the four short steps to the stage astounded him. He was supposed to be a pariah, a cheater, but here they acted like he was Johnny Depp on the red carpet.

Well, he thought grimly, Depp had his issues—maybe women around here liked bad boys. But he'd had his fill of being one. Reaching soul-deep for his inner calm, and making a desperate sweep of the crowd for Tori, he put on a smile and waved as if he couldn't wait to get started.

After that, the minutes blurred together into a frenzy. Tori wasn't the first to start the bidding, but she jumped in quickly and soon his going price was two hundred and fifty. Tori had confided that she had eight hundred dollars she was prepared to pay. He knew she wouldn't have to sacrifice that amount, but in the moments he allowed his masculine pride the slightest say, he told himself five hundred wasn't too cocky a goal.

At first five or six women warred back and forth to force up his number. He kept his eyes on Tori's happy smile. She'd be insufferable at the success of her plot, but suddenly he was enjoying himself. When he reached five hundred thirty bucks and three of the women dropped out, he even thought maybe her bragging would be worth it. How had he been lucky enough to connect with her?

Enjoyment morphed into downright vanity when he reached six hundred. One more girl shook her head with a laugh and it was down to Tori and one other woman.

"Six fifty!" Tori called.

"Six seventy-five!"

"Six eighty!" Tori began to laugh.

"Enough of this piddly bidding! Twelve hundred dollars!"

The voice from the back of the club stunned the crowd silent, and out of the atmospheric dimness Cynthia Gault appeared, weaving around tables as she strode to the front of the room.

"Cynthia, my goodness!" Rachel held her ceremonial gavel up in shock. "That's a very generous bid. Are you certain?"

"For this beautiful specimen of masculine talent? I am definitely certain."

Winn froze, his eyes on Tori who had rocked back in her chair, her mouth forming speechless "O." She started to raise her hand, and Winn shook his head furiously. She could not get into a bidding war with Cynthia, and he wasn't about to let her spend this kind of money.

"Girls? Ladies? Anyone else? Twelve hundred and one?"

Laughter sailed around the room. Reluctantly, with narrowed eyes, Tori put her hand in her lap. Rachel banged the gavel.

"Sold! And by far one of the most generous offerings in bachelor auction history. Enjoy your date Cynthia and Winn!"

On auto pilot, Winn gave a final wave and headed off the stage. From the corner of his eye he could see

Cynthia following him on the floor, and where she waited for him at the bottom of the stairs.

"Why hello there, Mr. Crosby. Are you surprised?" Her voice, a sultry purr he hadn't heard before, put him instantly on guard. And with the feeling came an idea.

"I am a little. I hardly think one date with me is worth twelve hundred dollars."

"You never know. Maybe there'll be more than one."

"Very flattering." He let her take his arm. "How would you like to make the first one immediate? I made reservations for dessert and wine to share with whatever intrepid lady won the bid tonight."

"Goodness, sugar, that is a dream date. A man who plans ahead for something romantic. I would love to accompany you tonight."

"In the spirit of honesty, I did arrive with Tori. She knew I might be leaving with someone else," he lied, "so if you'll forgive me, I'd like to say good-bye."

"Of course. I'm seeing more and more about you to like, Winton Crosby who they call Winn."

Tori awaited them at the back of the club, wearing a warm smile Winn could tell was completely faked.

"Tori is going to call and check on one of my horses while I'm busy. She heard there was a minor lameness issue. Excuse us for a minute while I give her some background on him. Then we can head right out."

"Absolutely, for the horses," Cynthia said.

"She's obnoxious," Tori whispered when they'd stepped out of earshot. "And I say that out of pure and spiteful jealousy."

"You're too honest for your own good." He grinned. "Look. I'm so sorry. I had a great night planned for us, but no way were you going to beat her."

"She was out for blood, and she's in heaven having bested me. Which she did fair and square I guess. I don't have to like it."

"Neither do I. But listen, this might not be a bad thing. Maybe I can get information straight from the horse's mouth. Forgive the pun."

"No pun, she's kind of a horse. One end of one anyhow."

"Oooh, Dr. Sterling. I'm seeing quite a different side of you."

"I know. I don't like it, but there you go."

"Tori." He touched her arm. "I'd kiss you but I think that would blow my cover and any chance I have of talking seriously with her. She's arrogant, she's entitled, she's not remotely attractive to me."

Her shoulders shook. "Thanks. You didn't need to do that, but I feel lots better. Go. I can play the game. Deep down I'm really a big girl."

He kissed her on the cheek. "That's because she knows we were together last night. I can't act too cold. See you later. If I get a chance to text I'll tell you where I am. Hey, why don't you send me a made-up text about a horse lameness in about an hour?" He stepped back. "Thanks, Tori. Let me know if you think it's serious."

"Glad you told me about that naturally weird gait. I'll ask Leo about it, and if I need to go over there I will. Have fun. Congratulations, Cynthia!"

"Why thank you, Tori. Thank you, as well, for placing your new friend up for auction. I needed a lovely distraction today."

Winn bit his lip as Cynthia led him to the door. He chanced one look over his shoulder and had to spin back or burst into laughter over the daggers raining into his date's back.

For a moment, when they reached the parking lot and Cynthia asked if she could get her wrap from her car, Winn morphed into a teenaged car junkie. The woman drove a blue Porsche 911. He couldn't stop the appreciative whistle.

"This is yours?"

"You like it?"

"That is the dumbest question ever asked a man. But you don't live here—how did you get it—"

"I wanted a road trip so I drove this time. Had to get my baby out of the New York sleet anyway, so I plan to store her here for the winter."

"Wow. Look, I'm all about chivalry, but I'm going to beg. Let's take your baby here on our date. Otherwise you're stuck in my 2005 Tundra. I am not too proud to have a woman drive if I'm sitting in this."

"Oh, honey, you have a deal. But I'm all about chivalry, too. Are you a good driver?"

"Tonight? I'm the Mister Rogers of nice guy good drivers."

She pursed her full lips into a pretty pout. "Now that's the most boring thing ever said to a woman. How about we try a little Jeff Gordon? He's retired. He ought to be safe enough."

The car was magnificent. Winn took the freeway for the ten miles between Chandlerville and Bourbonville at a fun, but modest for the Porsche, eighty-five miles per hour, betting the thrill against avoiding police long enough to reach the closest exit. He let himself forget for the few minutes it took that he was playing a potentially serious game with Cynthia Gault and fully enjoyed the experience. Didn't every guy dream of owning a hot sports car like this? Even a confirmed horse guy.

Once he left Highway 64, he found a backroad past Fire Lake and made the turn onto Bourbonville's main street, passing the Bluegrass Security building, the Depository bank and the Brass Rail where, because of Tori and the bar's famous chicken, he'd first decided Chandler County wasn't the hick, uncivilized place he'd imagined.

He skipped the bar, however, and pulled into the parking lot up the street at Swabbie's, a place supposedly top notch for fine dining. He'd had multiple recommendations—he hoped nobody had led him astray.

"This looks interesting," Cynthia said. "And you got us here safely. Good start to the night."

"That was fun, I have to admit," he said. "Thanks for trusting me with your baby. She's pretty sweet."

"She is that. So, we're here for dessert, you said?"

"Have you eaten yet?"

"Actually, no."

"Then we are here for whatever you want. I admit, I ate at the fair all day, but from what I understand, there's plenty of variety and a menu of fantastic desserts. Afterward, since it's a full moon tonight, we can get to know each other with some wine on the banks of the river."

"You have class. This is lovely."

A pang of guilt hit him. She seemed honestly impressed by his efforts, and now it felt disingenuous to be bringing her on a date he'd set up for Tori, knowing he had no intention of making a legitimate effort with her. She wasn't his type, and she was under suspicion. But she'd been nothing but pleasant on the drive. Maybe they were wrong.

Maybe the Porsche had gotten to him.

He asked her to wait, got out of the car and opened her door. He might as well act the part. It would do no good to be aloof.

He couldn't help but compare Cynthia to Tori while they ate. The conversation remained perfectly pleasant. Because she'd grown up around horses with her father, she knew a lot about Winn's job. Her questions were astute and interested. When she talked about her job as CFO of a mid-sized chain of retail stores, however, she talked about her successes, her quick rise in the company, and her goals. Where Tori was passionate about her clients, her animals, her job, Cynthia's passion centered on her accomplishments and fulfilling her goals. There was nothing wrong with her focus, but it seemed shallow after spending time around a woman who only cared about growing her business so she could spend more money on the loves of her life.

They left Swabbie's after sacrificing healthy eating for an enormous piece of chocolate lava cake with ice and whipped cream. He regretted the pig-out as soon as he had to drag himself and his loosened belt buckle back to the car. She handed him back the keys and told him she had no idea where their next destination was so he might as well keep driving. He stuffed himself behind the wheel feeling like Leo must have after all his pie.

Slowly he drove to a scenic pullout with grassy banks along the Cumberland River. There were several other cars in the lot, but he saw nobody as he and Cynthia exited the Porsche and took in the sweet scent of fall grass and wild water. It reminded him of the moments at Sanctuary Pond, and he wished it were Tori here with him. He couldn't imagine what he was going to learn from this night that would be of any help. The only avenue left to explore was asking her directly about her mother and the collection of B-covered items she'd mentioned at the ball. Maybe she would accidentally let something useful slip.

"Let's sit for a while and moon watch," she said. "It's so lovely here."

"Sure," he said, wishing he didn't have to keep playing the game. It suddenly felt like a ridiculous endeavor and that he had this theory all wrong. There was some other explanation for the box delivery. Cynthia was self-absorbed and a bit spoiled, and although she was clever, he couldn't quite see her as a saboteur.

"I have a blanket in the trunk," she said. "I'll get it."

"I can do that. You get settled in your coat. It's chilly tonight."

Despite his offer, Cynthia followed him to the trunk. "There's still a lot of stuff in here from the trip. We might have to dig for it."

She leaned over and for the first time he saw she was wearing the locket she'd gotten at the ball the night before. It swung free of her sweater and she absently tucked it back beneath the neckline.

"That's the necklace you got last night," he said. "Tell me about this collection based on B."

"It's a little bit 'B-for-boring.'" She shot him a questioning look. "What do you want to know?"

"What kinds of things have B on them that a person would keep?"

"Handpainted signs, decorative boxes, a couple of porcelain vases with monograms. Odd stuff. Why?"

"It's unusual, that's all. My grandmother used to collect moose statues. That's pretty weird, too, so I was only wondering. 'B' was for what again?"

"Bonner."

"But you don't have any B's in your name?"

"Not a one…" Her voice trailed off and once again she glanced at him. "Guys don't usually care about things like that. You're a little unusual, too."

"So I'm told on a regular basis." He laughed. "No worries, I'm just making dumb conversation."

She brightened. "Well, it's refreshing."

The trunk was filled with several good-sized boxes, and the alleged blanket wasn't in sight.

"Maybe it's in the car itself," Cynthia said. "Let me look around the back seat."

She left him searching the trunk, and when he finally saw the corner of a plaid blanket stuffed beneath two boxes, he set one aside and reached for the second. When he moved it, bottles clinked from inside. He ignored the sound and reached for the throw, then he stopped dead, his breath frozen in his throat. Nestled in the wool were two syringes, their needles covered by pink plastic caps. They were identical to the one Will had found the night Sunspot colicked. That meant nothing—the same size syringes were used for many things. But why would Cynthia carry them in her trunk?

Swallowing hard and checking to make sure she was still inside the Porsche, he lifted the flap of the box that had clinked. A dozen clear glass bottles, the kind containing prescription drugs, lay inside. He picked one up and peered at the white and red label. "Lutalyse Injection (dinoprost tromethamine)."

Shit.

He shoved the bottle quickly back into the box, flipped it shut, grabbed the blanket and put the first box back on top. He knew exactly what Lutalyse was.

"I found it!" he called and winced. He'd found it all right. More successfully than he'd dreamed.

"Great!"

A moment later Cynthia returned, all smiles. Winn slammed the trunk and turned, holding out the blanket, desperate to appear relaxed and casual when he was anything but.

"You all right?" she asked.

"Sure. Why?"

"You seem a little jumpy."

Shit again.

"Got a little cold standing there. Let's go sit with the blanket a few minutes, but I'm thinking maybe we'll cut this part short. Did I tell you I got submerged in freezing cold water this morning?"

"You did not." She took the blanket and then his arm. "But don't worry. There are plenty of ways to keep warm."

Any warmth he'd been starting to feel for her had vanished with his discovery. All at once, a date that had only been mildly uncomfortable was terrifying. He needed Tori. Lutalyse was a powerful drug used to bring on a mare's estrus cycle. Some mares reacted to it as if they had severe cramps. Some sweat profusely. Some colicked before the drug went to work. Negative effects were usually short lived, but they could be scary. He knew this because one of the farms he'd worked at had used the drug to synchronize six mares' cycles in order to breed them at the same time. What he didn't know was what would happen to a male horse if given the drug.

He didn't know, but the answer seemed pretty intuitive.

"Winn?" Cynthia's voice was the slightest bit plaintive. He looked down to see she'd already spread the blanket and was patting the ground beside her. "Are you really all right? You're a thousand miles away."

No, he thought, he was far too close to her, wondering how he could possibly find an excuse to end this date sooner than immediately.

He sat and she immediately curled her legs to one side and then snuggled into him, grasping his arm like a child's teddy bear, laying her head on his shoulder. It was all he could do to avoid recoiling.

"Nice," she said.

"It is nice here. I've driven past but never stopped."

"Get that full moon. Look how it's reflected on the water."

He was going to lose his mind making small talk. And then, like magic, he heard the sound of a text coming in. God bless her, Tori had read his mind all the way across two towns.

"Sorry," he said. "That's probably Tori about the horse. I should check."

"Of course." This time she was mildly miffed.

Horse is quiet. Sore in the right front. Isn't testing positive for abscess, tho'. Any thoughts?

He almost laughed. Nice to know if she was going to lie she was going to do it well.

"Trouble?"

"Lame horse. She needs a decision on something. Let me answer her quick and we'll get on with the moon watch. Sorry."

"Hey, what can you do?"

He bent over the phone and typed.

Me: Found several bottles of Lutalyse in Cs car. What the h?

Tori: Are you kidding?

Me: What happens to a colt if he gets dosed?

Tori: Cramping, sweats...damn! That's what I was missing. They were dosed with Lutalyse. Makes perfect sense. Now what?

He thought a second.

Me: Give me five minutes and manufacture an emergency.

Tori: Can do.

"Okay," he said, tucking the phone away and hoping his hands weren't shaking enough for her to notice. "So sorry. Life with animals never really rests."

"Don't I know it? It did my parents' marriage in long before my mother passed away."

"Sorry to hear that. This is not an easy life. Mama don't let your babies grow up to be racehorse trainers. Right?"

"My dad is great at what he does, but he sure wasn't home much. I think I see him more now than when I was little, and we live seven hundred miles apart."

She snuggled closer again and this time rested her hand on his thigh, giving a little squeeze. He shifted uncomfortably. The girl was certainly sure of herself.

"Thanks for a nice date," she said. "What's next, after we get too cold to sit out here?"

"Uh...well, that's up for discussion."

Tori came through with perfect timing. His cell phone chirped again.

"Good grief," she said. "I thought she was a vet. Seems like she shouldn't need your opinion on every matter."

"I asked her to let me know. Blame me not her."

Tori: Just got home. You need to come, so sorry. Sawyer fell and injured his leg—probably broke it. I need to go with him to the ER and someone needs to be here with the horse."

"Shit!" he cried aloud. "My groom was injured. I'm so sorry. I'm afraid I have to cut this short tonight. We can, uh, talk about another date for making up the time we're losing."

"Winn..." Her complaint this time hit him with shrill insistence. "Can't she handle this?"

"She's a vet, not an ER doctor. I need to go make sure someone is with the injured horse."

"One of your other workers. Or my father."

"She's looked for him, and he's not at the track. Look. A lot's been going on. You know that. We suspect someone has been dosing the horses with a drug. Maybe prostaglandin, like Lutalyse. I can't take any chances. Can I?"

She stared and he absolutely couldn't tell what she was thinking. Did she have any reason to suspect he'd poked her for a reaction?

"Fine," she said. "Take me back to your truck."

"Would you like to pick a time for a second date?"

"You let me know when you think you'll have a longer span of free time."

"After my hearing. Next week."

"Fine." She repeated the word, her voice tight.

"I'm sorry."

"Did she really need you to come home? Or are you trying to escape?"

He took a huge chance and centered the last message on the screen, then held it for her to read. She did and sighed.

"Sorry. Guess I'm a little envious that she has your attention despite our date."

"It's business."

"I see that. Come on."

He popped the trunk with the key fob and put the blanket back in. His eye caught something again and he halted. On the box containing the vials of Lutalyse he read a name. M. Bonner. With his blood boiling now, he couldn't keep silent.

"What's this?" He pointed. "Interesting to see your mother's name when we were just talking about her."

She paled slightly but covered it in a heartbeat.

"I have some of her stuff for my father."

"Can I tell you something really weird? About a week ago, I got a box mailed to me from an M. Bonner. I knew that name sounded familiar."

"Excuse me, what?"

"True. Do you find that strange?"

"I do." She paused and put her finger to her lips. "Wait, did it come from a P.O. Box in New York?"

"It did."

"I mailed a box, but not to you. It must have been delivered to the wrong place. I sent it to my dad."

"Really?"

"I did. He said he never got it."

"What was in it?"

"That one? Let's see, a couple of bags with some things he'd left. Odd things—some tape and scissors I think. No, a Leatherman tool he forgot at his last visit."

He didn't believe her for a moment. The box had been addressed to him. Her voice had grown silken, vixen-like. She was covering, he'd bet his license on it, but he found his calm again and nodded. He didn't need her to see his suspicion.

"That would explain a lot," he said. "I thought the name sounded familiar. Well, a mystery solved. Small world."

"Yes. Maybe it's a sign we were meant to find each other."

"Maybe."

Her voice returned to its normal measured tones, and that worried him. The easiness between them had tightened, and he had no idea whether it was because he was ending the date early or she didn't like that he'd discovered the Bonner connection. Either way he couldn't get home to Tori's fast enough.

"What do you think? Would you let me have one last turn at the wheel?"

"Honey. You still have the keys."

He opened her door and let out a nervous breath when he closed her in. He might have the keys, but he could only pray he was still in the driver's seat.

CHAPTER
Nineteen

"WE ARE NOT good influences on each other. We really should have called the police."

In the passenger seat of Heidi's little black Kia, Tori squeezed her hands together, crushing her own knuckles in agitation. Heidi had not hesitated to loan her the car after learning what Winn and Tori had discovered. Since the Kia was rarely at the track, it wouldn't be immediately recognized. Despite the fact that it was eleven at night, Tori didn't want her familiar vet truck anywhere near Churchill Downs. This time, however, she'd brought vet supplies with her just in case.

"We already talked about that," Winn said.

"I know. I know. We have no real evidence to convince the police the Gaults are doing anything wrong. It's becoming clearer the closer we get that being a cat burglar isn't my forte. I'm so nervous I think

I'm going to fill Heidi's car with everything I ate today."

"Sorry. You know you didn't need to come along. I'm glad you did, because there's nothing I enjoy more than getting a girl I like arrested on felony breaking and entering, but you could have stayed home."

"Wait. You like me?"

He sputtered. "You're insane, so we're a matched pair. And believe me, I liked you plenty before tonight. Spending two hours with Cynthia Gault only solidified exactly why."

"Sweet talker. Glad I make the cut."

"Baby, you're so far above the cut. You're the top of the measuring stick."

She settled back, smiling although her hands still clasped and unclasped spasmodically in her lap. At last Winn reached across and stilled her fingers with his.

"Five minutes and we're done. That's all. We can do this, Catwoman."

"With the luck I've had this week, yeah. Okay."

"I think our luck is changing. We have leads. That's a lot more than we have had. And we're going to find stuff in Fred's tack room. I absolutely know it."

"Catwoman and Psychic Man. What a team."

"More like Psych-o Man."

"I wasn't gonna say it."

They had a cover story prepared for the night guard at the backside track entrance, but when it turned out to be a guard they'd never seen, Winn patted her thigh with a grin.

"What'd I tell you? Luck's changing."

They flashed their security passes, and the guard waved them through the gate. Slowly, Winn made his way past his own barn and around the far end to Fred's operation. Nobody but Heidi knew their plan, and telling her had been necessary in case something went dreadfully wrong and somebody had to explain their actions.

"This is without a doubt the worst thing I've ever done," Tori whispered. "Unless you count the time I stole my friend Mary's favorite shoes so I could wear them to a party. You don't want to know how that debacle ended."

"Well we're definitely finished together after this gig," he said. "I can't be seen with a party shoe thief." He stopped the car and cupped the back of her head to bring her in for a kiss. When he pulled back he shook his head. "Tori, this doesn't even crack my top ten. It's you who shouldn't be hanging around with me after this."

"I'll think about it if we get out of here unscathed."

The fact that they'd dressed all in black and worn running shoes for a faster getaway was mildly hilarious, she thought as they walked down the empty barn aisle. Winn had told her he was nervous, too, but he seemed far more relaxed than she felt. Her quick-getaway shoes were ready to get her away before they even started.

"Here it is." Winn's whisper sounded like a klaxon as they stopped in front of Fred's tack room, and Tori winced.

"Ssh!"

"Relax," he replied. "We're here."

"And the door is locked."

"I promised it wouldn't matter, remember? Turn on your phone's flashlight."

She swallowed heavily and illuminated the pair of bobby pins he pulled from his jacket pocket. Before leaving home he'd fashioned them into angles she didn't understand, and now he bent over the lock like a cartoon robber. All he needed was a striped shirt and a bandit's mask. It took him three minutes to pick the lock, and he looked entirely too pleased with himself when he swung the door open.

"Okay, I admit I was a little worried," he said. "I haven't done that in about eighteen years."

"Like riding a bike is it?"

"I'll teach you some day. It's useful if you lock yourself out of the house."

"You weren't kidding about the felony B-and-E." The humor had been keeping them going but suddenly the reality hit her in the face.

"Tori. We're going to look around, take nothing, re-lock the door and leave. All we need is proof that the stewards will find something if they were to get an anonymous tip and come looking for themselves. Come on."

The room was immaculate. Tori marveled at the sheer amount of wall space filled with cubbies and cabinets. Twice as many saddles as Winn had in his tack room lined the end of the this one. Countless bridles, girths, pads and hoods were hung and stacked in precise order. They searched in every cupboard, and on every shelf. The space held nothing untoward.

"Winn, we're on a wild goose chase. There's nothing here. It was silly to think Fred would do this much less be careless enough to leave things out."

"It's here. I know it's here."

"What is here?"

"Whatever it is we need...Wait! Look."

The narrow cabinet was hidden in plain sight. The size of a high school half locker, it sat on the floor tucked beneath an overhanging shelf, painted to look like the wall. It had a small lock on it, but Winn squatted and tugged on the handle anyway.

"Luck is changing," he murmured as the door opened. "Holy here it is, Catwoman. I don't know whether to be elated or sad beyond belief."

She squatted beside him, her heart broken and pounding in disappointment. She hadn't realized until that second how much she'd wanted Winn to be wrong.

"Lutalyse." She pulled out one of five bottles. "Syringes. You know trainers aren't allowed to have these."

"Of course I do."

"What's this?"

She pulled out a heavy cardboard box. Inside were several buzzers and parts to make more. The finished models were identical to the ones they'd found in Winn's equipment.

"Damn it, Fred," Winn groaned. "What the hell is this for? Why?"

More searching turned up clippers, two more Leatherman tools, three seam rippers and duct tape, and several pieces of cut leather—everything that had been planted in Winn's tack room plus.

The final find was the most shocking.

"God, Winn, look." She held up a quart-sized bottle labeled "Cobalt Chloride."

He didn't say a word, just shoved the bottle back in the cabinet and closed it, then pulled Tori to her feet. "Okay, I'm as upset about this as you are," he said. "But we have him. Let's grieve later and get out of here now."

She didn't argue. They made sure everything was as they'd found it and headed for the door. Winn clicked the lock from the inside, pulled the door shut, and tested the knob to be sure it held. Tori dragged him into the aisle, but they were still directly outside the tack room when the barn flooded with light.

"My goodness, Winn. I thought our date was over for the night." Cynthia stood at the end of the aisle, her face a mask of cool satisfaction. "But here you are, and you brought a friend. What kind of kinky things do you think I'm into, you handsome thing?"

"What are you doing here, Cynthia?"

"No, no," she said firmly, her words icing over. "This is my father's barn. You aren't supposed to be at the track at all, as I recall. And even if you were allowed in, your barn is on the other end of the backside. So the question really is,'what are *you* doing here."

"Looking for your father."

"Oh he's not here. I believe you actually told me that yourself, although I don't think you had any clue you were right. He's off-site checking on a horse."

Tori's heart froze as Cynthia's pleased eyes fixed on hers an emphasized "off site." Fred only had one horse off site.

Cynthia sauntered toward them and switched her gaze to Winn. "You saw, didn't you?"

"Saw what?"

"In my trunk. In the box labeled with my mother's name. You acted so funny after getting that blanket, I had to go back and find out what you might have seen."

"Fine, Cynthia, I saw. Nobody needs half a dozen bottles of Lutalyse at one time. What's the deal?"

"You won't believe me, but I didn't put them there. I wouldn't have let you into the trunk had I known. I'm guessing my father thought it would be a good storage spot."

"You're right; I don't believe you. Even if you didn't know they were in your car, you know what they're for."

"I do. Dad uses it regularly on his mares."

"Then you also know the dosage needed for any given horse is tiny. The number of bottles he has would kill a stable full of horses." Tori ground out the words, anger dripping from each one.

"Don't be ridiculous. You don't kill horses with that stuff."

"You certainly can if you overdose. Especially on purpose."

Cynthia laughed. "I have no idea what you're talking about."

"Then how about this?" Winn asked. "You didn't mail that package to your father, did you? You mailed it to me, so it would be found—you hoped—and incriminate me."

"You have no proof. The box was taken away."

"Was it? How would know that?" Tori asked. "Unless you know who did take it?"

"I know the whole sad story of your imminent demise. I talk to my father."

"Yes, well your father is in a whole lot of trouble."

"And how would *you* know *that*? You have no proof he's done anything either, unless you've been in places you shouldn't be."

Tori closed her mouth over the retort that bubbled up. Cynthia had her there. The proof was behind the locked tack room door.

"We have someone following up on your doings in New York," Winn said. "He's not the kind who gives up easily, and whatever he finds is all the evidence we'll need to request an investigation. You might as well give up. We'll get your dad—he's hurting a lot of people."

"You don't know anything about my father." Cynthia's cool finally cracked visibly. "He's worked his entire life at running a good business and making other people a lot of money on their precious horses. Now when his time is running out and he has a big chance, everything is going wrong."

"Time running out?" Tori frowned. "What are you talking about?"

Cynthia's control gave way further. Her voice hitched. "Dad was diagnosed with Alzheimer's about a year ago. He's been doing well, but he made one final big business decision and bought a horse. A horse that has a very good shot at winning the Derby next year. Except that you brought Sunspot back from his injury, and Winn showed up with another huge contender. And that's making his hopeful look very bad."

"What horse?"

Cynthia walked to Full Monty's stall and stroked the gelding's eager nose. "This is going to be your next Derby champion. Dad's waited for this his entire life."

"That's what this is all about? He's trying to systematically sabotage his potential competition?" Winn's voice rose as he paced the aisle. "I've never heard anything so crazy in my life. One person can't control the entire outcome of a race like the Derby. Men and women have been trying that for a hundred years. One or two horses, maybe, but not a field of twenty. You don't even know who they're all going to be until right before the damn race."

"He's not in this alone. He's working with several other trainers here. You'd be surprised how many people want a piece of the Derby pie."

"Brett Mitchell," Tori whispered. "And Blue Moon's trainer. Oh my God."

"Nobody in the world is surprised by the greed," Winn said. "Look, Cynthia, I can't even begin to comprehend all this, but you have to tell us what your dad is doing now."

She didn't answer.

"You can't believe this is a rational plan." Tori appealed the only way she could think to reach a daughter. "You can't want this for your dad's legacy. Help us."

Cynthia's tears began to drip. "You can't stop him now. He wants Sunspot out of the way. When I called him half an hour ago and told him you were about to figure out his plan, we knew he needs to stop you as well. Yes, I want a legacy for him, so I'll help any way I can to make sure his final wish is granted. I can't let you two out of here to talk. Our plan to turn the two goodie-goodie children at the track into the perfect scapegoats has worked beyond our wildest hopes. It won't be any surprise to the world that you were caught breaking into Churchill Downs property looking for any way to clear yourselves. Accidents happen when you come upon intruders at night in the dark."

"Are you actually threatening to kill us?" Tori almost laughed.

Until Cynthia pulled the gun out of her pocket. It wasn't large, just a solid small gun meant for a woman, Tori thought. She'd hunted with her dad, but didn't even like that anymore, so all she really knew about Cynthia's weapon was that, at this range, it would indeed kill.

"Are you crazy?" she asked. "There are horses in here. One shot will bring a dozen people running."

"Like I said, I was pretty frightened when you came after me two against one in the dark. I live in the jungles of New York. I've learned how to protect myself."

"Cynthia, come on." Winn tried to step closer but she waggled the gun to halt him. "You don't want to live with something this stupid for the rest of your life. We're talking about a horse race."

"We're talking about every penny of my father's savings. Every single thing he has to help him through his years of illness is wrapped up in that horse."

"He could sell it."

"Not and get the price he would need to pay what he owes on him. So, we're going to make this horse make money. My dad knows how to do it."

Tori couldn't believe the woman had the deep-down chutzpah it would take to pull the trigger on a person. On the other hand, she sounded as crazy as her father's plan, so she wasn't quite willing to bet her life on it.

"You're going to shoot us in cold blood and pass it off as self-defense. Is that the plan?" Winn asked. "Have you thought this through?"

"I think when I tell you you're about to be out one barn and one very valuable horse, you might come after me, and I won't have to pass anything off."

"What are you saying?" Tori ached to strangle her. "What is Fred planning to do? Is he on his way to my farm?"

The malicious curve that pulled the corners of her mouth into a smile worthy of The Joker told Tori all she needed to know. She took a step toward the crazed woman without hesitation and Cynthia lifted the gun.

"What the hell are you doing, Cynthia? Put that thing down."

As quickly as Tori thought she was going to die, Nick Forge's strong arms pulled Cynthia's backward and up, pinning them behind her back. Winn sprinted forward and grabbed the gun. Tori bent double and rested her elbows on her knees.

"Nick. Oh Nick, thank God. How did you know to come?"

"Winn asked me to check on his horses. I just now made the rounds and found Fallon's stall door wide open."

"Where's the horse?" Winn glared at Cynthia.

"He's fine," Nick soothed. "He was standing in his stall perfectly happy, but I don't know how long ago the door had been opened; he mighta run off anytime. Got me thinking I'd best come check and see if Fred knew anything. Lo and behold, lookee what I've come across."

"Man, we owe you big time," Winn said.

"I learned this move straight from you, Dr. Sterling." Nick winked. "Gotta work together around here whenever we can. It doesn't happen often enough. I'm glad you called me. Glad nothing happened here tonight."

"Aw, you weren't really going to shoot us, were you?" Winn shook his head at Cynthia. Nick released her arms but held her left bicep tightly. She only glared.

"This is awful," Tori said, "but I have to go. I have to get home before Fred does something."

"You won't get there." Cynthia sneered. "He left here half an hour ago. He's there by now."

"Is your daddy up to something?" Nick stared down at Cynthia, dwarfing her and finally putting fear in her eyes. "If you know about it and don't tell us, you'll be an accessory. You know that, right?"

She hesitated and another tear rolled from her eye. "He's got gasoline." She shrugged. "If he can't get near enough to inject Sunspot with more Lutalyse, he'll start a fire."

"You two go," Nick said. "I'll call 911 and then I'll get security to deal with Miss Gault here."

"Nick I don't even know how to start thanking you," Tori said.

"Promise me again you'll never be my vet."

"It's a big fat deal."

After calling Sawyer to warn him, Winn pushed the little Kia Forte to ninety on the freeway back to Chandlerville. Tori watched the speedometer but didn't say a word. Please, God, make the police be busy somewhere else, she prayed. They didn't have time for a traffic stop.

And please, God, stop Fred before he hurts anybody or any of the animals.

"You know what I think?" Winn asked. "I think maybe Fred's already not himself. This makes no sense if he's fully in his right mind. After a career like his, he wouldn't risk it all unless his mind isn't working."

"It's really awful to say, but I hope you're right. I don't want him to have given up like this."

Her heart had already broken a dozen times tonight; she didn't know if she could stand anymore sadness. She prayed harder for the people and creatures at Sanctuary Pond.

A mile from the farm, the flashing lights and sonorous honking siren of a fire truck caused them to pull over until it passed.

"We're too late," Tori cried. "Oh please let everyone be all right."

They pulled in as firefighters scrambled to attach hoses to tanks on their truck. Two men with masks ran toward the barn, which, to Tori's relief wasn't in full flames. Still, smoke poured from the rear door. She ran for the opening, but a firefighter grabbed her.

"No, ma'am. You can't go in there."

She didn't waste time arguing but ran toward the other end of the barn in time to see Sawyer and Mallory each leading a horse. This end of the barn looked clear.

"Are you two okay?"

"We're fine. Sunspot is already in a paddock. The rest of the horses and the donkeys are back in the pasture. But I don't have the little guys out yet."

"I'll get them. How bad are things in there?"

"I think he started the fire only about five minutes ago. I'd already called the fire department and so had someone else. Good thing everyone loves you around here. When they found out it was your farm and we had word a guy with intent to start a fire was headed to us, they came even though there weren't flames yet. I fought some of them when they first started, but this is a barn. Fire spreads too fast."

"They'll get it pretty quick now," Mallory said.

"A hero's party later, you guys. Let's get the critters."

"Any sign of Fred?" Winn asked, as they dashed back into the barn.

Smoke filled the air but already flames were hissing as they got stung by blasts from the fire hoses.

"Mallory was down here beside Sun's stall, so he wasn't getting near the horse. I was outside watching. I caught sight of him running after the fire started, but I missed seeing him start the fire itself. I don't know if he's still here. I actually saw his car parked off by the garden. When I saw him he was headed for the house. Sorry, I figured the animals came first."

"Double hero medals." Tori gagged on the smoke and ran out with the two rabbits under her arm. "Quick, there's the fencing from the petting zoo. We can make a circle and put these guys inside."

Winn emerged from the smoke literally carrying four piglets. Mallory had the other three. From their hideous squeals it sounded as if they'd already been burned.

"Stella and Mike and the rest of the cats are the only ones left," Tori said.

"We'll get them," Mallory said. "Go see if you can find Fred. I doubt he's still here, but he doesn't move fast."

A chill ran up Tori's spine. "Winn. Remember Cynthia said something about Fred knowing we've discovered his plan and wants us out of the way, too? What if he thinks we're in the house?"

"Crap. The idiot probably has his own gun. And look, there's his car, still by the garden. Tori, we really shouldn't go after him."

"I have animals in the house, too. If he didn't care about murdering a Derby colt, he won't avoid hurting a dog."

They crept through the back door and let their eyes acclimate to the dark of the kitchen. Four eager dogs pooled around their legs, Tori knelt to pet them all and shush them. She let Things One and Two outside, but Axel and Zoom refused to leave. A floor board creaked above them.

"He's upstairs," Winn said, unnecessarily.

"I don't want to corner him there. He could easily trap us. I'll go lock the front door. You and Axel wait here, and Zoom and I will go to the porch. Hopefully we can surprise him when he figures out I'm not up there."

Through the living room and dining room Tori kept vigilant, in case the clunking upstairs wasn't Fred after all. Zoom followed her obediently. "Come on, girl, we have to surprise our visitor, okay? Wait with me now."

She was certain her nerves screamed loudly enough for others to hear as she looked desperately around her porch for anything that would help protect her. She had nothing. She kept no gun in the house and wouldn't have used it if she had. She looked quickly into Shaquille's cage to make sure she was okay and then the idea struck.

"Tell me I'm crazy, Zoom," she whispered, "'cause if you don't …"

The silly dog remained silent.

She heard footsteps on the stair tread moments later and took a deep breath. "Get ready guys." And then she called out loud. "Fred? Are you looking for me?"

"Victoria?" His voice echoed from the dark, rough and uncertain.

"I know why you're here. You didn't get Sunspot this time either, old friend. You might as well come in and talk about it."

"Half a million dollars," he called. "That's what that damn Curlin colt is going to cost me. Why did you have to tell Armand you could fix him? That crazy Kraut owns a quarter of Full Monty but he doesn't give a rat's asshole about him anymore. All the money and time is going to Sunspot." His voice changed to a sing-song, like a whiny kid. "Sunspot this. Sunspot that. I'm sick to death of Sunspot. I haven't got much time to fix it either. So I need you to leave me alone."

"I know, Fred. I think you're downright scared for the future. Come into the porch and let's talk about how to fix this."

His steps came closer.

"You in here, Tori?"

"Tori! Don't let him close to you! Don't do this by yourself." Winn, loud but calm, called from his spot in the kitchen.

"Stay there, Winn. Please. Hold onto Axel for a second, but get him excited—riled up. Fred, Winn isn't part of this. I'm the one who took care of Sunspot. Come and talk to me. Winn won't bother us."

His face appeared in the doorway, a little spooky in the ghostly shine of Shaq's aquarium light.

Tori startled but then nodded. "Hi Fred."

Zoom growled.

"You don't understand," he said. "You can't. You don't know what it's like to know that in a year or so you might not remember the great accomplishments from your life. I've never won the Derby. I need pictures to prove that I did. Pictures so I won't forget. Every penny I ever saved went into buying Monty. He's a good horse. He'll do it for me. If you and Sunspot are out of my way. And that meddling Crosby, too.

"Why the cobalt, though? I know that's you, too."

"Me and two other trainers. If we can get their middle-pack horses to win more. If they can start making any good competition look poor and maybe win a few of the qualifying races, then Monty has a good shot. I have a good shot."

"Those are tough odds, Fred. You know that."

"Cynthia is helping me. She knows the business and the numbers. She has the brains to pull this off."

"We know. But Cynthia got caught, too. She can't help you anymore. Let me help you instead. We can fix this."

He shook his head sadly and came fully into the room. Without a word his hand went to his pocket. Tori put her fingers to her lips and blew a shrill whistle. "Axel!" she cried. "Let him go, Winn. Axel come on, boy. Get 'im."

The mountain of black and brown galloped through the door and ran smack dab into Fred's back. "Kiss, Axel. Kiss boy."

She let Zoom go as well, and the two dogs barked and nipped around Fred's head. He shouted and pushed himself up to his elbows, flailing at the dogs who weren't truly biting him but thought he was playing. Grunting he propelled himself forward and Tori saw the pistol lying four feet from his hand.

She opened her jacket and reached for Shaq, wrapped securely around her waist. Carefully but quickly she set the long, boldly-colored snake in front of the gun. Fred screamed like a man in a bear trap.

Winn appeared at the doorway as Fred clawed his way backward. Nothing about this was funny, but Tori's nerves snapped and laughter spilled from her, bubbling and flowing until suddenly she was weeping.

"Aww, Tori, no, no. It's okay now. Thank God." Winn helped Fred to his feet and looked down at Shaq, slithering over the handle of the gun. "That's just wrong," he laughed.

He sat Fred on the sofa, and the man slid as far from the snake as possible. Tori picked Shaquille off the floor and kissed the shiny white head, letting tears drip onto the brown patch behind one eye. She set her gently back in the terrarium and fell into Winn's waiting arms.

"You're okay," he said. "You scared the liver out of me, but you're okay."

"I am. Fred's not."

"No," Winn agreed. "He needs a lot of help."

"Thank you," she said. "You made this happen."

"Oh no, not on your life," he said. "You and your crazy animals. Tori, I love you all. I love them all. Don't you ever let anyone tell you this isn't a house full of living miracles."

"Really. You mean that?"

He laughed and brought his lips to hers. "A snake," he said. "You brought down the bad guy with a snake. I think you have super powers I can't even comprehend."

"Nah," she said. "I have you."

Epilogue

AND IN THE far turn, heading for home now, it's Run 'Em Down in the lead, Getting the Gold is second and here comes Curly Sunspot taking it wide and bearing down on the frontrunners. Run 'Em Down still has the lead by two lengths but Curly Sunspot is passing Getting the Gold, and Derry O'Keefe looks like he's found another gear atop the big red bay colt. A hundred yards from home... and there he goes! Curly Sunspot has taken the lead! Now he's opening it up to a length, now a length and a half and they sweep past the finish. It's Curly Sunspot first, followed by Run 'Em Down and Getting the Gold...

The announcer's voice faded. Tori screeched with joy and jumped into Winn's arms to kiss him soundly. When she finally let him go, she turned to Armand. The man had outdone himself nearly to embarrassment today in a pair of two-toned blue and white diamond patterned plus fours, socks with narrow white and maroon horizontal stripes, and a matching blue sweater vest adorned with four large white diamonds running diagonally up the front. She threw her arms around him as well.

"There you go, Armand," she said. "Your colt is back, good as new."

"You are the miracle vorker, Tori. I put my faith in you, and you delivered on your promise."

"I wish Fred could have seen this." Winn reached to shake Armand's hand. "It sounds like he's doing a little better."

"It's a good place he's in because you lobbied for care instead of prison. I thank you for zat, Winn. And I thank you for stepping in to take over my horses. I think we will get along fine."

"It's been a good two weeks to start. Thanks for the opportunity."

"And congratulations on our first win together."

"No. No. The kudos go to Fred. He started this guy out right. He did all the work to this point."

"And you will take him all da way to the Triple Crown. Come. Ve must go meet our champion at the winner's circle."

"We're right behind you!"

Tori squealed again, her heart thumping with wild happiness, and Winn hauled her back for another kiss.

"My miracle worker," he said. "Congratulations, you. He's an amazing horse. And you're an amazing doctor."

"Just stubborn. And don't sell yourself short. You've been through a lot to get back here. I'm so proud of you. I love you, you know."

"Just in case I didn't catch it the other twelve times you've said it today?"

"That's right."

"Come on, let's get in the picture."

Everyone crowded into the winner's circle. Armand and Winn held Sun's bridle. Derry raised a hand in triumph from his winning colt's back. Tori slipped in under Winn's arm, Mallory and Sawyer, Leo and Renee and Jocelyn each took a spot, and even Tori's parents joined the group. The official track photographer snapped the shot but he wasn't the only one. Waving wildly for attention, Will lifted his camera and took his own photo. It was the finish to a story he'd started a month earlier when he'd shown up at the track thinking to write a small article about a come-back colt. Now, Tori had heard, he was up for an award at the paper for breaking the biggest scandal story in two years at Churchill Downs—and for playing a part in convicting Cynthia Gault by tracking down her post office alias and confirming her collusion in attempting to frame Crosby Racing.

In the span of a few weeks, Tori had gained more honorary family than she'd ever imagined possible.

The group started to disperse, congratulations still flowing when Winn caught her hand.

"Tori," he said, concern etching his face. "Would you take a look at this? Did Sun bang his head somewhere? What's this bump?"

"What? No! Let me see."

"Hey, William-the-Reporter, come over here," Winn called. "I might have a breaking story for you."

Tori frowned, not understanding when Armand directed Will to stand in front of her, and Winn took her hand to place her fingers on the supposed lump. She felt along the cheek piece of Sun's bridle and scowled at the rough bump. But it wasn't on the horse... Will's camera shutter snapped, and snapped again when Tori peered more closely and gasped. She glanced at Winn in confusion, but he only nodded before handing her a small scissors.

"Cut it loose," he said.

"It's…" She looked again. Zip-tied to the leather was a ring, sparkling silver, catching the Kentucky sunlight in a diamond far bigger and brighter than any Armand had on his sweater.

With shaky hands she cut the plastic tie and let the ring fall into her palm. Winn took it.

"Don't tell me that ran the whole race." She couldn't think of anything more intelligent to say.

"It did," he said, and the camera shutter snapped once more. "Win or lose, Sun was going to bring this to you on my behalf. He knows that if it hadn't been for him I never would have asked you to be my vet. And if I hadn't ever done that? I don't even want to go there. So…"

Right on the bricks of the Churchill Downs winner's circle, he knelt and held up the circlet of silver.

"Dr. Victoria Sterling. It hasn't been that long, barely a heartbeat really, but it's been long enough for me. Will you and your dogs, your horses, donkeys, sheep, cats, pigs, rabbits *and* your snake marry me?"

As if her heart hadn't been through enough crazy rhythms in the past month to hospitalize her for a-fib, it leaped now into a beat she'd never experienced before—the one that thundered into joy right before she said yes.

The End

About the Author

Award-winning author Lizbeth Selvig writes heartwarming contemporary romance. Whether set in a small town, on a huge western ranch, or at a Kentucky racetrack, her strong, fun and funny characters don't mind poking at societal norms even while they're finding their ways home to family and love. Lizbeth turned to fiction writing after working as a newpaper journalist and magazine editor, and raising an equine veterinarian daughter (handy, since there are usually too many horses in her stories) and a talented musician son (also handy because she's been known to write about rock stars). She shares life in Minnesota, where her first book series is set, with her best friend (aka her husband, Jan), an under-ridden gray Arabian gelding named Jedi, two human grandchildren, and her four-legged grandbabies, of which there are nearly thirty, including a wallaby, three alpacas, a mammoth-eared donkey, a miniature horse, a pig, and many dogs, cats and regular-sized horses. In her spare time she loves to hike, quilt, read, and horseback ride.

Lizbeth also loves connecting with readers, so contact her anytime. *www.lizbethselvig.com*

Welcome to Chandler County

Chandler County is a unique place situated in the heart of Kentucky's world famous bluegrass country, midway between Louisville and Lexington. The county consists of two towns, Chandlerville and Bourbonville. Horse farms and a world class bourbon distillery are the area's main claims to fame, and the towns come alive twice a year: once for the Kentucky Derby in May and again for Chandler County's birthday bash celebration in November.

All the goings-on in this lively place have been chronicled in the Chandler County novels—a branded author series featuring some of today's most popular authors. All the books are available in e-book format from online retailers.

You can find a list of current titles at the end of the book after you enjoy the following excerpt from *Missing My Heart*, by Tina Susedik.

Missing MY HEART
By Tina Susedik

Bourbonville, Kentucky
February 1975

The vacuum cleaner roared, overpowering Eleanore Farrell's confusing thoughts. Shaped like a silver bullet, heavy to maneuver, and loud enough to drown out the roar of a 747, Ellie figured it was built around the time of the first rocket launch. It certainly looked like something from outer space. Every week as she cleaned the house she and her grandmother had shared, Ellie had tried to convince her to replace the monstrosity. But her grandmother's words echoed in her mind, "If it isn't broke, why replace it."

Careful not to bump the antique furniture packed into the stuffy, pink living room, Ellie gave the too-short cord a yank, pulling it from the wall plug. The cord flipped through the air, snapping like a lion tamer's whip. Ellie leapt over the couch to grab a priceless lamp standing helpless in the way of the wild, snake-like creature. Her foot snagged on the coffee table and with a resounding thud her grandmother's absolute favorite treasure fell to the pink and red floral, carpeted floor.

'The Horse.' Not just any horse, but a heavy brass horse, complete with saddle and a chain for reins. Bright from Miranda's weekly polishing, the horse now lay on its side, its bottom glowing in the lamplight. For the first time in her twenty-eight years of life, Ellie finally knew 'The Horse' was male.

She sat cross-legged on the floor, leaned over and reached out her hand, then drew back. As long as she could remember, 'The Horse' had been off limits. The last time she'd dared touch it, she'd been four and had been soundly whopped on her rear for her disobedience. Everyone knew you never, ever touched 'The Horse.'

Tears pooled in her eyes. Now there wasn't anyone left to chastise her for touching the object. The last of her relatives, her grandmother, had passed away two weeks ago, leaving Ellie alone. Still, guilt whipped through her like the vacuum cord snapping through the air. Surely Miranda was watching from heaven, ready to slap her hands.

Memories washed over her, building inside until she wanted to scream. How many times had she accidentally come across her grandmother holding the horse in her arms, polishing it, caressing it like a lover? Several times tears had streamed down Miranda's face. If Ellie dared ask why the horse was so important, Miranda would say it as none of her business, that young girls should keep their noses to themselves.

The piece wasn't large. Twelve inches from nose to tail; ten inches from ears to hoof. With shaking hands, Ellie picked up the horse, surprised at how much heavier it was than it looked. And cold. So cold. Why had her grandmother cherished something that had no warmth to it?

Ellie turned the horse over. Something rattled. She shook it. A distinct sound of metal hitting metal came back at her.

"What the heck?" She wiggled it back and forth. Except for an old crack in one leg, nothing seemed to be broken. Maybe it was the saddle. She tugged and pulled. Jiggled and twisted.

"It *is* the saddle." She bit her bottom lip. "I. Almost. Have. It."

"Ellie. Ellie? Are you home?" her best friend, Pam Hackett called through the front door.

"Darn." Why was Pam here? Had they agreed to meet? Keeping the horse in the crook of her arm, she pushed herself from the floor, her knees creaking in protest. Pam pounded a few more times before Ellie opened the door.

In her usual whirlwind way, Pam brushed past her, her long, blonde hair sweeping against Ellie's arm. In the fifteen years they'd known each other, Ellie had never figured out what an outgoing, popular girl like Pam had seen in a shy, awkward, unpopular person like herself. Since the day Pam had yelled at a group of kids taunting Ellie because of her parents, they'd bonded. Ellie would be forever grateful.

After her father's suicide and her mother's breakdown and subsequent death, if she hadn't had Pam, she probably wouldn't have survived. Although she loved the grandmother who had taken her in, the loss of her son had shaken the woman, and turned her inward. The loving, caring woman Ellie remembered from her childhood was gone.

"I was getting worried when you didn't. . ." She stopped and threw a hand to her mouth. "Oh. My. God." She glanced around the room as if waiting for someone to jump out at her—probably Miranda. "You're actually touching 'The Horse.'" The last two words came out in a whisper.

"I know. And I feel so guilty." She led the way from the foyer into the large, but cramped, living room and sat on the end of a bold floral, forties-style couch. She waved Pam to the other end. "I keep waiting for Grandma to come into the room and slap my hands silly."

"You're a brave woman, my friend—even if she is six feet under." Pam hooked her arm over the back of the couch, toed off her shoes, and tucked her legs to her side.

"Not that I'm not happy to see you, but did we have plans for the night?"

Pam shook her head. "No. I just wanted to see how you were doing."

"I'm fine—I think. There's so much to do."

"Can I help?"

Ellie set the horse on the coffee table and laughed. "I don't even know where to begin. I don't think Grandma ever threw anything out. While Grandpa was alive, he held down her tendencies to keep everything, but once he died, she got a bit out of control."

"What are you going to do with the house?"

Even though it was only late afternoon, answering her friend's question required a drink. "You want some wine?"

"Sure. Barrett has a town council meeting tonight and is going there from work, so he won't be home for supper. Want to order a pizza?"

Ellie laughed and wove her way through furniture to the kitchen. Still decorated with large black and white checkered floor tile, an ancient Frigidaire, and a wide stove she remembered Grandma saying Grandpa had bought for her in the 1940s, the room was as cluttered as the rest of the house. Cupboards were packed with gadgets, spices, and dishes her grandmother never used. Countertops littered with pristine cookbooks. Red and white flour, sugar, and spice containers. A Hoosier cabinet trimmed in red and white. Matching gingham curtains hung over the sink and back door windows.

Eventually she was going to clean everything out. Maybe have a garage sale. Then update the kitchen and the rest of the house to bring it into the seventies. Eventually. When she had the energy and desire to weed through her grandmother's belongings. The extra money would come in handy, too.

"We're not in Chandlerville. Where do you think you're going to get a pizza delivered in Bourbonville?"

"Sometimes I forget you still live in the boonies."

"Like Chandlerville is such a metropolis." Ellie opened the refrigerator and pulled out a bottle of her favorite wine, then dug in a drawer for a corkscrew. "Maybe we can go to Sadie's Cafe later for burgers." She tugged on the cork. Some day she was going to get the hang of using the old contraption. Miranda had said it only took muscles. Ellie thought it took a new corkscrew.

Pam took the glass of wine from Ellie. "You haven't answered my question. What are you going to do with the house?"

Ellie returned to her place on the couch and folded one leg beneath the other. "I spoke with the lawyer the other day. Grandma willed the house to me, lock, stock, and barrel."

"Lucky you," Pam said, taking in the stuffed room. "Will you stay here?"

"Since the house is paid for, it would be silly of me not to." She paused and sipped her wine, letting the sweet flavor tease her taste buds. "Once I go through and get rid of her stuff, it could be a cute place."

"You have a better vision than I do." Pam pushed aside a stack of magazines and set her glass on the table.

"Look around you. Once I remove the heavy drapes and sheers and put up something lighter, think how much brighter it'll be in here. Since it's just me, I only need a couch and a chair, so I can get rid of most of the furniture. I've always hated having to dust her knickknacks, so those will go." She pointed to a wall between two windows. "Put a television console and stereo there, and paint the bookcases on either side of the fireplace for my books. Think how cute this'll be."

Pam frowned. "Can you afford all of that? Because if you can't, I'll help."

"I'll be fine. Besides the house, Grandma had a little money set aside. I'll keep that in the bank for taxes and repairs." A tiny glimmer of excitement built inside her. This was *her* house now, not her grandmother's and she could do anything she wanted with it. "If I have to, I'll pick up a few cleaning jobs to help."

"You're going to go back to cleaning houses?" Pam's shook her head. "You're so damned smart. Too smart to be cleaning up after slobs who are too lazy to do it themselves."

Pam thought she was smart? No one had ever called her smart. Dumb. Ugly. The joke of Bourbonville High. But never smart. "Hey, wait a minute. I did more than clean houses. Some of my people were elderly, so I cooked some meals, ran errands. Now that I don't have to take care of Miranda anymore, I can return to them."

"Do you get paid extra for all that?"

Ellie sighed. Of course she didn't and since they'd had this discussion before, Pam knew it. For a few minutes, the only sound in the room was the ticking of the clock on the fireplace mantle.

Pam snapped her fingers. "I know what you should do."

Ellie mentally cringed. Sometimes Pam's ideas weren't the best in the world, but she'd bite. "What's that?"

"I know how much you like helping people. Maybe you should go to school and become a nurse. You'd make more money."

The idea held merit and was something she'd thought about in the past, but when Miranda's health deteriorated, she gave up her dream. "The problem is, it takes money to go to college. Money I don't have."

"Oh, pooh." Pam flapped her hand at Ellie. "There are loans and grants out there. And I said I'd help you."

Pam's family was rich, one of the richest in Bourbonville. Her father owned one of the biggest horse ranches in the area. His horses placed every year in some of the biggest races in the country, not to mention the world. On top of that Pam married a successful surgeon and had her own degree and business as a psychologist. Once again, she wondered why someone like Pam would be friends with someone like her.

Pam's svelte form was taller than her own 5'8". Her friend was beautiful with sparkling blue eyes and long, blonde hair. Ellie, on the other hand, had average brown hair, average brown eyes, and an average build. Nothing at all exciting about her. Take into consideration her family's past and the fact that she was a house cleaner, well, there was no comparison. But, lordy, she was glad for Pam's friendship getting her through some rough stretches in her life.

"Ellie? Are you there, Ellie?" Pam waved a hand in front of her face.

"Sorry. I was woolgathering. I do like the idea of becoming a nurse, but you know I can't take your money. Once I get this place cleaned out and settled, I'll look into it."

Pam's frown showed how dubious she thought Ellie's comment was. "Just make sure you do.

Barrett is always saying how they need good nurses. Nurses who are mature, not these kids the schools are producing today."

Maybe Pam was right. "I'll think about it."

"Hey, what's up with "The Horse."

Ellie laughed. "Do you realize every time you say, "The Horse," you whisper?"

"I was always afraid if I said it louder, I would get in trouble with Miranda. I remember the time I *almost* picked it up. Thought my head was going on the chopping block."

"Yeah. I have no idea what the big deal was about it. I knocked it over with the vacuum cleaner cord, which, I might add, I'm going to replace as soon as I have some extra cash." She picked up the horse and wiggled the saddle. "It's making a clunking noise. I think the saddle might come off, but it seems to be stuck." With one last tug, the saddle came off, flew from her hand, and hit a particularly ugly, rose lamp matching the couch, sending it crashing to the floor.

"One less thing you have to get rid of." Pam brought her attention back to the horse. "Hey, is that a hole in its back?"

"Well, I'll be. It is." Ellie turned the horse around in her hands and moved the horse closer to a lamp matching the broken one. "I think there's something in there."

"Turn it upside down."

Ellie's hands shook. What could Grandma have hidden in a hollow horse? And more importantly, why? A small piece of folded paper fluttered to the carpet. Another followed floating like a paper airplane. "What in heaven's name?" Neither was bigger than her thumb. She picked one up, while Pam took the other. As if it were as fragile as a hummingbird feather, she opened hers up. The writing was so small and faded, deciphering it was almost impossible.

My dear Randi. Who the hell was Randi? *I miss you so much my heart aches. XX Bert.* And who the hell was Bert? "What does that one say?"

Pam opened hers. *Randi. Love you to the moon and back. XX Bert.*

"Who are Randi and Bert?"

"Beats the hell out of me." Ellie tipped the horse again. Piece after piece of paper dropped to the floor. "There have to be several dozen here."

Pam rubbed her nose. "They look like love notes. I know your grandmother's name was Miranda. What was your grandfather's name?"

"John. That's not even close to Bert."

"Wow. I mean. Why would your grandmother keep all these love notes?" Pam opened a few more.

"What the hell?" Ellie flopped against the back of the couch. Heat rose to her face. "This one asks how their son is doing and to give him a hug and kiss."

"And this one says his wife is getting suspicious, but he can't give up the love of his life."

Ellie closed her eyes and bit the bottom of her lip. "Do you suppose Grandma was keeping these for someone and that's why she wouldn't let anyone touch the horse?"

"Or..."

What was that speculative look on Pam's face about? "What are you thinking?"

"Oh, Ellie." Pam opened another note, but before reading it, set it on the coffee table. "What if these are Miranda's?"

Good thing she hadn't taken a sip of wine at that moment, or she would have spewed it across the room. "Are you kidding me?"

"Think about it. Randi could be a nickname for Miranda. I have no idea who this Bert guy is, but *that* could be why she was so protective of the horse. Your grandmother had an affair."

Ellie's stomach flipped. Her heart raced. Was it possible? "But who would their son be? I never heard of Grandma having a son besides my father."

Pam's silence spoke more than if she'd yelled.

"You think this Bert guy is my real grandfather and not John?" Ellie scooped up the notes and rushed to the kitchen. "That's plain crazy." She yanked open cupboards, ignoring items from the over-stuffed shelves dropping to the counter, until she found a ceramic, gray cookie jar shaped like a cat. A pink ribbon separated the cat-head top from the bottom. When she was ten, she'd saved her money and bought it for her mother for

Christmas. After removing the head, she dropped the notes inside and took the jar into the living room.

"Here put the rest in here. I can't deal with this right now."

"I'm sorry, honey." Pam dropped the remaining notes into the cookie jar. "This is a lot to take in after going through the funeral and everything."

Ellie pushed a stack of magazines to the floor. Why had her grandmother subscribed to so many of the damn things? She never read them. A piece of her heart broke as she set the jar in the center of the coffee table.

"Let's go get a hamburger." Maybe food would stop her rambling thoughts.

Pam stood and slung her purse over her shoulder. "I'm buying."

"You always buy." Ellie held the front door open for her friend.

"Yes, I do. That's why you're such a good friend."

Ellie laughed. "*I'm* a good friend? That doesn't make sense." Even though Bourbonville was a small community and everyone knew everyone, she locked the front door. It was better to be safe than sorry. There had been a few strangers seen in the area. Someone said a redhead was asking a lot of questions. She hadn't heard what he was asking, but with the celebrations of the founding of Chandler County coming up in a month, he was probably interested in the event.

Pam hooked her arm through Ellie's. "Let's walk instead of drive. Yes, you're a good friend. Good friends let their friends do what they want. And I want to buy you supper."

"Tonight, I'll let you, but one of these days…"

"Sure. One of these days I'll let you buy."

Not likely. They strolled arm in arm down Main Street. A breeze made the early evening temperature bearable. The fall heatwave, with temperatures in the upper eighties with the humidity sticking around, had stretched for nearly a week. She longed for the temps to drop back into the seventies.

At least, the tree-lined street kept them out of the direct sunlight. When her grandmother's house, no, make that hers, was built in the 1920s, there were no houses between hers and town. In fact, Main Street didn't even stretch that far. Now, fifty-five years later, houses lined both sides of the street, many built during the post-WWII boom. When her father lost their ranch because of his drinking and gambling, a developer scooped up their property before the owners of the Balmoral Ranch could, tore down the barns and their home, and started constructing small residences. Now, instead of being surrounded by pastures filled with horses, she was surrounded by people. She missed the seclusion.

Ellie mentally shrugged. Life went on. Things changed, just as Bourbonville had changed. As they got closer to downtown, the trees thinned out, making room for more businesses. Stores that had once served the community had gone by the wayside, with others taking up the slack. Thank goodness the Rexall Drugstore and Miller's Grocery were still there, but with more and more people heading into the larger Chandlerville to shop, who knew how long they'd survive. They passed an old, red brick blacksmith shop being restored into an auto repair shop.

"You're quiet." Pam interrupted her thoughts.

"Just thinking about how this town has changed."

"You sound like an old fogey." Pam nudged her in the shoulder. "Heck, if you're old at twenty-eight, then so am I. And I'm sorry, my friend, I am not old, so neither are you."

"Sometimes I feel old." Ellie stopped in front of Blooming Petals Flower Shop and peeked through the window. She loved flowers. Her grandmother had hated them. Now that the house was hers, maybe she'd put in flower beds.

"That's because you lived with Miranda for so long. And what happened to your parents and how the kids in school and this community treated you, would have aged anyone." Pam tugged at her arm. "Let's get moving. I'm hungry. I hate to say it, but now that you're free, you can start living your own life. And I plan on helping you."

The bell over Sadie's Café door jingled as they entered the establishment. With its red and white booth seats and matching décor, sometimes it was like walking into her grandmother's kitchen—reminiscent of the fifties.

A few people waved and yelled out greetings to Pam, but ignored her. Even after all these years, people hadn't forgotten her father. Like Pam had told her over and over, she needed to put the past behind her and get on with her life. Easier said than done. The taunts and meanness were hard to get out of her head, even though the taunts had ended, but not the snubs.

"What are you going to have?" Pam asked, as she flipped through the table-top juke box, dropped in a few coins, and pushed buttons. In a few seconds, a toe-tapping rock and roll song blared through the café's speakers.

"My usual. Hamburger with fried onions, fries, and a chocolate shake."

Melva, a waitress who'd been at the café for as long as Ellie could remember and was one person who hadn't sided with the town's people, came to the table. Her hair was cut like a man's. She was short and thin. Her voice was like a lumberjack's, but had a smile so warm, it was like being enveloped in a hug.

"What'll it be ladies?" Her pencil poised on her pad,

she grinned at Ellie. "Wait, I bet you'll have the usual. And, Pam," she tipped her head to the side. "You'll have the same?"

"Right as usual, Melva." When the waitress left to slip the order on the round, metal order rack, Pam leaned against the back of her seat, the leather creaking against her weight. "So, what are you going to do about the notes?"

Until their food arrived, they went over what the notes could mean. Once their mouth-watering burgers were in front of them, Ellie changed the subject to the county's up-coming birthday celebration. She wanted to think about what the horse had contained on her own, in her own time.

"Why do you keep looking over my shoulder?" Pam asked.

"There's a guy," she nodded in the direction past Pam, "who keeps looking over here. I've never seen him before." Ellie averted her eyes when the man smiled at her. "Wait, don't look," she whispered when her friend turned.

Pam tossed a fry onto her plate. "Well, how on earth am I supposed to know who you're talking about?"

"He's got reddish hair."

"I'm not into red hair on men. Is he cute?"

She slapped Pam's arm. "You're married, remember?"

"Married, but not blind. So, is he cute?"

"I guess. He's rather thin. I can't tell the color of his eyes from here. I think I see a dimple."

"Not looking much, are you?"

"It's hard not to when he's facing this way and keeps staring at me. This is creeping me out."

"Anything else, ladies?" Melva said, interrupting their conversation and blocking the view of the mysterious man. "Here's your bill." She placed a piece of paper on the table and took their empty plates.

"Hey, Melva," Pam said. "Do you know who that red-headed guy is?"

"Don't know his name, but I hear he's some reporter or writer or something looking for information on bootlegging going on around here during prohibition."

Ellie frowned. "Why would he want to know that?"

Melva shrugged and stacked the plates on top of each other. "Beats the heck out of me. Guess he's staying in Chandlerville. Have a good night, ladies."

When Melva left the table, the man was gone. A shiver skittered down her spine. How had he disappeared so fast?

On their walk home, she couldn't help but keep checking over her shoulder to make sure they weren't being followed. Even Pam was spooked. This entire day had been strange.

Patton Trullinger leaned against the café wall, waiting for the two women to leave. He had a strong feeling he'd freaked the woman out, but he couldn't keep his eyes from her. Probably in her mid to late twenties, there was something about her that drew his attention. Her sultry laugh made him think of hot, summer nights, legs entwined in cool sheets, and sex.

There was nothing extraordinary about her. Her long, dark, brown hair was in a pony tail that brushed her shoulders and swayed during an animated discussion with the other woman. The café lights picked up its auburn hues. High cheekbones, trim arms, and delicate ears put together to form an intriguing face. Since she was sitting, he couldn't tell how tall she was, but shapely calves beneath the table caught his attention.

Patton, or Stretch as his friends called him due to his height, patted his shirt pocket for a pack of cigarettes no longer there. He'd quit smoking a year ago, but the urge came upon him now and again when he was nervous. And for some reason this woman made his nerves jump.

It had been a long time since a woman caught his attention. His work as an investigative reporter for a large newspaper in Milwaukee, Wisconsin, had kept him busy. He ran a hand through his hair—or what was left of it after getting the longish locks trimmed a few days ago before arriving in Kentucky. He knew how some people felt about men with long hair, and since he was in the more conservative south, he thought it would be better to trim it off. With this heat, he was glad he had. Now it was almost as short as when he was in the military.

Thankfully the café door opened before his thoughts snapped him back from his time in Nam. He so didn't want to go there. A stream from the restaurant of light hit the sidewalk as the two women left the café and headed north. When they walked beneath a streetlight, he recognized the ponytail swinging back and forth. It was the woman who piqued his interest.

He ignored the temptation to follow. There would be other ways of getting to meet her. With that thought in mind, he strode to his 69 Malibu and headed back to his hotel in Chandlerville.

Missing My Heart
is available at all online retailers

CHANDLER COUNTY

**Complete your collection of
Chandler County books:**

Missing Alaska by Cherime MacFarlane
Missing Desire by PJ Fiala
Missing Out by Trish Edmiston
Missing By a Heartbeat by Lizbeth Selvig
Missing My Heart by Tina Susedik
Missing the Gate by Aubree Lane
Missing Us by Traci Wooden-Carlisle
Missing Home by Stephany Tullis

Missing Pieces by Stephany Tullis
Missing the Point by PJ Fiala
Missing: The Lady Said No by Jacquie Biggar
Missing Destiny by Traci W. Carlisle
Missing the Crown Jewels by Valerie J. Clarizio
The Missing Ingredient by Debbie White

Made in the USA
Columbia, SC
19 January 2018